Dear Reader,

Do you ever wonder what it would be like to be Cinderella? To go from being a lowly companion to being a wealthy duchess, with men fighting for your hand in marriage? I know I've thought about it. I've imagined myself dressed in the finest gown, poised at the top of the ballroom stairs, while below me, everyone marvels at my beauty. Then reality intrudes, and I realize I get nervous when people stare at me, then I get clumsy, and I would probably fall down those marble stairs and knock myself silly.

Reality is overrated.

Which is pretty much what shy Miss Eleanor de Lacy discovers when she changes places with her cousin, Madeline, the duchess of Magnus. Madeline's father has lost her in a card game to a rogue by the name of Mr. Remington Knight, so Eleanor travels to London to confront Remington. She finds herself facing a handsome, heartless man who believes her to be the duchess and intends to marry her. He ruthlessly romances her, dresses her in great clothes, takes her dancing every night, and what's worse, Eleanor likes it. She likes him. She wants to keep him—and she's lying to him about who she is. Did I say reality was overrated? So is being Cinderella.

I hope you enjoy.

Christina Dodd

Books by Christina Dodd

CHRISTINA DODD

One Kiss From You

AVON BOOKS
An Imprint of HarperCollins*Publishers*

This is a work of fiction. Names, characters, places, and incidents are products of the author's imagination or are used fictitiously and are not to be construed as real. Any resemblance to actual events, locales, organizations, or persons, living or dead, is entirely coincidental.

AVON BOOKS
An Imprint of HarperCollins*Publishers*
10 East 53rd Street
New York, New York 10022-5299

Printed in the U.S.A.

To my mother, Virginia Dodd—
you're the best mother in the world, my only parent,
and words can't convey
how much I appreciate your sacrifices,
your kindnesses and your constant support.
I cherish and love you.

One Kiss From You

Chapter 1

London, 1806

The coach belonging to the duchess of Magnus pulled up to the tall house on Berkley Square, and an imposter stepped out.

The imposter's long, sturdy traveling cloak covered plain, dark, modest traveling clothes. Like the duchess, she was tall and well-rounded, and she spoke with the duchess's aristocratic accent. Also like the duchess, she wore her black hair smoothed back from her face.

Yet for the discerning eye, the differences were obvious. The imposter had a sweeter, rounder face, dominated by large blue eyes striking in their serenity. Her voice was husky, warm, rich. Her hands rested calmly at her waist, and she moved with serene grace, not at all with the brisk certainty of the duchess. She was slow to smile, slow to frown, and never laughed with glorious freedom. Indeed, she seemed to weigh each emotion before allowing it egress, as if sometime in the past every drop of impulsiveness had been choked from her. It wasn't that she was morose, but she was observant, composed, and far too quiet.

Yes, a knowledgeable person would recognize the differences between the duchess and the imposter. Fortunately for Miss Eleanor Madeline Anne Elizabeth de Lacy, no such person was in London at that moment, with the exception of her groom, her coachmen and footmen, and they were all devoted to her cousin, the real duchess, and to Eleanor, the duchess's companion. They would never betray Eleanor's mission.

They would never tell Mr. Remington Knight the truth.

Eleanor's heart sank as Mr. Remington Knight's stern-faced butler made the announcement into the large, echoing foyer. "Her Grace, the duchess of Magnus."

To hear herself presented in such a formal manner made her want to glance about for her cousin. If only Madeline were here! If only she hadn't turned aside from this mission for a more important task!

If only Eleanor hadn't agreed to impersonate her.

At the far end of the room, a liveried footman bowed, then disappeared into an open doorway. He was gone only a moment, then returned and inclined his head to the butler.

The butler turned to Eleanor and intoned, "The

master is busy, but he will receive you soon. In the meantime, ma'am, I'm Bridgeport. May I take your cloak and bonnet?"

Although noon had passed, the mists outside subdued the sunlight into a wash of gray. The light of the candles couldn't illuminate the dark corners of Mr. Knight's enormous entry, an entry built to communicate, in the surest way possible, the owner's wealth.

Eleanor's nostrils quivered with scorn.

Bridgeport jumped a little, as if anticipating her ripping at him as a substitute for his master.

Of course Mr. Knight would take this house; he wanted everyone to know he was rolling in riches. He was, after all, nothing more than an upstart American who dreamed of marrying a title.

Yet the entry was decorated with velvet draperies of evergreen and gold, and with a profusion of cut glass and beveled mirrors in marvelous good taste. Eleanor comforted herself with the thought that Mr. Knight had bought it in this condition and was even now planning to gut it and install gilt in the Chinese fashion, a style fully as vulgar as—Eleanor's mouth quirked with humor—as vulgar as was adored by the Prince of Wales himself.

Bridgeport relaxed and returned to his stolid demeanor.

He watched her much too closely. Because he thought she was the duchess? Or because his master had so instructed him?

She removed her bonnet, stripped off her gloves, placed them in the dark bonnet, and handed them to the butler without a trace of outer trepidation. After all, what was the point of showing trepidation? It would merely be another proof that, although Eleanor had traveled across war-torn Europe as the duchess's companion, she hadn't acquired the verve and confidence that characterized Madeline's every move. This wasn't from lack of trials; the two women had faced trials aplenty. It was because— Eleanor sighed as she allowed the butler to take her cloak—Eleanor was born timid. She never remembered a time when her father's shouting hadn't paralyzed her with fright, or when her stepmother's narrow-eyed glare hadn't had the power to turn her into a bowl of quivering blancmange. Which is why Eleanor cultivated a serene facade—she might be a coward, but she saw no reason to announce the fact.

"If you would follow me, Your Grace, to the large drawing room, I will order refreshments," Bridgeport said. "You must be tired after your long journey."

"Not so long." Eleanor followed him through the tall door off to the left. "I stayed at the Red Robin Inn last night and spent only four hours on the road this morning."

The butler's impassivity slipped, and for a moment an expression of horror crossed his countenance. "Your Grace, if I might make a suggestion. When dealing with Mr. Knight, it's best not to tell him that you failed to obey his instructions with all speed."

Turning from her contemplation of the elegantly appointed room, she raised her eyebrows in haughty imitation of her cousin and gazed at the butler in a frigid silence.

It must have worked, for Bridgeport bowed. "Your pardon, Your Grace. I'll send for tea."

"Thank you," Eleanor said with composure. "And more substantial refreshments, also." For she suspected Mr. Knight intended to keep her waiting, and it had been five hours since breakfast.

Bridgeport left Eleanor to scrutinize her grandiose prison.

Tall windows let in the timid sunlight, and the candles washed the walls with a pleasant golden glow. Books lined one wall, reaching all the way to the twelve-foot ceiling, and the furniture was stylishly striped in an austere pattern of crimson and cream. The Oriental rug was crystal blue and crimson flowers on a cream background, and crimson roses nodded in the tall blue-and-white Oriental vases. The scent of leather bindings, fresh carnations, and oiled wood blended to create a familiar smell, a smell that seemed to Eleanor to be uniquely British. This room had been created to put a guest at ease.

Eleanor would not relax. Such a lack of vigilance could not be wise, and in truth, when she thought about meeting Mr. Knight, her stomach twisted into knots. But neither would she dance to Mr. Knight's tune. He no doubt imagined she would grow more anxious the longer she waited.

Well, she would, but he would never know.

With every appearance of airiness, she wandered to the bookshelves and examined the titles. She found the *Iliad* and the *Odyssey*, and sniffed in disdain. Mr. Knight was a barbarian from the Colonies and therefore unschooled. Probably the former owner had left the books. Or perhaps Mr. Knight had acquired the books so he could sniff the richness of their bindings.

Yet a worn title caught her eye, a book by Daniel Defoe. *Robinson Crusoe* was an old friend, and she reached up, trying to pull it down off the shelf just over her head. She couldn't quite touch the spine, and, glancing about, she found a library stool. Dragging it over, she took the long step up and in triumph retrieved the book.

This book had been read, and read again, for it fell easily to the page where Robinson found Friday. That was Eleanor's favorite part also, and she couldn't resist reading the first few lines. And the next few lines. And the next, and the next.

She didn't know what dragged her from the lonely island where Robinson survived and despaired. She heard nothing but experienced a sensation that prickled along her spine like a warm touch caressing her skin. Slowly, with the care of prey beneath a predator's survey, she turned her head— and met the gaze of the elegant gentleman lounging at the door.

In her travels, she had seen many a striking and charming man, but none had been as handsome as this—and all had been more charming. This man was a statue in stark black and white, hewn from rugged granite and adolescent dreams. His face wasn't really handsome; his nose was thin and crooked, his eyes heavy lidded, his cheekbones broad, stark and hollowed. But he wielded a quality of power, of toughness, that made Eleanor want to huddle into a shivering, cowardly little ball.

Then he smiled, and she caught her breath in awe.

His mouth . . . his glorious, sensual mouth. His lips were wide, too wide, and broad, too broad. His teeth were white, clean, strong as a wolf's. He looked like a man seldom amused by life, but he was amused by her, and she realized in a rush of mortification that she remained standing on the stool, reading one of his books and lost to the grave realities of her situation. The reality that stated she was an imposter, sent to mollify this man until the real duchess could arrive.

Mollify? Him? Not likely. Nothing would mollify him. Nothing except . . . well, whatever it was he wanted. And she wasn't fool enough to think she knew what that was.

The immediate reality was that she would somehow have to step down onto the floor and of necessity expose her ankles to his gaze. It wasn't as if he wouldn't look. He was looking now, observing her figure with an appreciation all the more impressive for its subtlety. His gaze flicked along her spine, along her backside, and down her legs with such concentration that she formed the impression he knew very well what she looked like clad only in her chemise—and that was an unnerving sensation.

Well. She couldn't keep staring at him. She snapped the book shut. In a tone she hoped sounded serene, she said, "Mr. Knight, I was indulging myself in your formidable library." *Very calm. Immensely civilized.* She waved a hand along the wall. "You have a great many titles." *Inane.*

Still he said nothing. He failed to respond to her conversational gambit by word or gesture.

His silence made her lift one shoulder defensively.

If he was trying to intimidate her, he was doing a first-rate job. Just when she was going to say something else—she didn't know what, but something that would crush this beast and his pretensions—he started forward.

At once she realized she had named him correctly. He was a beast. He moved like a panther on the prowl, all smooth and leggy—and he prowled toward her. The closer he got, the bigger he seemed, tall and broad at the shoulder. He seemed an element of nature, a rugged mountain, a powerful sea—or a beast, a huge, ruthless beast who kept his claws hidden until he chose to use them.

In a moment of panic, the imposter thought, *My God, Madeline, what have you let me in for?*

Then he was beside her. Eleanor looked down into his face, framed with hair so pale it looked like a halo around his rugged, tanned features, and wondered if he would use those claws on her now.

Slowly, he reached up and wrapped his big hands around her waist. The touch was like the heat of a fire after a long bout of winter. No man ever touched her. Certainly not a beast of such epic proportions, a man of ruthlessness who imagined he could buy his way into the tight-knit heights of English society. Yet he did touch her, pressing his hands into her flesh as if measuring her for fit, and from his expression, he found the fit acceptable. More than acceptable, enjoyable.

And she . . . her senses absorbed him with an eagerness that left her embarrassed and gratified. She found herself breathing carefully, as if too deep a breath would cause her to spontaneously combust.

The scent of him added to her discomfort. He smelled like . . . oh, like the crisp, still air at the top of the Alps. Like a cedar grove in Lebanon. Like a man who could give pleasure. . . . and how did she know that? She was as pure as the driven snow, and likely to stay that way to the end of her days.

Men did not wed twenty-four-year-old companions who had no dowry and no chance for one.

Tightening his grip, Mr. Knight lifted her off the stool.

Incredulous, Eleanor dropped the book. Grabbed for it. Almost overbalanced.

The book landed with a thud.

He tipped her body against his.

Reeling and operating totally by instinct, she clutched his shoulders. Shoulders immovable and strong as a boulder in a storm.

Slowly, gradually, he allowed her to slither down him, as if he were a slide and she an artless child. But she didn't feel like a child. She felt . . . she felt like a woman, confused, overwhelmed, driven by an absurd desire for a man whom she had never before seen. A man she knew to be a scoundrel of extraordinary audacity. She, who had been so careful to steer clear of those very emotions!

Just before her toes touched the floor he stopped her and gazed into her face.

His eyes, she saw, were a pale blue, like chips of frozen sky. They disconcerted her in their directness and lavishly complimented her without him ever saying a word.

She blushed. She knew how very well her fair skin showed color, and she must be positively crimson.

Embarrassed, intrigued, and in more danger than she'd ever faced in her life, she tried to think what the duchess would do in this instance. But the duchess, direct, brisk and managing, would never find herself in such an iniquitous position.

In the dark, smoky voice of a veteran seducer, he said, "Your Grace, welcome to my home." He let her slide down those last few inches and waited, as if to see if she would run away.

Instead, she stepped back with the self-possession of the real duchess.

His hands lingered on her waist before slipping away, and this time his voice contained a razor-sharp edge of menace. "I have looked forward to this day for a long, long time."

Chapter 2

*W*hatever confusion Eleanor had felt on seeing Mr. Knight dissipated. He despised her . . . no, Madeline . . . and Madeline hadn't given her instructions on how to handle him. Madeline had only said that they should switch places, that Eleanor should masquerade as the duchess, and that Eleanor should stall him until Madeline could arrive and straighten out this infernal mess her father, the duke, had created.

At the time, Eleanor had thought it a foolish idea. Now she knew it was, for she hadn't the slightest idea how to handle Mr. Knight.

Picking up the book, he looked at the title. *"Robinson Crusoe.* One of my favorite books, also. In fact, this is my copy." He ran his long finger down the leather spine. "It's good to know we have something in common."

She wanted nothing in common with this man.

And she worried that he knew it, for he observed her, a cool and handsome man with far too much poise.

Finally, she clasped her hands together at her waist, and by some effort of will managed not to nervously twist her fingers. "I don't believe that you've looked forward to meeting me for a long time. You didn't even know of my existence a month ago."

"But I did. I've known of your existence for over eight years, ever since my man of business returned to Boston from England and told me that the duke of Magnus had been blessed with a daughter. A most beautiful daughter." He placed the book back on the shelf, and he didn't need the stool. "My man of business did not exaggerate."

Disconcerted, Eleanor said, "Well . . . thank you." Although he was speaking of Madeline, he was looking at her. She knew, without conceit, that she was attractive. One less-than-honorable Englishman, who'd seen an opportunity to seduce a pretty girl, had told her she was more handsome than her cousin. But when Mr. Knight gazed at her, that tiny flame his touch had ignited spread through her veins.

That flame, and the attendant warmth, were bad things. *Very* bad things.

Then he took her arm, cupping her elbow and leading her inexorably toward the small sofa.

How did such a small contact make her feel that this man would sweep everything before him in his determination to possess her?

He seated her, and as he withdrew his hand, she was relieved—and worried. Because if Mr. Knight was as ruthless as she suspected, Madeline had no chance against him.

But Madeline had given Eleanor some advice. She had said, *Whenever you are in doubt, think, What would Madeline do in this situation? And do it.*

Madeline would attempt to take charge. So would Eleanor. "Why would you investigate my family?"

"Because I need a wife."

And there it was. The crux of the matter, the reason Madeline had determined to come to London. Because her father, the duke of Magnus, an inveterate gambler, careless and charming, had wagered Madeline's hand in marriage against Mr. Knight's fortune, and His Grace had lost.

"I imagine you were quite surprised when your father told you you were betrothed." Mr. Knight circled the sofa like a panther circling for the kill. "To me."

Eleanor weighed her words carefully. "I had not imagined a betrothal of any kind."

"Why not?" Mr. Knight purred like a huge cat as it toyed with its prey. "You're a wealthy young woman with an exalted title. Surely it must have occurred to you you would have to wed."

"The duchess does not *have* to wed," Eleanor said with an echo of Madeline's haughtiness. "She makes her own decisions."

"Not any more." That smile, the one that made him look like a dark angel, hovered on his lips. "The duchess has me to make those decisions for her."

No. No, this match would never do. This man

would make Madeline miserable with his cool assumption of authority and that scorn, which underlay his every word. And Madeline, Eleanor knew, loved another. Mr. Knight would not tolerate that misplaced affection lightly.

"I can imagine how you feel, coming into my house under such circumstances." Mr. Knight's gaze flicked about the room. "I had expected your father would travel with you."

"No, the duke is off on his own errands." Or so Eleanor suspected. And if those errands included gambling away the last precious remnant of his daughter's inheritance, what did he care? The duke of Magnus was a careless man, inconsiderate of his own daughter's health and well-being—and that was why Eleanor found herself here, in Mr. Knight's possession, pretending to be someone she was not.

Glancing up at the prowling Mr. Knight, she wanted to be anywhere but here. When she'd traveled the Continent with Madeline, she'd occasionally found herself in difficult situations. French soldiers had threatened them. Avalanches had almost sent them careening down the Alps. Worst of all, there had been that imprisonment in the harem in Turkey, surrounded by eunuchs and concubines and every sort of dissipation, while she'd wondered if they would ever escape. They had done better than that; Madeline had made so much trouble they'd been escorted out of the country.

But none of those situations had held the terrors that being here, alone, with Mr. Knight, held for Eleanor.

"Why . . . the duchess?" she asked. "Why this family, specifically? What were you thinking?"

"The future duchess has holdings all over Britain, and a great personal fortune. What was I thinking? I was thinking I would win her. I was thinking I would wed her. I would control her vast fortune and be the father of her large brood of children." Mr. Knight smiled, a slight upturn of his lips, but his eyes warmed not at all. "Who wouldn't covet the position of husband to one of England's richest women?"

He sounded absolutely reasonable, and of course men wanted to marry Madeline for just those reasons. But there was something about Mr. Knight . . . the glint in his eyes, the insolent way he stood, the faint half-smile . . . that made Eleanor think he was lying.

In a tone that ridiculed, he asked, "Yet I must ask why we're speaking of the duchess in third person, as if you aren't here."

She swallowed. Had she, in her ineptitude, divulged the truth already?

But if she had, he gave no real indication. At the rap on the door, he said, "I believe Bridgeport has brought our tea."

Followed by a maid, the butler walked in, as proper and unobtrusive as he had been before. He placed the tea tray before her.

"Thank you, Bridgeport," she murmured.

The maid placed a tray of cakes and sandwiches beside that.

"Thank you," Eleanor said again.

The girl was an adolescent, new and raw, and wanted to know what Mr. Knight's future bride looked like, so she ogled Eleanor as if she had never before seen an aristocrat. Eleanor had witnessed that kind of open examination before, but only toward Madeline. Eleanor had always before been hidden in the corner, the invisible companion.

Bridgeport was about to remonstrate when, with crushing authority, Mr. Knight said, "Milly, that will do."

The maid jumped, cast him a frightened glance, curtsied and scurried from the room.

Bridgeport bowed, then in ponderous steps left and shut the door behind them. Shut Eleanor in with Mr. Knight.

Eleanor's gaze lingered on the closed door. "You didn't need to frighten her."

He stood on the fringe of the carpet, a tall, broad gentleman who dominated the room without effort. "She was making you uncomfortable."

That startled Eleanor. Of course it was true, but how had he pierced her serene facade?

More important, why had he taken the trouble to do so?

"I take sugar, no cream," Mr. Knight advised.

Eleanor considered the plump china pot, decorated with porcelain blue flowers, a faint gasp of steam slipping from its spout. Two matching cups with their saucers had been placed on doilies beside the pot. The tray was everything that was civilized and normal. Furthermore, she poured tea on a regular basis. Madeline didn't care to, while Eleanor found comfort in the scent, the warmth, the routine.

But right now, with all of Mr. Knight's attention focused on her, the task became an ordeal. The pot seemed to weigh too much. The cup rattled in the saucer as she picked it up. She tilted the pot, aimed the spout toward the cup—

And in that same, smiling, deceptively pleasant voice, Mr. Knight said, "I like having a duchess wait on me."

Both of Eleanor's hands shook. The hot liquid splashed on her fingers. She dropped the cup. As she reached for it, it shattered against the table. A shard jabbed into her palm.

She yanked her hand back and closed her fingers.

In a rush, he came and knelt beside her. "Are you hurt? Did you burn yourself?"

"No, no, I'm fine." She wasn't fine. She was embarrassed. She cultivated the graceful moves of a lady for a reason. She hated making a spectacle of herself—and now her nerves had betrayed her. "Please, Mr. Knight, stand up."

For all the notice he took of her, she might not have spoken. Turning her hand to the light, he at once detected the slight cut beneath her little finger, oozing a sullen drop of scarlet blood. "You've cut yourself."

"Only a little." She tried to tug her hand back. "I was clumsy. I broke your beautiful cup."

"To hell with the cup." He pressed his finger lightly on the cut.

She winced.

"You're lucky. There's nothing in there." Lifting her hand to his mouth, he sucked the small wound.

Shocked, she stared at him. His head bent over

her hand, his chiseled features were intent, serious. His mouth was warm, wet, and the suction he used made her feel . . . odd. More animal than human, pain and intimacy mixing . . . never, ever had a man's mouth touched her on any part, in any way. How, after so short a time, with all the accoutrements of culture around her, had she come to such a pass in Mr. Knight's drawing room?

Glancing up, he caught her looking at him. "What? Do I scandalize you?"

Did he really not realize? Was she expected to explain the matter to him? But no. She couldn't do that. So she grasped at the least of his sins. "Hell."

His frozen blue eyes narrowed. "What?"

"You said *hell*. You said, 'To hell with the cup.' You're an American. You're ignorant. Here in England, one doesn't swear in mixed company."

He laughed. It wasn't a pleasant laugh. More of a snort or a bark, unwilling and involuntary. But it was genuine, and for the first time, his eyes warmed. "I shall teach you to swear."

"No, sir, you will not!" But she didn't know if she was replying to his words or his actions. "If you continue to curse in society, you'll find you're welcome in none of the best homes."

"There you're wrong." Pulling out his pristine white handkerchief, he wound it around her hand and tied it securely. "As long as I am well dressed, wealthy, and betrothed to the future duchess of Magnus, I'm welcome everywhere. Even sought after. I am, in fact, an original."

"Oh . . . no."

"You sound dismayed. Don't you want me to be acceptable?"

Naturally, she didn't want him to be acceptable, to know that the English hostesses were unable to see beneath the surface of his handsome features and wealth to the dangerous beast beneath. But she couldn't admit to such unkind contemplations, so without looking him in the eye, she said, "It's not that. It's that when the best hostesses pluck someone to be their new original, they can sometimes drop him as swiftly."

"I hold in my palm a guarantee they will not." Lifting her hand to his again, he pressed his lips to the back of her fingers.

This was awful! Awful that he flirted with her. Awful that she relished his attentions. "I wish you wouldn't . . . court me. It makes me uncomfortable."

Taking no notice of her appeal, he remained on his knees before her. In a voice both low and curious, he said, "You're not what I expected."

"No," she whispered. "I suppose I'm not."

Time seemed to slow and stretch. He observed her with intensity, as if she were a songbird he had trapped and would cage forever.

Yet she wasn't the duchess, she was a poor relation who lived in the shadow of her strong-willed cousin and was happy there.

His tone was seductive, his words prosaic. "I had my men bring your luggage in."

It took a moment for his words to sink in. Then, desperate to get away from him, she scooted back along the seat. "In? Here? Into your house?" He retained her hand, and because he did, it seemed as if she dragged him onto the sofa beside her.

Nothing was further from the truth, of course. She could never budge this man without his assent.

"Of course, into my house." He sounded mildly surprised.

"Why?" Merciful heavens, *why*? What was he expecting of her? Or, more precisely, what was he expecting to do to her?

"Where else would you stay?"

"I . . . we have a town house in Chesterfield Street."

"You misunderstand. Now that you're here, you cannot leave." He leaned close and whispered, "My future wife stays in my house—with me."

Chapter 3

Trapped.
Eleanor was trapped in this man's house. "I can't stay here." She shrank from Mr. Knight, from the visions he inspired. Visions of villainous seduction and of social banishment. And beneath it all, a desperate excitement, an excitement that she wouldn't admit to, but it was there nonetheless. If he came to her bedchamber in the dark of night, would she do the proper thing? Would she fight?

In a soft voice, she said, "I'm . . . unwed."

"For the moment." His words, his voice, his gaze made clear his intentions toward her—or rather, toward his bride. He intended their marriage to be not one of convenience but one created of passion and tangled emotions. "We *will* be wed. That I promise you."

If she believed that, she wouldn't fight his seduction at all.

Her mouth dropped open at her own lascivious notion.

His eyebrows veed in a demonic scowl. "You look stunned. Surely you knew I would wed you, regardless of any obstacle."

"It's not that." *It's so much worse.* In the clear, careful tone of a teacher explaining fractions to an eight-year-old, she said, "I don't know how matters are handled in America, but in England, if I stay here with you, my reputation will be ruined regardless of your future intention."

"If you stayed here alone, more than your reputation would be ruined." His gaze dropped to her lips, her breasts, and lingered.

Eleanor knew very well her traveling clothes were dark, sturdy and covered every inch of skin up to her throat, but his scrutiny made her want to check her buttons to see if they'd somehow disappeared. Her breasts swelled, and her nipples pressed against her bodice. It was an odd sensation, breathtaking in its boldness, and proved without a doubt she must banish her meekness and demand her freedom! Instead, she could only falter, "You mean . . . you would . . . ."

"Sneak into your bedroom in the dark of night and seduce you? Yes, my darling girl, without a qualm."

She didn't want him holding her hand anymore. Her palms were sweaty.

"That's why I brought you a chaperon." Leaning over, he rang a bell sitting on the table.

Torn between relief and misery, she asked, "A

chaperon? Are you mad? There isn't a chaperon in the world respectable enough to protect my reputation while I live here."

From the doorway, a merry, feminine voice proclaimed, "My dear niece, of course there is."

Eleanor swiveled and gaped.

"And here I am!" The lady in the doorway stood with arms out to embrace the room. She was short and plump, dressed in a gown of modish lavender, which gave a sheen to her swirl of white hair. "My first advice to you, dear Madeline, is that you not hold hands with Mr. Knight while you're alone in a room with him. In fact, until you're married, I would not recommend that you be alone in a room with him at all, for I believe he is a scoundrel of unparalleled guile."

Eleanor closed her fist over the handkerchief that bound her palm, and she rose slowly to her feet. "Lady . . . Gertrude?"

Lady Gertrude bustled in, and in her own indefatigable way, burbled, "You remember! It has been too long."

It had been longer than she realized, for Lady Gertrude, the countess of Glasser, was the sister of Madeline's mother, and not related to Eleanor at all. Not that the dear lady had refused Eleanor her affection on the rare times they'd met. Quite the contrary. Lady Gertrude's kind heart had embraced Eleanor as surely as it did her own niece.

But now Lady Gertrude would destroy this masquerade before it had even started.

As Lady Gertrude swept forward to embrace the duchess, Remington watched them.

So this was Madeline de Lacy, the marchioness of Sherbourne and the future duchess of Magnus. From his observation so far, she was not the typical English noblewoman. He had been prepared to break her, like a spirited horse who had never worn saddle or bridle. Instead, when he looked at her, he saw a diffident woman without any sense of her own consequence. Her face was gently rounded, with dimples in her cheeks, an indent in her chin, and full, supple lips. She swept her black hair into an unfashionable roll at the back of her head, and if he knew his women—and he did—when unpinned it would reach to her waist with a natural wave that made a man want to coil his fingers in the living strands. Her body was bound in dark, unsightly clothes, but that camouflage couldn't conceal a generous bosom, and when he had wrapped his fingers around her waist, he had discovered how narrow that waist was, and beneath that, the graceful flare of her hips.

He looked down at his hands and smiled. The feel of her had burned through her petticoats to his flesh, and he thought—no, he knew—the same flame had licked at her, for she'd examined him as if he were wild and unruly.

Ah, if she knew how cold and deliberate his actions, how important she was to his plans, she would be more than wary, she would be frightened. But of course she didn't, nor would he let her know. Not until it was too late for her family—and for her.

She was *his*. His duchess.

Lady Gertrude had portrayed the relationship between her and her niece as warm, and he thought it must be, for Lady Gertrude was pleasant, kind, and she knew everyone in English society.

Yet his duchess looked aghast to see her aunt.

"Dear child, I'm so happy that you've returned from the Continent at last. With that dreadful Napoleon marching around, and all his disgraceful soldiers imprisoning good English citizens, I was worried about you and"—Lady Gertrude looked up at his duchess, and her eyebrows rose—"Eleanor . . ."

Eleanor glanced over the top of Lady Gertrude's head at Remington, and he clearly saw her swallow. In a rush of words, she said, "Eleanor stayed behind this time. She's quite fatigued from the journey."

"Well! Of course. She must be." Lady Gertrude sounded brisk—and amused. "Who wouldn't be fatigued after four years traipsing across every country in Europe? But Eleanor's absence makes it an especially good thing Mr. Knight requested I chaperon you." Lady Gertrude leaned up and patted his cheek. "Dear boy."

The amazing thing was—she meant it. She was kindliness personified, and in the five days of his acquaintance, he had developed an affection for Lady Gertrude. She had that way with people. Everybody liked her, even those who found themselves on the wrong side of her very frank tongue—as he had. She might have consented to be the young lady's chaperon, she might now be pleasant and caring, but on their first meeting she had made her opinion of this match clear.

In return, he had made his indifference to her opinion clear, and so they'd come to neutral ground, with Lady Gertrude agreeing that she wouldn't interfere with his marriage plans as long as he abided by the rules of her chaperonage.

Seating herself on the sofa, Lady Gertrude tugged Eleanor down beside her. "What an extraordinary event has brought you to this moment, eh? What do you think about the duke of Magnus and his latest folly?"

On that subject, his duchess spoke decisively. "I think it's a shame he can't control his urge to gamble long enough to think of his only daughter."

The flash of her eyes startled Remington. "Am I so bad a match, then?" he asked, and waited with bated breath and ill-concealed humor to hear her thoughts on his self.

Still in that tart tone, his duchess said, "I don't know, Mr. Knight, I know nothing about your character. But while perhaps few young women in this day are allowed to wed whom they wish, all at least meet their future husbands before the betrothal is announced. It's a shame that a duchess is denied that privilege."

"Exactly my notion! Your sentiments do you honor, dear." Lady Gertrude shot Remington a glance. "I thought that Mr. Knight was a victim of his own urge to gamble, also, but now that I've met him, I suspect he knew exactly what he was doing when he won my niece in a game."

Remington lifted his eyebrows in supercilious innocence.

Lady Gertrude concluded, "He's a dear boy, and a good match."

"For whom?" his duchess snapped.

Then he would have sworn she bit her tongue. "For you," he answered. "Only for you."

"Sit down, dear boy," Lady Gertrude said. "You make me nervous, looming about like a great, leggy brute."

Reflecting he had never been called a great, leggy brute before, he sat on a chair that placed him so he could best view his bride.

Touching the side of the teapot, Lady Gertrude said, "I was hoping for a spot of tea, but it's cold." She frowned at the shards scattered on the table and the floor. "Did you break a cup?"

Madeline blushed a miserable red, and hid her injured hand beneath her skirt. "I did."

Lady Gertrude blinked. "That's so unlike you! Or at least as I remember you. Ah, well, no use crying over a few pieces of porcelain. Will you ring for more hot water?"

"With your permission, Mr. Knight," Madeline murmured, lifting the bell.

He gestured his acquiescence. "Please. I want you to think of this house as your home now."

"I . . . I can't . . . that's not possible. I must return home!"

He bent his gaze, impressing his will on her. "If I have my way, you'll never return to your father's house."

She turned her head away, rejecting him with every movement.

That was fine. He liked a challenge, and this duchess, with her modesty and shyness, tested him. He watched as she rang just loudly enough to bring a footman running. He watched, too, as she spoke to the footman firmly but quietly, like a woman who had been trained to get results without calling attention to herself.

He crossed his legs. "Would you ladies be so kind as to enlighten me how Her Grace has so exalted a title when she's as yet unmarried?"

"Because of Her Majesty, Queen Elizabeth," Lady Gertrude said, as if that clarified everything.

He waited, but when nothing more was forthcoming, he said, "I find that so simple an explanation eludes me."

"Probably because you're an American. Not that I have anything against Americans. No, not at all. I find them refreshing, with their odd way of speaking and their open manners." Lady Gertrude lifted her lorgnette and peered at him. "Although holding my dear niece's hand while unchaperoned is a little *too* open, may I tell you!"

"Yes, ma'am." It was too open in America, also, but he had no intention of admitting that, or that he always pushed every matter as quickly as he could toward its natural conclusion—and that conclusion was always predetermined by himself. He was not a man who allowed fate to take its winding path to God-knew-what destination. He shaped his own destiny—and now he shaped this young duchess's, too.

"One of my ancestors was lady-in-waiting to Queen Elizabeth, and she saved Her Majesty's life. In gratitude, Her Majesty granted a dukedom to the lady, one which of course always comes to the eldest son, if there was one—but if a daughter is the first-born, then the title falls to her." Madeline spoke slowly, choosing her words as if she considered every syllable, and her voice sounded like . . . like heartbreak.

And what had the future duchess of Magnus to be heartbroken about? She was born to privilege and wealth, and he'd learned only too well the way English aristocrats dealt with those they considered to be their inferiors. Nothing got in their way. No ethics held them back. They thought nothing of ruin . . . or murder.

Yet he would get his revenge, and in the end poor Madeline would know the true meaning of heartbreak.

He allowed none of his thoughts to appear on his face. In a properly respectful tone, he asked, "Such a title is very rare, is it not?"

"My family is the only one to be so blessed," Madeline answered. "But no one could gainsay the will of Queen Elizabeth."

"A strong woman," he said. Not like this meek, impressionable girl.

Oddly, she shot him a hurt glance. He would almost have thought she'd read his mind.

So, although it felt a little like kicking a puppy, he pressed his advantage. "As long as your father's alive, you aren't yet the duchess. All that deference isn't truly warranted, is it?"

In an oppressive tone, Lady Gertrude said, "My niece is the marchioness of Sherbourne and the future duchess, a position that warrants great respect among the ton. She is, in fact, frequently called Her Grace, and given all the privileges of her future rank."

He had been soundly rebuked, and he bowed his head in recognition of a worthy adversary.

"Whether or not he gives me the respect due to a duchess is of no importance," Madeline said with a flick of scorn. "Americans are not impressed with the aristocracy, or so they claim. One hopes, however, Mr. Knight behaves with suitable courtesy to other women he encounters—in all walks of life."

Yes, Lady Gertrude had rebuked him, but it was the contempt from his future wife that stung. "I'll do my best not to embarrass you."

"Do your best not to embarrass yourself," she said with icy composure. "Now here is Bridgeport with our tea."

The butler entered with a clean tea tray, a new pot of tea, and the maid, who carried a fresh platter of biscuits and cakes. This time Milly didn't make the mistake of staring at the duchess, but with a nervous glance at Remington, quickly deposited the platter and departed.

Madeline considered him reproachfully.

What had she expected him to do? Allow a little chit of a maid to stare? Sometimes, he didn't understand women.

But worse, sometimes he did.

She picked up the pot, and this time her hand was quite steady. She poured for him, for Lady Gertrude, and for herself.

When she was finished, Lady Gertrude indicated the handkerchief still wrapped around Madeline's palm. "What have you done?"

"A small injury," Madeline said. "Nothing more."

Rising, he came as if to get his tea. Instead, he took

her hand in his, unwrapped it, and examined the mark. "You should be careful in my house. There are dangers here, and I don't want you hurt."

Her gaze flew to his. Her lips parted, and again she looked properly anxious.

What a dichotomy she was! She seemed timid until he spoke derisively of her title, and then she spoke in an icy ferocity. A few minutes later, with a few words artfully couched to sound like a threat, he once again reduced her to diffidence.

If he was not careful, this woman would fascinate him.

Taking his cup, he returned to his chair. "On Lady Gertrude's advice, I have accepted invitations on our behalf to a number of parties."

Madeline sat up straight, and her hand went to her throat. "You didn't!"

So. At last she showed the snooty behavior he'd expected. She didn't want to be seen in public with him. He stirred his tea. "No doubt you object because you didn't bring the proper clothing."

Taking a relieved breath, she grasped onto the lifeline he had thrown her. "Yes! That's why!"

Coolly, he yanked it from her hands. "I have a seamstress waiting to fit you into the gowns worthy of my wife."

"You can't . . . I can't . . . that wouldn't be proper." She turned to Lady Gertrude. "Would it, ma'am?"

Lady Gertrude frowned at him. "You didn't tell me you had taken the liberty of getting Madeline clothes."

"I thought you would object, and I find it easier to ask forgiveness than beg permission." An explanation that covered many sins. "For the next few nights, we'll be attending parties all over London, being introduced as the duchess and her most devoted fiancé."

"Oh." Madeline scarcely breathed the word.

He could have sworn this new development horrified her more than any of the rest of the shocks that had come before. How much he would enjoy dragging the little snob about on his arm, forcing her to face London's hostesses with a smile.

But this week held more and bigger shocks for her—starting now. "Then, three nights hence, we'll be hosting our own party right here. The invitations have gone out. The acceptances are pouring in."

"A party. Here." Her dark lashes fluttered as she tried to maintain eye contact. "Why . . . why is that necessary?"

He seldom smiled, but he smiled now, and with a great deal of charm. "We must have a party. We must celebrate our betrothal—and our upcoming nuptials. And on that night, I will present you with your betrothal ring, and place it on your finger. As a symbol of our eternal love, never will you remove it—until your death."

Chapter 4

*E*leanor stared in frustration at the flint she usu-ally handled with such dexterity. She snapped it again, but no spark appeared. "This stupid thing must be broken," she said aloud, talking to the empty room, trying to convince herself.

Of course, she knew that wasn't true. The onset of evening deepened the shadows that lurked in the corners of the luxurious bedchamber Mr. Knight had assigned her, but her fingers trembled too much to successfully light even one of the candles. She tried again to ignite the wick. A spark sprang from the flint, but the candle remained stubbornly dark. "It's the wick. The wick must be damp."

A knock sounded, the door swung open, and Lady Gertrude stuck her head in. "Dear girl, may I enter?"

Eleanor jumped in alarm, then stared wildly at

Lady Gertrude's kindly face. "Yes! Please! Do!" She didn't know when she had started speaking so emphatically, but she would wager it was soon after she'd laid eyes on the inscrutable Mr. Knight. She looked over Lady Gertrude's shoulder, half-expecting him to be there, lounging in the corridor and waiting for his turn to enter . . . which, if she had her way, would never happen.

Unfortunately, since she'd arrived in this household, she'd not had her way even once.

"I hope I'm not interrupting your unpacking." Lady Gertrude seated herself on one of the elegant chairs near the fireplace. She was so petite that her feet dangled, and she pressed her toes to the floor to stay in her chair. "I understand you didn't bring a maid. So unlike you, dear Madeline! When I knew you, you were unable to mend a seam or fix your hair. You depended on Eleanor for everything!" Lifting her lorgnette, she examined Eleanor. "Of course, that's the Madeline I remember. Probably you're quite different after the rigors of travel in such difficult circumstances."

Eleanor stared at her and wondered what to say. How much to say. Lady Gertrude was a kindly woman with a delightful sense of mischief, but this trick Eleanor and Madeline had perpetrated could only be called ramshackle.

Lady Gertrude prattled on. "I must tell you why I accepted this position of chaperon when you must be dreadfully unhappy about the betrothal to Mr. Knight. I always said your father could make a cake of himself better than any man I ever met . . . excuse me, dear, I know you're fond of him, but if he didn't have his ducal title, people would call him a fool to his face. Not that he would take offense, he's too amiable by half, but nevertheless . . . I say, this is quite a lovely room. Mine is beautiful, too, but not nearly so elegant."

Eleanor peered around. "It's grand," she said flatly. Sky blue walls and midnight blue drapes presented a sense of the outdoors, and the abundance of fresh flowers on every surface gave the room a fresh, country scent. The rug was rich with amber and azure hues mixed in a Persian's graceful pattern. The furnishings were delicate, ladylike, and airy . . . yet she added, "It's oppressive."

"It's dark, certainly. Why don't you ring for a maid to light the candles and make up the fire?"

Eleanor stared at Lady Gertrude. Of course. Ring for a maid. For someone who had done everything for herself and the duchess for eight years, using a maid for such a simple task was unprecedented. Eleanor hurried to the bellpull and gave it a yank. "An excellent idea. Thank you, Lady Gertrude." Faintly she heard a jingle beyond the door.

Almost at once, a sturdy young girl appeared and, with a curtsy, proceeded to efficiently use the recalcitrant flint. "I'm Beth, Yer Grace, the upstairs maid, an' Mr. Knight says I'm t' serve yer every need. If ye need anything, anything at all, please let me know."

"Thank you." Eleanor hoped she didn't need another thing ever. She hated being waited on. Most of all, she hated being called Your Grace.

But Lady Gertrude broke into the conversation. "Her Grace seems to have left her lady's maid behind. Do any of the girls below stairs have training in clothes and hair?"

Beth broke into a wide grin. "Aye, ma'am. I 'ave. I'm good with an iron an' never put 'oles in the silk stockings. Best o' all, I can cut and arrange 'air in the newest styles. I coiffed Lady Fairchild's 'air until she went lunatic and 'ad t' go t' Bedlam."

Lady Gertrude tapped her cheek as she thought. "Lady Fairchild was well turned out." She looked Eleanor over with a critical eye. "And, my dear, your hairstyle could be freshened."

Eleanor touched the severe bun at the base of her neck and brushed her fingers around the wings of hair that framed her face. "I like this." This coiffure was proper for a companion, and regardless of what anyone in this house thought, a companion was what she would always be.

"But if I trimmed it a little around the face." Beth made a clipping gesture with her fingers. "The color's so grand, an' tis so thick."

"Yes." Lady Gertrude stroked her chin. "A cut would give you a whole new look."

"Not that ye need one," Beth added hastily. "But every lady likes a change now and then."

"I don't," Eleanor said.

"Think about it," Lady Gertrude urged.

"Why did Lady Fairchild go insane?" Eleanor couldn't help asking. Had Lady Fairchild been trapped in such a crazy situation, too? Had she perhaps been exposed to Mr. Knight?

"All of the Fairchilds are insane one way or the other," Lady Gertrude said.

The maid made a humming noise that sounded like agreement.

"Very well, Beth, you can wait on Her Grace." Lady Gertrude gestured the girl out the door, and when she had gone, Lady Gertrude said to Eleanor, "The Fairchilds' family tree doesn't split, you know. Now, where were we? I remember. I was going to explain why I took the position as your chaperon."

"You don't have to explain yourself to me," Eleanor said, and wondered, should she admit her true identity to Lady Gertrude? Or should Eleanor have faith that Madeline would appear at any moment and make confession unnecessary?

"How very unlike you, Madeline! You've always been so properly aware of your position and your title. Even as a child, you understood your importance and demanded clarification for the least of matters." Lady Gertrude slid down on the hard cushion until her toes touched flat on the floor, then sighed and used her arms to scoot back up.

"Here, ma'am." Eleanor brought a stool and placed it beneath her feet. "That will help."

Lady Gertrude brightened. "Thank you, dear. How kind of you to notice. Such a tribulation to be short. One wants to saw the legs off of all the chairs."

"I can imagine." Actually, she couldn't. Eleanor hadn't been so petite since she was eleven.

"I must explain myself and my position to you, and besides, you'll want to know what happened to your uncle. Uncle Brinkley, remember him?"

"No." Eleanor had never seen Lady Gertrude's husband. He had a nasty reputation for arrogance and womanizing, and he did not deign to visit the family even for Christmas.

"Well, he died."

Startled by that blunt declaration, Eleanor halted in the process of seating herself. "I'm sorry."

"Don't be. He was shot in Lady Bertelot-Stoke's bed by Lord Bertelot-Stoke, although why his lordship took exception about Brinkley when so many others had usurped his place, I will never know. At any rate, Brinkley left me in penury. Dreadful place. Worse than Cornwall. So I've spent the last two years living in genteel poverty. Mr. Knight's offer came at just the right time. I was about to get a"—Lady Gertrude glanced around as if fearing listeners—"job."

Eleanor covered up her half-hysterical laugh with a fit of coughing. "Heaven forefend."

"Exactly, since I have no skills except needlework and gossip."

Eleanor picked up her own needlework and stared at it. Needlework was her cure for worry, for idleness, for any kind of problems. Any time she faced a dilemma, she worked on a pattern of flowers, and eventually the solution presented itself.

She didn't think a solution to her current dilemma was going to present itself.

Lady Gertrude continued, "At any rate, Mr. Knight is paying me well, providing me with a clothes allowance, and I am to lend your presence here countenance."

Without the supervision of the girl's parents? Impossible! Eleanor picked up her needle and in the politest tone possible, said, "I apologize, Lady

Gertrude, but betrothed or not, the fact Mr. Knight and I are living in the same house is going to cause talk."

"And I will crush it. I am not without influence, you know. My bedchamber is right next to yours." Lady Gertrude gestured at a hitherto-unseen door. "Our rooms connect. Also, I made Remington move upstairs. Until your wedding day, when he may move his things back into the master's suite, he is banished from this floor. I take my responsibilities seriously. Your person is completely safe."

"I'm glad to know you'll be sleeping so close." Eleanor was, for otherwise she hadn't a doubt Mr. Knight would ensure the marriage in a most physical way. The man, for all his elegant clothing, was a primitive to his bones.

Leaning forward, Lady Gertrude lowered her voice. "Although I must warn you, my dear, I believe Remington has underlying reasons for his deeds, especially concerning you."

To hear her own suspicions echoed by Lady Gertrude sent a chill up Eleanor's spine. "I believe you're right."

In a salubrious tone, Lady Gertrude added, "Furthermore, I fear they may be shady."

Eleanor wanted to be sarcastic about the obviousness of that observation, but Lady Gertrude nodded so earnestly and seemed so serious that Eleanor could only say, "I'll be careful."

"I know you will, Madeline. You were always such a forthright and levelheaded girl, running your estates and trying to keep your father from running amok, and you should continue to be sensible with

Mr. Knight. I'm convinced that's the way to handle him, with a firm hand and strong convictions!"

"I have the very strong conviction I shouldn't go to any society events with him." Because, despite the years that she and Madeline had been gone and their strong resemblance, surely someone would recognize that Eleanor was not the duchess. Even if Eleanor successfully made her way through those dangerous waters, when Madeline did appear, it would be obvious they had made a monkey of Mr. Knight. That, Eleanor was convinced, would be a bad idea. He would wreak a terrible vengeance.

Lady Gertrude shifted uncomfortably in the chair. "I don't see that you have a choice, dear. He isn't touchy about his consequence, he has too much self-worth for that, but he would take your refusal badly." Fretfully, she said, "I don't know what you were thinking when you came here alone."

Eleanor had hoped, had prayed, that Lady Gertrude would realize the switch she and Madeline had pulled, but apparently she had not. And she had to be told. Surely *she* would know what to do. Taking a quivering breath, Eleanor made the plunge. "I have something to confess."

Lady Gertrude held up her wrinkled hand. "Don't!"

Startled, Eleanor stammered, "Wh . . . what?"

"I've pledged to keep Remington informed of everything about you, and you must admit that's what a proper chaperon should do."

"If he were my guardian!"

"He's worse than that. He is your future husband. He holds you in the palm of his hand. He can control you, he can discipline you, he can clutch your purse strings so tightly you go to bed hungry or rob you of your inheritance." Clearly, Lady Gertrude was remembering her own circumstances. Considering her own well-being.

But more than that . . . she knew. Eleanor saw the truth now. Lady Gertrude's frown, her emphatic refusal, her reasons—all pointed to the fact that she knew!

And she couldn't—or wouldn't—help Eleanor.

In a kind but firm tone, Lady Gertrude said, "Mr. Knight is my employer, the man who pays my wages. I owe him my loyalty. So please—if you have secrets, keep them to yourself."

Chapter 5

$\mathcal{T}$he dining room was the perfect example of pretentiousness, with a long, polished table, a celadon Chinese salt cellar and stately paintings that marched along one wall. Eleanor would have hated eating in that echoing chamber, and she would have taken secret pleasure in laughing at Mr. Knight's posturing.

Unfortunately he, Lady Gertrude, and Eleanor dined in a small antechamber. The round table was not crowded, and at the same time seated them at a comfortable distance. The polished wood paneling reflected the candles' warm glow, the heavy drapes kept the draughts at bay, and most important, the room sat nearer to the kitchen stairs, so their food arrived piping hot.

The silverware clinked, the silence loomed, and

Lady Gertrude made a valiant attempt to break it. "What are our plans for tomorrow, Mr. Knight?"

"Tomorrow I'll be at the bank, making some transactions." He bowed his head to Eleanor. "I beg your pardon, but since I've arrived from America, such business is sometimes unavoidable."

"It's fine," Eleanor mumbled. "I don't mind."

"How good of you." Beneath his polite words, he obviously didn't give a damn.

Mr. Knight dominated the room with his size, but more important, with his presence. He continued, "Tomorrow night, we have an invitation to go to Lord and Lady Picard's ball. I understand it's the grandest of the Season."

"So it is, Mr. Knight." Lady Gertrude clasped her hands. "I can't wait. I haven't been for over three years."

"I'm glad you're pleased." Again he bowed his head, this time to Lady Gertrude, and waited as if to hear Eleanor heap praise upon him.

She couldn't. She wasn't pleased. She was dismayed. The grandest ball of the Season, and she had to go as the duchess? She wanted to cover her face with her hands. Whether she was recognized as an imposter or not, she would be the center of attention. She would be trembling and fearful all evening.

As she was now. She couldn't even lift her spoon to her mouth for fear of drenching herself with clear oxtail soup.

She had to discover a way out of this house. She had to escape.

Once again, the silence stretched on until the footman removed the soup and replaced it with the seafood course.

Lady Gertrude said, "Mr. Knight, your cook is excellent! I can't remember when I've enjoyed such fine dining as I've had in this last week." She turned to Eleanor with an expression that demanded a reply. "Don't you agree, dear?"

"Yes, I especially liked the, ah, the soup." Eleanor's voice trailed off. After all, that had been the first and only course. *Think of something else to say. Anything else. The weather.* "Do you think the fog will last until morning?" *Not that.*

"This is London, so yes," Mr. Knight said. "If we were in Boston, I would say I smelled a storm brewing. But I fear my senses can't be trusted in this new land."

Eleanor sneaked a glance at his harsh and handsome features. No matter how much she wanted to dislike his presumption and his arrogance, she found herself drawn to him. She would have noticed him if he'd been courting Madeline, and quivered over the most careless glance. But with all his attention focused on her in the belief she was Madeline, her mind was a blank. She couldn't taste her food. She could only see and smell and crave to taste Mr. Knight.

"I'm sure your senses are fine," Eleanor said.

Both Mr. Knight and Lady Gertrude turned to look at her.

Eleanor stared down at her plate, where the cold, dressed crab waved its claws at her, and she thought that it, too, gawked at her from its beady little pep-

percorn eyes and wondered at her incredible trite-
ness. Then she thought about what she'd said, and
she slumped in her seat. *His senses?* She had commented on his senses?

In a deep, controlled voice, which, she feared,
masked his amusement, he said, "I trust your bedchamber is to your liking."

He wasn't supposed to be talking about her bedchamber. He was her . . . Madeline's . . . betrothed!
Those who weren't married didn't mention bed-
chambers or beds or anything of a personal nature.

Yet he was her host. It was proper he should ask.
"Yes, it's lovely. It . . ." Eleanor realized she was being conciliatory when she should be taking a stand.
As Madeline had said, *Whenever you are in doubt,
think, What would Madeline do in this situation? And do
it.* Straightening up, Eleanor stared forbiddingly at
Mr. Knight. "It's in the wrong house, however. I
should be in my father's home in Chesterfield
Street."

He stared back, waiting . . . waiting. The silence
stretched out, long and dreadful.

As he must have known she would, she began to
crumple. "That is, I liked the colors. The chimney
draws well. It's clean. It's . . . it's very clean. I do like
it." Eleanor had warned Madeline that she was unable to talk to men. Eleanor had warned Madeline
she was timid and easily cowed.

As if there were nothing at all unusual about this
conversation, he asked, "And the upstairs maid?
What's her name?"

"Beth. Her name is Beth."

"She came to us with impeccable references. I hope you'll feel free to take her as your lady's maid."

"Yes, I . . . did." Eleanor stared at his hands as he expertly lifted the red-tinged crabmeat from its shell. His palms were broad and strong, his fingers long, his nails perfectly manicured. She liked his hands. She wished she didn't. She wished she were as indifferent as she had always been with every other man. But there was something about Mr. Knight that made her notice him. Demanded that she notice him.

"I hope she proves satisfactory. If she doesn't, please tell me at once and I'll rectify the matter."

"I wouldn't want to trouble you." Eleanor's voice dropped lower with each word she uttered.

"You're going to be my wife. Nothing I do for you is *trouble.*" He looked sincere. He sounded sincere. And for a woman whose early life had been bound by neglect and malice, that sincerity was seduction in itself. "It is simply the kind of assistance you may rely on for the rest of your life."

Did that sound ominous to anyone else? Eleanor cast a glance at Lady Gertrude.

But she was smiling and nodding. "Your sentiments do you honor, Mr. Knight. So few men remember that their wives should be coddled and cared for. The poor helpless male creatures prefer to think it should be the other way about."

He was the type of man whom other men liked for his skills and abhorred for his authority—and his appeal to women. "My wife will be as pampered as a princess in an ivory tower."

"It's cold in an ivory tower," Eleanor murmured.

"But a duchess lives in an ivory tower from the day she's born. She always has someone to take care of her. A husband is required to do only one thing— to watch over her with consideration." Mr. Knight took a sip of his wine and settled back in his chair to allow the footman to remove the crab and replace it with lamb cutlets and French beans. "Oh, and ivory towers are good for one other thing. When a wife's in her tower, her husband knows her location."

"That smacks of imprisonment," Lady Gertrude said good-humoredly. "I'm sure you don't mean that."

But as he gazed at Eleanor, she thought his expression most peculiar, like a miser's when he was gloating over his gold.

Nor did he address Lady Gertrude's comment. Instead he poured them all a new, ruby wine to go with the meat. "Your Grace, I've settled the problem with your groom."

This time, Eleanor had the good sense not to glance around for Madeline. "Dickie Driscoll?" She'd forgotten about Dickie. Clearheaded, steadfast, and good with horses, forty-year-old Scotsman Dickie Driscoll had been Madeline's groom for as many years as Eleanor could remember. He had traveled the length and breadth of Europe with them, getting them out of scrapes, protecting them from rifle-wielding bandits, and proving himself a rock of loyalty and integrity. "There's a problem with him?"

"Dickie Driscoll objected to leaving you in my custody, so I sent the coachman and footmen and the travel coach back to your father's house, and Dickie is putting up in a room over the stable."

Dickie was here in Berkley Square. He hadn't abandoned her! She was not so alone as she imagined.

"What an expression of relief, my dear fiancée. However did you make your way through London society with such a revealing face? Not that I object, you understand." Leaning toward her, Mr. Knight smiled with the kind of intimate bewitchment that made her swallow to relieve her suddenly dry mouth. "When a woman is as beautiful as you are, she's usually adept at hiding her emotions. With you, I'll always know what gives you pleasure, and strive always to do as you wish."

Eleanor heard a voice in her head, whimpering, *Oh, Madeline, what did you get me into?* It was Eleanor's own voice, of course. When her cousin had suggested this mad scheme, for good reasons, of course, Eleanor had warned that Mr. Knight might try to flirt with the woman he considered his future wife. Well, Eleanor had been right on that account, and so she would tell her cousin when next they met.

But that wouldn't be, couldn't be soon enough, for tonight Eleanor would have to sleep in Mr. Knight's house, in one of his beds, and know that one floor up, he was there, thinking of her. . . . She realized he was talking, and she jerked her attention back to the dining room.

His smile had disappeared, and he watched her as if he really could read her mind. "Since you arrived this afternoon, I've been waiting for you to try and explain to me that it would be ridiculous for us to wed."

Eleanor didn't know what he was intimating, but by his expression she knew she wouldn't like this. "I beg your pardon, sir?"

Even Lady Gertrude looked confused. "Whatever are you talking about, Mr. Knight?"

"According to my source, those were the exact words you used on the morning when your father told you he had wagered you and lost you. You said, *I shall go to London and explain to Mr. Knight it would be ridiculous for us to wed.*" Mr. Knight covered Eleanor's hand with his. "Isn't that right, dear girl?"

Beneath his palm, Eleanor's hand curled into a fist. "Are you saying that someone *told* you I had said that?"

"Indeed. Just as someone told me your father blustered that he had a solution to the problem of marrying me, but you assured him you could handle me. You collected your steadfast companion and cousin, Miss Eleanor de Lacy, and after a late start, stayed last night at the Red Robin Inn rather than continue on your way . . . to me."

In horror, Eleanor pulled her hand free. He had repeated the turn of events for the last two days exactly as they had happened. "Sir, I don't understand."

Relentlessly, he continued, "A respectable inn, but rather rough with the men Mr. Rumbelow hired for his house party, wasn't it?" Mr. Knight asked, but it was obvious he knew the answer. "You ate dinner with a Lady Tabard and her daughter Thomasin, got a good night's sleep, and this morning dispatched "

your companion to Mr. Rumbelow's gaming party—
I didn't quite comprehend the reason why, but I
thought perhaps it had to do with your father's insa-
tiable gambling?" Lifting his eyebrows, Mr. Knight
waited for an answer. When she returned none, he
continued, "Perhaps you can enlighten me later. But
you hurried forthwith to London and my house on
Berkley Square."

"You have been watching me," Eleanor breathed.
He knew everything—except the one most important thing. He didn't realize the cousins had changed
identities.

"I've been having you watched," he corrected.
"As much as I would like to do it all myself, I fear I
must occasionally labor for a living." He put his finger to his lips in a mocking signal for silence. "But
don't tell the ton."

When Eleanor had time, she would feel sorry for
Madeline for imagining she could manipulate this
man, but at the moment, all of Eleanor's pity cen-
tered on herself. She was in a mess that grew bigger
and more complicated every moment. "Why would
you spy on me?"

"Have some wine, Your Grace, you're looking a
little pale." He waited until Eleanor had raised her
shaking glass to her lips and sipped.

Lady Gertrude did not sip her wine; she swallowed in great gulps, for she looked a little pale,
also. "Yes, Mr. Knight, why would you have Madeline watched?"

"With all apologies to you, Lady Gertrude, I'm
afraid I've found the treachery and arrogance of the
English aristocracy to be monumental." As he

turned to Eleanor, the ice in his eyes made his blue eyes paler and more menacing. "Your Grace, I don't trust you not to betray me. Before you try, I wanted you to know—it is impossible. I know your every movement. Soon I will know your every thought— even before you think it. Remember that, my dear Madeline, before you make any more plans to eliminate me from your life."

Chapter 6

*A*s Eleanor furtively hurried out the back door of Mr. Knight's town house, she muttered to herself, *"With your permission, Mr. Knight, I would like to speak to Dickie Driscoll.* No!" Shaking her head, she tried again. *"I wish to speak to Dickie if you don't mind."* Fretting at her own diffidence, she said, "That's not it, either." Drawing her cape tighter about her shoulders, she glanced behind her as she made her way through the small garden.

Ever since last night when Mr. Knight had told her he'd spied on her—or rather Madeline— Eleanor had had the creeping sensation of being watched. She'd looked at Beth differently, seeing not an eager-to-please lady's maid but a shifty-eyed informer. She'd heard footsteps behind her when no one had been there. Last night, she had even placed a chair under her door handle to ensure her privacy, and she'd woken frequently to listen to the night's silence.

Now, as she slipped through the fog-tinged air toward the stable, she practiced being glib in case someone caught her.

In case Mr. Knight caught her. He was supposed to be at the bank, but she didn't trust him to do as he said.

"I'm going to speak to Dickie and see if he's comfortable in his quarters. Better. No, still too conciliatory. *I'm going to speak to Dickie.* That's it." She nodded decisively and tried to appear the confident duchess everyone thought she was.

She had never been more miserably aware that she was merely Miss Eleanor de Lacy, impoverished cousin and shrinking violet.

The garden gate opened with a creak of the hinges, and she peeked across the mews toward the stable. An urchin swept desultorily at the stones. No one else was in sight.

With every evidence of equanimity, Eleanor walked to the stable door and slipped inside the dim, warm building. She'd come this far. Not bad for a coward.

Now all she had to do was find Dickie, and she would be as good as free. Compelled by an itching between her shoulder blades, she peeked around the door and again scanned the mews. It was now empty. She *had* to escape Mr. Knight before the Picards' ball. Dickie was her only prospect.

"Can I 'elp ye, Yer Grace?"

She jumped at the sound of a respectful male voice and whirled to find herself facing one of the tallest men she'd ever seen in her life. He held a pitchfork, and he towered so far above her that, in the gloom, she had trouble discerning his respectful tug of his forelock. With her hand at her tight throat, she stared until her voice returned. "I'm looking for Dickie Driscoll."

The stablehand turned and bellowed, "Dickie! The duchess is alookin' fer ye!" With a return to his quiet tone, he said, "He be acomin', Yer Grace."

"Thank you," Eleanor faltered. It would be a miracle if Mr. Knight hadn't heard the shout all the way in the house—and she was giving him credit for more powers than it was possible for any man to possess. He was a bully, that was all. A gambler, a stalker, a man distrustful of everyone and everything. He didn't deserve Eleanor, and he most certainly didn't deserve Madeline.

Eleanor heard the thump of boots on the wooden floor, then Dickie walked out of the gloom.

Broad-shouldered and broad-bellied, his rounded physique hid a pugnacious nature and a stubborn loyalty to Madeline and, by extension, to Eleanor. He was fast with a fist, good with a pistol, and he could make any horse follow him with doglike devotion. He'd gotten Eleanor out of scrapes before, scrapes of Madeline's making, of course. Never had Eleanor been so happy to see him.

Dickie placed his hand on the big man's arm. In his pronounced Scottish accent, he said, "Thanks, Ives. The grooming is na done on Mr. Knight's horse. Ye might want t' finish that fer him."

With a nod, Ives stumped away, the floor shaking beneath his feet.

As soon as he was out of earshot, Eleanor and Dickie spoke at the same time.

"Dickie, you've got to get me out of here."

"Miss, I've got to get ye oot of here."

"Now," she said.

He stared as if her vehemence took him aback. "What aboot yer things? Or rather, Her Grace's things. Ye two changed luggage, did ye na?"

Bluntly, she said, "He's having me watched."

"Watched?" Dickie glanced around, as if expecting to see someone lurking in the corner. "What do ye mean?"

"Someone has been spying on me—or rather, Madeline—since we returned to England, and reporting back to Mr. Knight."

"Ach, that Mr. Knight, he's a villain, and so I told Her Grace as soon as she made her foolish plans." Dickie ran his hands through his hair, making it stand up in bright red strands. "All right, then. Did anyone see ye leave the house?"

"No." She barely refrained from looking over her shoulder again. "I don't think so."

"Very well." He took her arm. "Let's go."

They moved quickly toward the back of the stable, past the horses to the door.

"Hey!" Ives thundered. "Where are ye agoin'?"

Eleanor jumped and shivered.

Dickie squeezed her arm encouragingly. "The lady wants to know her way to the street," he tossed back.

Lying was not one of Dickie's strong suits.

"Who's agoin' t' clean the stalls, I'd like t' know!" For a big man, Ives managed to sound peevish.

"I'll be back in a minute," Dickie called. In a quieter tone, he asked, "What made ye run now, Miss Eleanor? The blackguard didn't make advances, did he?"

"No." No one would call lifting her off a stool "making advances." Only a silly virgin like her would weave fantasies about the press of his body against hers. "I wanted to come last night, but he never left the house, and I didn't dare try to make my way to the stables in the dark. I'm sorry, Dickie, I knew Madeline would find a way to do so, but I feared getting lost in the house or finding the wrong stable. . . ." She had no trouble keeping up with Dickie's long strikes. She would have run every step of the way to escape Mr. Knight and his insidious seduction.

"Timid, ye are, but that's all right, miss. 'Tis our bold duchess who gets ye into these fixes."

"Mr. Knight wants to take me to a ball tonight." Eleanor gestured down at herself. "I can't go into society as the marchioness of Sherbourne and the future duchess of Magnus."

Dickie looked properly horrified. "Nay, that ye canna."

Besides, if she stayed in Mr. Knight's house, before long she'd think of nothing but how handsome he was, how any woman who wed him would be well-pleasured indeed, and how darling his children would be tucked into the curve of her arm . . . "Hurry, Dickie."

They burst out of the stables. With a swift glance up and down the empty alley, they rushed toward the corner. They strode over the cobblestones, past piles of garbage, past two cats fighting over a fish bone. Ahead, through the narrow gap between the buildings, she could see the stylish pedestrians, hear the carriages rumbling past and the call of vendors.

Eleanor's heart pounded. If they could just make it through the gap, they could blend with the crowds and disappear.

She would disappear, and never see Mr. Remington Knight's handsome, cold, sensuous countenance again as long as she lived. It had to be that way, for her own peace of mind.

She tugged the hood of her cloak up.

"That's guid, miss," Dickie said approvingly. "We're almost there."

They rushed forward the last few steps.

And with silent menace, a black-clad figure stepped around the corner and blocked their path with a long, barbarically carved cane.

Eleanor stopped short. Her heart pounded, her fingers crushed her reticule.

It was him. Mr. Knight.

Of course.

Chapter 7

*T*wo henchmen stepped around Mr. Knight, grabbed Dickie Driscoll by the arms, and lifted him off his feet.

Eleanor lunged for the groom.

Seizing her around the waist, Mr. Knight held her back and snarled, "Dickie, listen to me now. You're not to come back here. You're never to see her. You're not to try and take her away from me again. If you try, I'll kill you. Do you understand? I'll kill you."

"Ye don't understand, sir, she's na for ye!" Before Dickie could say more, one of the thugs punched him hard enough to jerk his head back.

"Get rid of him," Mr. Knight commanded.

Dickie was leaving. They were taking him away. "No. No! Where are they going with him?" She watched as Dickie twisted around, trying to see her, trying to get free.

"Damn ye, Knight, don't ye hurt her," he yelled.

Mr. Knight watched, his pale blue gaze frozen, his hand gripping the tall, old-fashioned cane he held, a cane carved with barbaric elegance and topped with a heavy, gold ball.

Visions of violence and blood filled her mind. Grabbing his lapel, Eleanor jerked so hard she brought his head around. "What are you doing with him?"

He stared down at her as if he'd forgotten that he gripped her.

"Don't hurt him!"

"We're throwing him into the street." Still Mr. Knight stared at her, his gaze ferocious.

She didn't believe him, and she grasped him tighter, using both hands to command his attention. "He's in my employ. You can't dismiss him."

He laughed unpleasantly. "I just have."

She desperately glanced at Dickie, then back at Mr. Knight. "Promise me you won't have him beaten."

Without inflection, he asked, "Do you think me a thug?"

She did, and more than that—she was vitally aware he hadn't answered her. "Just promise me."

"He'll be fine."

"That's not good enough." Dickie was her friend. He was in trouble because of her. He could be killed . . . because of her. "Promise me you won't hurt him. That you won't have him hurt in any way, by anybody."

Knight's eyebrows lifted, as if surprised by her forcefulness. With care, he placed his cane against the wall. Pinching her chin between his fingers, he lifted her face to his and studied it as he might an unexpectedly feisty pet. "On one condition."

She thought she knew very well what that condition would be. He wanted in her bed.

But whatever the price, she would pay it. She'd seen too much violence in Europe. She'd seen the results of battles: the wounded, the dying, the agony. She hadn't known any of those men. She knew Dickie, and she couldn't allow him to be hurt now, after they'd been through so much together. "Anything."

Mr. Knight's black brows made his frown more ferocious, and his mouth curled into a sneer. He looked handsome and enraged, like some magnificent dark angel come to bargain for her soul. "Promise me you won't try to run away from me again."

Her heart stopped, then started beating too quickly. Didn't he want . . . ? She looked at him again, trying to see inside his head. But that was impossible. He showed her his wrath, but not his desire, and only her instincts told her that the man was all the more dangerous for his self-discipline.

"Decide now, Madeline."

The use of her cousin's name reminded Eleanor; she was playing a part, but she was playing in earnest. Dickie's well-being, perhaps his life, depended on her. Taking a quivering breath, she said, "I promise."

"*What* do you promise?"

Trust Mr. Knight to demand the exact words. "I promise not to run away from you."

He weighed her words, as he feared he'd been paid in fool's gold.

He didn't trust her. Very well. She didn't blame him, but she had to convince him. "I swear I won't leave until you tell me to go."

He slid his fingers around her throat, just lightly, so she could feel his heat and his strength. "I will never tell you to go."

Of course he would. As soon as he found out she was an imposter. But until that time he had bound her to him. Staring into his cold, pale eyes, she felt the chill of the future.

Slowly, as if irresistibly drawn, he slid his fingers into her hair, loosening the already drooping chignon at the base of her neck. Leaning his face toward her, he spoke, his voice gravelly with desire. "I love your hair. It's as thick and as rich as sable. I'll see this spread over my pillow before a fortnight has passed. I'll bury my face in it and drink in the scent. I'll use it to hold you in place while you thrash beneath me and moan with pleasure."

She was shocked by every word. By every threat and every promise. But more than that, she watched his soft, tempting lips move with his words, and she wanted those lips on hers.

He was going to kiss her, here, now, in the alleyway off a busy London street. She felt the heat of his desire. She knew, she feared, that that heat would melt her reservations and give her over to him, at least for the moment. She couldn't allow that. She daren't. Before his lips touched hers, she said, "Go now and save Dickie."

He halted, and for a moment, she thought he would kiss her regardless of her command. But she held his gaze and silently demanded that he do as she wished.

His hands slipped away from her, inch by inch, as if he released her only grudgingly.

And she hated the loss of his warmth and hated more that it mattered to her.

With an abrupt nod, he strode after his henchmen.

The wall between the buildings was grimy with soot, but she leaned her hand against it, light-headed now that the crisis had passed.

She had committed herself to remain with Mr. Knight. It didn't matter that she had given her word as Madeline; Eleanor's lips had formed the words, and when she gave her word, she kept it.

That was why she'd come to such grief eight years ago when her stepmother had tried to bend Eleanor to her will. Eleanor had refused to give her word.

"Welcome, Remington, welcome!" As his secretary ushered Remington in, the president of the bank, Mr. Clark Oxnard, rose from his desk. "I've been looking forward to your visit. Did our shipment turn a profit?"

Remington didn't bother to reply as he settled into the high-backed, cushioned chair the secretary dragged out from the corner of Clark's luxurious office. The place smelled of money and looked like a gentleman of leisure's study, but Remington knew very well the kind of exacting, conscientious work Clark did here.

"Of course it did," Clark answered his own question. "You've made me a rich man."

"A richer man," Remington corrected.

Clark pulled a moue. "Wealth is a relative term. Henry, please bring Mr. Knight and me a pot of tea. Or Remington, would you rather have a brandy?"

"Tea will be best. I need a clear mind. I've got a ball to attend tonight."

Henry exited, shutting the door behind him without a sound.

"Picard's? Good, I'll see you there." With a broad smile, Clark said, "I hope for the day when my bank balance equals yours."

"And on that day, I plan to have twice what I have now." The two men were about the same age, but other than that, they had nothing in common. Clark was English-born, the fourth son of an earl, given over to business to help support his aristocratic but impoverished family, and doing so very well.

Yet despite Clark's aristocratic connections, Remington liked the stout, balding, dignified gentleman. The two had exchanged letters long before Remington had come to England, and they found their thoughts and goals to have much in common. "I've come to ask a favor," Remington said.

Folding his hands over his paunch, Clark leaned back in his leather chair. "Certainly."

Remington recognized some apprehension in Clark's manner and hastened to reassure him. "It has nothing to do with money. It's a personal favor."

Valiantly, Clark ignored the reference to filthy lucre. "Anything within my power, dear boy."

"I'd like you to stand as my witness and best man in my marriage to Madeline de Lacy, the future duchess of Magnus."

Clark beamed. "Good heavens! Yes, of course, what an honor you bestow on me!" Rising to his feet, he extended his hand.

Remington stood also and shook it. "Not necessarily such an honor. The duchess is a prize of unparalleled wealth and beauty, and you know as well as I there are men who would kill to be in my shoes."

Clark guffawed. "Yes, of course. Kill to be in your shoes."

Remington didn't smile back. "As in olden days, I need you to watch my back."

Clark's merriment faded, and he sank down into his seat. "You're serious."

Remington seated himself also. "Indeed I am."

Henry arrived with a quiet knock and the tea tray. He poured for the two gentlemen, fixed it as they liked, and disappeared out the door.

Taking a sip, Remington took up the conversation where it had left off. "The de Lacy family, especially, is treacherous."

"The . . . de Lacy family?" Clark's brow knit. "Are you speaking of your bride?"

"No, I don't think so." Remington thought of Madeline, of the deal they'd struck that morning. He had known she was not to be trusted, of course, for last night, when he had informed her she was being watched, he had seen the hunted shadows in her eyes. This morning, he hadn't been surprised when she had proved her deceitfulness by sneaking away with Dickie.

Yet she *had* surprised Remington with her loyalty to her servant. She had feared for Dickie. She had demanded Remington release him. And when Remington had demanded a boon, she had, without knowing what it might be, agreed to pay the price. "My bride seems to be quite genuine in her emotions."

Clark rocked back in his seat, and the leather squeaked beneath his weight. "Quite right, quite right. Not that I know her well at all, but she has a reputation for sincerity."

"Yes, I imagine she does." Very soon, she would pay her bridegroom the same allegiance she paid to her horsegroom, for he would bind her to him with kisses, with long, slow strokes on her bare skin, with a union that would leave her in no doubt of his possession. And she would live for him. She would die for him. She would be his, and all his plans would be complete.

Yet even today, when he'd vanquished the last of her allies, he still wasn't sure she wouldn't somehow escape. She was going to be a duchess; she had resources he might not have identified.

Still, she had given her word, and the de Lacys always kept their word—or so it was said. Not that he would call off his watchdogs, but her promise did give him a measure of security.

"What de Lacy do you think treacherous?" Clark asked curiously.

"Her father, certainly."

"The duke of Magnus?" Clark's mustache quivered with astonishment. "I don't know him, although my father does. But I've never heard anything lethal about him."

"Still waters run deep." The tea soured in Remington's mouth, and he put down the cup. "Do you recall hearing about his sister's murder?"

"His sister's? . . . Lord, yes. Brutal, vicious slaying. My parents whispered about it when I was young. They said Lady Pricilla was one of the beauties of the day."

"Yes, and cut down in the bloom of her youth on the same night her betrothal was to be announced." Remington had heard the tale many a time, and he could recite it without thinking.

Clark's bushy eyebrows shot up. "Magnus had nothing to do with that. Someone else was convicted, some commoner."

"By name, Mr. George Marchant. He was accused, but the testimony of three noblemen who swore they were with him at the time of the murder made it impossible for the magistrates to convict him. Because they had no one else on whom to pin the crime, and because the crime was so heinous, he was deported to Australia."

"Probably did it," Clark muttered, but he didn't meet Remington's gaze.

"Your father was one of the men who swore that he didn't."

Clark's teacup rattled in his hand, and he hastily placed it on the desk. " 'Pon rep! You're joking."

"Not at all. Does your father make it a habit to lie?" Remington already knew the answer, but he enjoyed watching Clark puff up in indignation.

"Never heard him tell a bouncer for any reason." Clark rubbed his bulbous nose. "But I still don't understand why you mistrust Magnus. He was Lady Pricilla's brother!"

"In crimes like this, my friend, it almost always is a member of the family."

"No, really. Family members are supposed to care for one another."

Clark's ingenuous belief brought a smile to Remington's face. "Sometimes they do. And sometimes, they hate with all the ferocity that familiarity brings." When Clark would have disputed with him, Remington said, "Come now. Don't you have acquaintances where you're afraid to go to their homes for fear a fight will start?"

Clark conceded, "Yes. I suppose you're right."

"Ask a Bow Street Runner. Murder is usually a family affair." Remington toyed with changing the subject just to relieve Clark's uneasiness. Yet he admired Clark's intelligence, and he'd never had the chance to examine the crime with anyone. "Someone killed Lady Pricilla. It wasn't George Marchant, so the killer hasn't been caught."

"Dreadful thought." Clark looked deeply unhappy. He was a man who liked everything clearcut and orderly, like the rows of figures in his accounting books.

"Rumor says she was going to elope with someone, a gentleman less suitable than her wealthy lord.

Who else would take violent exception, except one of her family?"

"Her fiancé?"

"The earl of Fanthorpe."

Clark slumped in his chair. "Ohh."

His reaction surprised Remington. Clark so seldom openly expressed aversion. "You don't like him."

In exasperation, Clark said, "He's such an old school aristocrat. He banks here, and he won't speak directly to me. *I* have muddied my hands with *commerce*."

Remington's lips twitched with amusement.

"He comes into my office, he sits in that chair"—Clark pointed at Remington's seat—"he tells his secretary what he wants done with his account, and his secretary tells me. I, of course, do exactly the same thing in reverse."

"You speak to the secretary, and—"

"Exactly."

"Would he have killed Lady Pricilla?"

"Only if he could have had his secretary kill her." Clark laughed, then looked guilty. "Pardon me, that is an insensitive jest. Was he not a suspect?"

"He was, but he, also, had an alibi." Remington toyed with his spoon. "I used to think it was the old duke of Magnus."

"I never met him. He died before I was out of Oxford, but he is a possibility." Clark seemed fascinated by the unsolved mystery. "He had a reputation for temper, rages that rampaged out of control."

"He was famous for them, and after Lady Pricilla's betrothal he was heard shouting at her on several occasions. He could have killed her, but witnesses said there was no blood on him." Although he could have hired the job done, the attack apparently had been one of impulse and rage. "The violence was so malicious, he should have been covered with blood."

"All right. It wasn't her father." Clark sounded almost regretful. "And I stick by my contention it wasn't the current duke of Magnus. But I would say it could easily be his brother, and hers, Lord Shapster. Have you met him?"

Remington shook his head. "I've not had the pleasure."

"No pleasure at all. The bastard's a cold fish. Married that dreadful Lady Shapster." As if unpleasant memories were connected with her name, Clark pulled out his handkerchief and wiped his forehead. "When she tried to force Eleanor, as fine a girl as ever I met, to marry, Lord Shapster paid no attention. Let Lady Shapster brutalize his own daughter. So long as he's not forced to cease hunting, he cares nothing for anything or anybody."

Clark had piqued Remington's interest. "I had no idea you knew the family."

"I come from Blinkingshire, just a few miles down the road from their home. I knew Eleanor from the time she was a bit of a girl. She's a good deal younger than me, of course, but she sits an excellent seat on a horse. Never makes a scene, never says a peep unless she's forced to, and that's Lady Shapster's fault." Clark passed his hand over his balding head. "So Lord Shapster is a good suspect."

Regretfully, Remington said, "He hasn't enough money."

"He doesn't need money to stab a woman to death."

"He needed money to wreak vengeance on George Marchant from afar."

Aghast, Clark said, "He wouldn't do that. Send somebody to Australia to kill the man who he knows perfectly well *didn't* kill his sister? Doesn't make sense."

"George Marchant had a genius for making money, a genius he passed on to his son, by the way." Remington kept his expression bland, taking care not to show the anger unfurling in his gut. "After George served his term, he made his way from Australia to America, where he married a shipping heiress, had two children, was widowed, and built a fortune, all with the idea of coming back to England and wreaking vengeance on the man who had killed Lady Pricilla."

Uneasily, Clark asked, "Why would George care so much? If he had money, family and reputation in America, why come back here?"

"Haven't you discerned the truth?" Remington rose and paced over to the desk. Leaning over, he looked Clark in the eyes. "He loved Lady Pricilla, she loved him, and they were going to elope that night."

"Dear God." Clark stared at Remington intently. He was starting to figure out the connection.

"Yes. About the time George, in America, was ready to act against the nobleman who had killed Lady Pricilla, his home and business were set afire, his daughter was brutally murdered, and he was beaten almost to death. When his son returned from school, grieving and horrified, George was clinging to life. George told his son who had done the horrible deed."

The two men stared at each other across the glossy expanse of Clark's desk. Finally, Clark asked, "Why do you know this?"

Remington walked to the door, and before he opened it, said, "Because I am George's son. Magnus will never rest until all the Marchants are dead—and I will never rest until I have vengeance."

Chapter 8

That evening, Remington sat in the drawing room, watched the clock, and leafed through his well-read copy of *Robinson Crusoe*. But he couldn't concentrate on the story.

His fiancée was late. This morning, as he'd marched her back across the garden and into the house, he had informed her she was to be downstairs at seven o'clock. It was now almost eight.

He usually accepted, with weary tolerance, the peccadilloes of beautiful women, and making a belated entrance was surely the most common transgression. But he would have never suspected his duchess of such petty dramatics—which proved he understood her not at all.

After the incident with Dickie, Remington had thought she would faint from alarm. He'd taken her into the house, wet his handkerchief, and pressed it to her cheeks. She'd pushed his hand away, and with silent dignity had made her way upstairs. He hadn't seen her since, but he had believed her sufficiently cowed to submit to his plans without further insubordination.

A woman, his father used to say, would always prove a man wrong when he least expected it. It appeared his father was right.

The brief sparks of originality and kindness he saw in her were nothing more than the polished performance of an aristocrat who thought she could manipulate him. Much to her own dismay she had learned he was in command.

Yet she was late, and that left him to ponder the events at the bank.

Clark had been shocked at Remington's revelation, but he'd proved his mettle when he'd answered, "If this is the truth, if Magnus truly is your enemy, then I'll take a weapon to your wedding and watch for treachery every second." Before Remington could thank him, Clark had added, "But on the same token if, for reasons of vengeance, you ever harm the duchess, I'll consider it my responsibility to hunt you down and bring you to justice."

Remington liked Clark—for his bravery, and his candor. "I won't harm her. What is mine, I keep, and I swear you won't regret your decision."

The two men had solemnly shaken hands, and Remington had departed.

Now Remington again glanced at the clock.

Madeline's new defiance boded ill. Probably she was sulking, but Beth would have let him know if she was refusing to dress. His duchess would be downstairs in ten minutes—he glanced at the chiming clock—or he would go up and get her.

Finally, from the floor above, he heard the faint, pleasing chime of women's voices.

At last. Her Grace had consented to make her appearance.

As Lady Gertrude descended the last few stairs, she was saying in a distraught tone, "Dear girl, my point is, I don't think he's going to like this."

She didn't think he was going to like . . . what? Rising, he made his way into the foyer.

When Lady Gertrude caught sight of him, dismay chased across her soft features. Her tone changed to chipper. Excessively chipper. "Oh, sir, Her Grace looks beautiful, absolutely ravishing."

The duchess stood one step up from the foyer, her hand on the rail, her gaze distant.

And her magnificent mane of hair had been cut. *Short.* Wisps curled around her face, caressing her forehead and her cheeks, and longer strands of hair clung to her neck. *Short.* She had shorn her hair.

Striding furiously to the foot of the stairs, he stood directly below her, and in the voice which made subordinates cower, he demanded, "What the hell have you done to yourself?"

Turning her head, she looked down at him with calm indifference. "Mr. Knight, I warned you—one doesn't swear in mixed company. Not in England."

She dared reprimand him . . . now? Now, when she looked so different? This cut changed her appearance from that of a soft, timid, gentlewoman to one of a daring hoyden, and by God, he wanted his other fiancée back. "I'll damned well swear if I want to, especially when faced with this kind of desecration."

Lady Gertrude wrung her hands. "Oh, dear. Oh, dear. I told you he would be—"

Turning, he glared at her.

She shut her mouth and backed away.

"Mr. Knight, do not intimidate her," the duchess commanded. In a softer tone, she said to Lady Gertrude, "Hush, my lady, I don't require Mr. Knight's approval."

His blood rose at Madeline's cool dismissal of his opinion. "The day will come, Your Grace, when you'll want my approval."

"Really?" she drawled, and for the first time he thought she sounded every inch an English aristocrat. "You won't mind if I don't hold my breath."

As she stood on the step, their heights were almost comparable. His eyes were only a few inches below hers, and he viewed too clearly her pale, cool face and studied unconcern. His hands itched to take hold of her and show her how very quickly he could make her want him, and his approval.

But what new defiance would that provoke? He spoke slowly, weighing each word with significance. "Where is your hair?"

"A good bit of it is on my head." Lifting her fingers, she sifted them through the strands, as if still marveling at the transformation. "But Beth carried most of it away. A great long mare's tail, it was. Now it's gone."

The hair he'd imagined spreading over his pillow, clutching in his fist, using as a rope to bind him to this woman . . . that hair now adorned a trash barrel in the kitchen. "This is Beth's doing?" He would make the maid sorry.

"I took the scissors and hacked off all of the length," Eleanor informed him.

He winced at the picture that called to mind.

"I cut it crooked, too. Poor Beth had to fix matters, and her hands are still trembling with fear of what you'll do."

"So they should." His fingers flexed. "She should tremble."

"I told her she had nothing to fear. I told her you were a great many things, but unfair was not one of them." Eleanor's dark blue eyes watched and assessed him while she spoke. "Am I wrong, Mr. Knight?"

Of course she was not. He wouldn't dismiss a maid for doing as her mistress commanded. But he didn't have to, didn't want to, admit that now. In a guttural tone, he asked, "What made you do this?"

She leaned toward him, close enough that he could smell the faint perfume of some exotic flower. Close enough that her plump, pale breasts strained against her bodice. "I think you know."

He did. She'd cut her hair because he'd told her how he would use it to subdue her. He leaned forward, too, until their noses almost touched. "You'll grow it again."

"If I wish it."

"You'll grow it again, and quickly."

She smiled, a smooth, satisfied tilt of the lips. "I promise you, Mr. Knight, whether I do or not will have nothing to do with you." She sounded so certain.

He didn't understand why, and he didn't like it.

She was timid, meek, frightened of him. He'd seen evidence of her caution at every turn. Didn't she realize how thoroughly he held her in his power?

Searching her face, he sought the reason for her composure. But as she met his gaze, he got lost in her eyes. They were beautiful eyes, wide and deep blue with long, dark, curling lashes that fluttered. He could almost see the soul she held so privately, and he wanted to know her. All of her. Her mind as well as her body.

To his astonishment, what started out as a furious visual interrogation changed. Softened. As they gazed at each other, each remembered that moment in the alley when he'd almost, *almost* kissed her. The remnants of the morning's passion grew between them, and he wanted to taste her, here, now . . .

Lady Gertrude's voice intruded with all the subtlety of a marauding bandit. "Mr. Knight, what do you think of Madeline's gown?"

He started.

The duchess straightened abruptly. She stared at her hands as they nervously smoothed her skirt over her thighs.

He watched, too, unable to look away from that revealing introspection.

Lady Gertrude intruded again, and this time with more success. "I especially like the neckline, and the austere cut, and the way the little sleeves puff up and show her fine white arms."

Remington listened to Lady Gertrude and observed the gown. The duchess wore a cream muslin evening robe, crossed across her bosom and opening to show a burgundy satin petticoat. The edges of the robe were embellished with a rich green trim in a subtle Greek pattern. Her satin slippers matched her petticoat, and a burgundy ribbon was threaded through her dark hair. A cream-colored fan dangled from her wrist. The effect was arresting. Not at all what he would have chosen, but with her height and her slender proportions, it was an excellent selection. Yet . . . yet . . .

Grimly, he said, "Correct me if I'm wrong, but this gown isn't one of the garments I had purchased for you."

"No. It's one of mine." Madeline sounded so composed, the moment between them might never have happened.

"You said you didn't have the proper clothing."

"What a surprise," she said, deadpan. "I found them in my trunk."

She said nothing else, no matter how pointedly he waited, and so he scrutinized her without subtlety. "Very handsome." He thought, for a moment, he saw relief in her eyes.

Then he delivered an ultimatum. "But I beg that you go change. On your first appearance as my betrothed, I would have you wear a more fashionable outfit." His gaze flicked to her hair. "If not a more proper coiffure."

In what was the perfect illustration of noble haughtiness, she said, "I am the future duchess of Magnus. I set the fashion."

He wouldn't tolerate her defiance. "Go change."

Pulling on her cream, over-the-elbow gloves, she

said, "I fear that's impossible. It offends every convention to arrive at the party after the Prince of Wales, and we're already late."

He didn't know if that was true. English society had so many rules and mores he couldn't comprehend, not to mention those interminable titles and their hierarchy and their different methods of address. He had perfected the abashed apology for the many times he'd said or done the wrong thing, called someone by the wrong title, entered a room before or after the proper time. So far the English had tolerated his mistakes. He doubted they would tolerate an insult to their prince. "You did this on purpose."

For the first time, he saw the flash of anger in her blue eyes. "Of course. Did you really think I would meekly wear the clothing you had procured for me, as if I were some light-o'-love you rented for the month?"

Lady Gertrude gasped and covered her mouth. Gradually, her shocked expression changed, and her eyes began to twinkle.

Then the truth was borne in on him.

He had lost.

It was a small battle, unimportant among his schemes, but he lost so seldom he could scarcely comprehend it.

He had lost. Lost to this quiet, diffident, stubborn duchess.

Very well. He would remember, and in the future, he would fine-tune his tactics and never underestimate her again. "I would never make the mistake of thinking you a light-o'-love, Your Grace. I would more likely think you a chess master."

She inclined her head, accepting his tribute as a matter of course.

He accepted his black evening cape from the waiting butler and swung it around his shoulders. He took in hand his tall, carved wooden cane, and with a flourish, planted it on the floor, looking every inch a proper British gentleman while knowing he was every inch a thoroughly American barbarian. In a tone as soft as velvet and as harsh as winter, he said, "Be warned, my duchess. The next move is mine."

Chapter 9

"What a crush!" Pink with excitement, Lady Gertrude peered about the crowd with her lorgnette. "Lord and Lady Picard always have everyone to their ball, absolutely everyone! Some people complain they have pretensions, with the way their footman announces everyone as if this were a royal reception. They have a ballroom that covers almost their entire ground floor, but pretensions *are* acceptable in people who have five large estates." With a shake of the finger at Remington, she added, "But I'm giving you a crass view of the English, Mr. Knight. Social acceptance does not depend on having wealth."

"Of course not, ma'am," he said to the petite lady on his left arm, while he thought, *But it helps.*

A cacophony of voices and music spilled through the arch that led to the ballroom as the duchess,

Lady Gertrude, and Mr. Knight inched forward in the line to be introduced. Around them, the other guests pressed close, jockeying for position, everyone wanting to be first into the ballroom. They stared at the trio and whispered behind raised fans and gloved hands.

"Look, Madeline," Lady Gertrude said, "everyone's gaping at you!"

"I know." The future duchess stared straight ahead, her shoulders stiff, her back straight.

Never had Remington seen a woman less comfortable with her own distinction. Never had he enjoyed the success of his own plan quite so much. The ton adored only one thing more than a romance, and that was a scandal. He had—and would—give them both. "Maybe it's because of your hair," he murmured.

Madeline shot him a glare.

"Everyone's absolutely avid to discover all about you and dear Mr. Knight." Lady Gertrude peered around him at her niece. "Dear girl, you'll be the belle of the ball!"

"That's putting a good face on it," Madeline said. She seemed very aware that people strained to hear their conversation.

With a suave assurance he thought would put her at her ease, he said, "I'm sure my fiancée is the belle of any ball she ever attends."

She barely glanced at him. Barely seemed to hear him. If he didn't know better, he would say she had stage fright.

He wasn't used to having a woman, any woman, ignore him, and now, tonight, she had done more than that. She had defied him, and now she tried to pretend he wasn't here, at her side, as her fiancé.

In a deep voice, he called her name. "Madeline." Still she ignored him. Taking her hand, he lifted it to his lips and, at the last minute, he turned it and kissed her wrist.

That got her attention. She looked at him, her eyes as wide and startled as those of a doe who had never seen a human before.

All around them, the tittle-tattle of gossip grew louder.

"Mr. Knight!" Lady Gertrude used her most disapproving tone. *She* didn't care whether she was overheard. "You will not do such a thing again. That is quite improper."

"Until we are wed," he answered. He didn't care, either.

"Ever," Lady Gertrude said with crushing certainty. Then she amended, "In public."

Madeline said nothing but ducked her head and blushed, and he would have sworn he saw the glitter of tears on her lashes.

For a moment, just a moment, he felt guilty. Damn her. Most women of his experience used weeping like a weapon, to get their own way. His duchess seemed embarrassed by her tears and wanted no one to see. Not him. Not anyone else in the crowd.

He had investigated this woman thoroughly before he'd made his bid to win her hand, and everyone had told him she was at ease in society, bold and open, very aware of her importance but not snobbish with it. Why had the years abroad changed her so much? Or was this a game to win sympathy for her plight?

"La! There's Lord Betterworth, and that's not his wife." Lady Gertrude fluttered her fingers in greeting. "Mr. Knight, can you behave yourself long enough for me to go talk to Mrs. Ashton? She always knows the newest on-dit, and she can bring me up to date on everything."

"I'll be the perfect English gentleman." *Bloodless and boring.*

"You don't mind, do you, dear niece?"

Clearly, Madeline didn't want her to go. But Lady Gertrude's eyes were shining, and he watched as his duchess lost the battle between desire and kind-heartedness. "Do go, ma'am. Since I've been out of the country, I'm quite ignorant too, and will need to be caught up on every matter."

"I'll be back in time to be announced. Hold my place, Mr. Knight!"

"Don't be late." He utilized his command voice.

Lady Gertrude started to toss off a giddy reply. Then she saw he was serious and, recalled to her duty, said, "Of course I'll be here. I haven't forgotten that I'm the chaperon." She almost skipped, so anxious was she to be away.

Quietly, Madeline said, "There's no need for you to be mean to her. She intends no harm."

Her reproof surprised him. "I'm not being mean to her. I hired her. I'm paying her well to make sure your reputation doesn't suffer from our premarital association. I was reminding her of her duties. Furthermore, I believe you're more comfortable with me when she's close." He heard Madeline's quick intake of breath. "Aren't you?"

Turning her head away, she didn't answer.

He found himself distracted by the wisps of dark hair that caressed the pale skin at the back of her neck. Perhaps he could learn to live with this new cut . . . well, he had no choice, did he? At least until her hair grew back.

"Remington!" Clark battled his way to his side. "A pleasure to see you so soon."

"Good to see you, too." Remington turned to Madeline. "May I introduce her ladyship, the marchioness of Sherbourne, the future duchess of Magnus and my future wife? Your Grace, this is Mr. Clark Oxnard, president of Whittington Bank, and a man I'm proud to call my friend."

Madeline stared at Clark in what looked like frozen dismay.

But Clark bowed and chuckled. "My lady, if I may say so, I had heard you look like your cousin, Miss Eleanor de Lacy, and you do. You do, indeed. I was acquainted with that young lady years ago before she left Blinkingshire, and if I didn't know better, I would say you are her twin."

Madeline bobbed a curtsy that looked as if she'd lost her balance. "Not twins. No, we're not."

"Of course not," Clark said comfortably. "This fiancé of yours has asked me to be his best man at your wedding. I can't tell you how honored I am." He placed his hand on Remington's arm. "One of the best chaps a man ever knew. You're a lucky young woman. Of course, he's one lucky man, too."

"That I am," Remington said.

"I'll be at the church, prepared for every eventuality." Clark nodded meaningfully at Remington.

At that reassurance, Remington experienced an upwelling of camaraderie unlike any he'd ever experienced. "Clark—thank you. You restore my faith in mankind."

"Not at all." Clark grinned. "I daren't lose the bank's most profitable client."

Remington chuckled.

Madeline stared at the two men as if they were speaking a foreign language. She said nothing. No small talk. No courtesies. If Madeline was going to act like this to all of Remington's associates, he would have a long discussion with her about the proper courtesies.

Clark seemed not to see anything wrong. "I'd best get back. Mrs. Oxnard is a tiny thing, and the crowd will shove her all over if I'm not with her. If we never see each other again tonight, I'll see you at the wedding ceremony. A pleasure, Your Grace."

"A pleasure, sir," she echoed, and stared after him as if the back of him fascinated her.

Remington spoke softly into her ear. "Is it so dreadful to be seen on my arm?"

"What?" She glanced up at him and blinked at him in seeming amazement. At his question. At seeing him so close.

"You barely glanced at Clark, and you haven't looked me in the eye since we arrived." She was looking at him now. She was *seeing* him, for her lips opened slightly, and her lashes fluttered as she tried to maintain eye contact.

"You're embarrassed to be seen with me."

"I most certainly am not!"

"I'm properly dressed and, except for the occasional kiss on your wrist, fairly well behaved, so perhaps you're worried that your reputation as an aristocrat will fail beneath the strain of your association with me."

"The consequence of the duchess of Magnus is so great, even arriving at a ball on your arm, Mr. Knight, cannot damage it." She smiled as she made the claim, as if she were amused by her own temerity. Under the influence of that merriment, her skin glowed, her eyes lit up, and her delightful dimples quivered in her cheeks.

With a start, he thought, *She's charming.* He had expected to be challenged by this woman, not captivated. She surprised him, and surprise made him vaguely uneasy. Yet she was only a woman, and a woman whose father cared so little for her that he was willing to gamble her life away. Remington needed to remember that. He had the matter well in hand.

Touching his white gloved finger under her chin, he lifted her face to his. "You smile too seldom. I wonder why."

Her amusement failed her. She wiped her hand down her skirt, as if, beneath her glove, her palm was sweaty. "I don't enjoy balls."

"You're nervous."

"It's not every day I'm notorious."

He knew better than that. He had heard the truth of the scandal that had driven her from England. "I would have thought you were used to it. You caused quite a lot of gossip when you ended your last engagement."

Madeline blanched. She'd made a scene when she'd broken her betrothal to the earl of Campion, and now she knew that he was aware of her past. She recovered her composure and snapped, "When my past becomes your business, sir, I will let you know."

"You're going to be my wife." He smiled down at her, playing to the crowd and at the same time letting her see his false affection. "Your past is *now* my business."

"Marriage, they tell me, is a mutual exchange. I'll tell you my secrets when you tell me yours." She smiled at him with the same false affection he showed her, and with a gesture at the milling throng, invited, "Do go ahead. This *is* the appropriate place."

"So the dormouse does roar, after all." They moved to the front of the line. "You needn't worry you'll see Campion here. He's out of town."

She sounded excessively fervent as she said, "Good. I don't want to see him."

"Even if you did, it wouldn't matter." They stood at the top of a stairway that descended into the immense ballroom. Below them, black marble pillars rose to the blue-and-gilt ceiling. Windows rose, tall and narrow. The room was so packed that people could scarcely walk. Certainly no one danced to the music of the small orchestra that played in the corner, trying furtively to cover the babble with music.

The stage had been set. The play was afoot. Everything was going as planned.

Chapter 10

As Eleanor stared into Mr. Knight's cold, clear eyes, she saw the fallacy of Madeline's scheme. Madeline had determined to come to London and talk Mr. Knight out of this misbegotten betrothal. Madness, for Mr. Knight would do as he wished—and he wished to marry the duchess. *Poor Madeline*, having to wed him on so flimsy a pretext as a wager!

And *poor Eleanor*, who would have to watch, then slip away.

"I will get what I want," he warned her.

Eleanor squeezed her hands together. He wanted her . . . would he easily transfer his affections to Madeline? Flattery, perhaps, but she thought not. All their plans were askew, and only heaven knew what would happen now.

Lady Gertrude squeezed her way back through the crowd. "I'm here, I'm here!" Glancing between the two of them, she said, "I sense an atmosphere. Should I leave again?"

"Not at all. We're about to be announced." Mr. Knight gave the herald their names.

In a lower tone, Lady Gertrude told Eleanor, "The tales I have heard." She winked and nodded, and in a theatrical whisper, said, "Later, when we're alone."

"Yes, ma'am." Eleanor's throat was dry, her palms were wet, her head felt light and shorn. "Later."

Dimly, she heard the herald say, "Yes, Mr. Knight. I know who *you* are." Turning, he faced the noisy, crowded ballroom and shouted, "Her ladyship, the marchioness of Sherbourne and future duchess of Magnus!"

Heads in the ballroom turned.

"Lady Gertrude, the countess of Glasser!"

Conversations began to die.

"And Mr. Remington Knight!"

As they descended the stairway, the silence grew greater and more profound. Even the orchestra fell silent. Never in Eleanor's quiet life had so many people paid her heed. Worse, she recognized a good many in the crowd. Did they recognize her in return? When would she be revealed as a fraud?

Unaffected, Lady Gertrude chatted, "We are making quite an entrance, and just as I expected, it is a terrible crush. Isn't this exciting?"

Not exciting. *Dreadful.* Eleanor's hand clutched Mr. Knight's elbow. Step by step, the length of the stairway stretched. All those eyes . . . staring, staring. Her feet grew too large to fit on the steps. She would surely trip and fall. Yes, she would fall, and even if she didn't get thrown out as an imposter, she would make Madeline a laughingstock.

At last they reached the shining, black-and-white marble floor. Those staring eyes looked away. The buzzing conversations resumed. Eleanor breathed again.

Lord and Lady Picard stood receiving their guests, the lady a consummate hostess, the lord a consummate fool.

Eleanor had met them during Madeline's first Season four years ago, but Lady Picard had scarcely looked at Madeline's companion, while Lord Picard had done more than glance. He had leered as he did with every young lady—although not at her face. Eleanor felt sure they wouldn't recognize who she was. But would they recognize who she wasn't?

She braced herself, but Lady Picard considered her without the slightest sign of recognition. "My lady, how good of you to make our ball the first party you attend on your return to England. And Mr. Knight. Dear sir, I had hoped you would come to make my evening"—she fluttered her lashes— "complete."

He bowed. "I wouldn't have missed this for the world."

"No, of course not. Your first ball with your new fiancée." Lady Picard almost gloated over Eleanor, but she apparently noticed nothing different about the duchess. Eleanor had cleared the first hurdle. "Your betrothal was such a surprise to come home to, wasn't it, Your Grace?"

The question set Eleanor's teeth on edge. "His Grace, the duke of Magnus, always holds his daughter's best interests at heart."

It wasn't so much an answer as a rebuke, and Lady Picard acknowledged it with a tight smile. "Lady Glasser, how good to see you. You're the guest of your niece?"

"And her chaperon," Lady Gertrude said firmly. "I'm near her day and night. I don't leave her alone for a minute."

Lady Picard adored Mr. Knight with her gaze. "Such a good idea. Mr. Knight is an excessively dangerous man."

"How can you say such a thing? I'm a lamb," Mr. Knight protested.

Both Lady Gertrude and Lady Picard giggled.

Eleanor couldn't even smile. A lamb. Absurd. He was a wolf who didn't even bother to disguise his teeth and his claws—and his ruthless nature. And if anyone here knew she lived in his house, all of Lady Gertrude's protestations would be for naught and Eleanor would be ruined. Every direction she turned, she found trouble, and all that trouble related to Mr. Knight.

Worse still, when she looked at him, she no longer perceived an upstart American. No matter that he threatened her, spied on her, coerced her. Tonight he looked absolutely smashing. He wore formal black knee breeches and a fashionably cut black coat in the way every man should—but most men lacked the form. His snowy white cravat had been tied in an intricate knot. His silk vest was a subdued pattern of gold fleur-de-lis on a blue background, and his shoes were plain and dark. Mr. Knight didn't need tall heels—he towered over the other men already. He was, in her eyes, the perfect specimen of man and, glancing around, Eleanor realized she wasn't the only woman who thought so. A great many lascivious and flirtatious glances were being lavished on Mr. Knight.

"Your Grace, how did you find Europe?" Lady Picard asked.

"In a rumpus," Eleanor said.

"That dreadful Napoleon." Lady Picard lifted her snub nose. "I'll host a little soirée later for just us women, and you can tell us all about your adventures."

"That would be lovely." Eleanor planned to be long gone.

Gesturing at the stairway behind them, Mr. Knight said, with a question in his tone, "The Regent must arrive very late to your parties, or a great many people will be turned away."

"Oh, dear," Lady Gertrude murmured.

Eleanor held her breath and prayed that Lady Picard would pretend to understand him.

Instead the lady frowned in obvious confusion. "Whatever do you mean?"

"No one can arrive after the prince—"

Lady Picard chuckled indulgently. "No, no, I'm afraid you're confused, Mr. Knight. Once the prince is here, no one can *leave* until he does. There are no rules about *arriving* after the prince."

"Ah. My American ignorance is revealed again." Mr. Knight shot a sideways, killing glance toward Eleanor.

"There are so many rules"—Lady Picard rested her hand on his in a presumption of intimacy that revealed only too clearly why he was society's darling—"and you remember them very well."

Mr. Knight smiled, showing all his perfect teeth. "I have a perfect memory. I remember everything." Especially, he said without words, Eleanor's falsehood.

Behind them, people coughed and shuffled.

Lady Picard decided she had made enough of a show of them, and she should move them along. "A pleasure to have you with us tonight. Dinner will be at midnight. Please dance and enjoy yourselves!" She dug her elbow into her husband's ribs.

He dragged his contemplation away from Eleanor's bosom. "Eh? What? Yes, the wife was saying today that if the notorious Lady Sherbourne and that lucky bastard Mr. Knight didn't come, the ball would be declared a disappointment and she might as well hang herself."

"We couldn't have that," Mr. Knight said. "Such a loss to English society."

Lady Picard beamed. Lord Picard nodded. Did neither of them hear the sarcasm in Mr. Knight's tone? Smoothly, Eleanor intervened. "Thank you for your invitation. We wouldn't have missed the event of the Season." With a small shove, she moved Mr. Knight along.

People waited to pounce on them, but Mr. Knight glared, and they backed off—for the moment.

Gracelessly, he said, "Lady Gertrude, find your friends and have a good gossip." Lady Gertrude looked doubtful. "But I just told Lady Picard I never left Madeline's side."

"I'll care for my fiancée for the rest of the evening. She can't come to harm here in the ballroom."

If he only knew!

Lady Gertrude looked to Eleanor. "Go on, Aunt. I'll be fine."

He waited until they stood alone, then in a voice both cold and furious, he said, "Lord Picard had no right to leer at you. In the future, you will let me handle these situations."

"We've made an entrance, sir, guaranteed to attract attention. It was of your making. You can't now complain that it worked." She thought herself the voice of logic and good sense and was startled to see Mr. Knight glower with even more ire. "As for Lord Picard, he's already tipsy, and he'll be snoring by midnight." She took a fortifying breath and prepared to face the crowd.

Mr. Knight took her hand and tugged her to face him instead. "I have another reason to be enraged." Painstakingly, he repeated her earlier instruction. "We're not allowed to arrive after the prince?"

If she hadn't been so nervous, so aware of their observers, she would have grinned at her small victory. "I've been gone from England for a long time."

"So long you forgot such a basic decree?"

"No, so long I forgot I'm supposed to tell the truth."

His expression made Eleanor wish Madeline were here to handle him. Obviously, Eleanor couldn't. She was an imposter who would surely be unmasked tonight, on the arm of the most charismatic man she had ever met. He was going to marry her cousin—and after tonight, he would hate her.

A female voice called, "Your Grace!"

Eleanor turned in relief, and came face-to-face with a woman that looked familiar. Very familiar.

"Your Grace, don't you remember me?" The woman's voice hit a high note that made Mr. Knight flinch. "I was Horatia Jakeson."

Horatia Jakeson had come out during Madeline's debut Season, a fresh-faced girl who'd suffered from spots, narrow lips, and a traditional father who demanded she dress conservatively and never, ever, wear cosmetics.

Apparently, she was out from under her father's thumb, for tonight she wore rouge in circles on her cheeks and paint on her lips. Her hair had been cut and frizzed across her broad forehead, and she'd gained three stone, most of it across her behind. "Horatia?" Eleanor blinked in amazement.

Horatia clapped her beringed hands. "You remember!"

Horatia had been one of the girls who had spent hours trying to inveigle herself into Madeline's inner circle. She hadn't succeeded, but she had spent hours confiding her ambitions to Madeline's companion. Surely she would recognize Eleanor, and Eleanor told herself it was better to get the unveiling over with now, right away, and end this nerve-twisting anticipation. She waited, chin up, feet braced, for Horatia to look at her, really look at her, and see that she was not the duchess.

Instead, Horatia babbled, "I married Lord Huward on a dreadful day, you should have seen the rain, and everyone said it was a bad sign, but we have two sons, so I guess they were wrong, so now I'm Lady Huward. But you and I were best of friends before you left England. You do remember that, don't you?"

Eleanor now remembered how Horatia rambled in incoherent circles. She remembered that Horatia's conversation was enough to make one want to shriek. She didn't remember how unobservant Horatia was.

As Horatia peered up at her, her face remained content. "The Continent certainly appeared to have agreed with you. You're looking beautiful. Not that you weren't beautiful before, but a little gaunt, you know. Now your cheeks are all round. Is that hairstyle new from France?"

Eleanor started. In the last hour, she'd forgotten about her hair. She touched the short ends of her hair with her fingertips. She wasn't used to the cut yet; she would probably never be used to the cut. But if this kept her from being recognized, it was worth the sacrifice of her beautiful, waist-length hair. Her hair . . . her one vanity.

She glanced at Mr. Knight. And the cut had infuriated him. To her surprise, she'd rather enjoyed his rage.

She didn't understand why. Normally those kinds of scenes made her stomach hurt, made her want to run and hide. But when Mr. Knight had stormed toward her, she'd been conscious of only one thing. He cared enough to make a scene.

Her own reaction had been interesting.

His had been fascinating.

Horatia babbled on. "But you probably didn't go

to France. That dreadful Napoleon. Doesn't he ever think of anyone but himself?"

How could Horatia not see the difference between Madeline and Eleanor? After four years, had Eleanor changed so much? Or had the years erased the sharpness of Horatia's memory and left her to see what was presented to her?

Horatia's bug-eyes darted to Mr. Knight, and the surprise she hadn't shown Eleanor she now demonstrated for him. "Good evening, I didn't see you standing there, and how I could miss the most handsome gentleman of the Season, I don't know. Lord Huward says I'd forget my head if it weren't attached to my neck, but I say, Huie—I call him Huie—Huie, that's absurd, everyone's head is attached to their neck, and he says that could be rectified. He's so droll!"

Eleanor risked a glance at Mr. Knight, and his expression of mingled horror and fascination made her release a stifled explosion of laughter.

It was probably relief that made her give way, but Mr. Knight's darkling glance only added to her mirth. With a bow and a murmured, "Excuse us," he led her away. "That's a friend of yours?" he demanded.

Eleanor had difficulty maintaining her sobriety. "No, don't be ridiculous. She is someone who would like to call the duchess her friend." Someone who had just established first contact and not shrieked out a revelation. Right now, Eleanor almost liked Horatia.

"You always speak of yourself in the third person, as if you were royalty," Remington commented.

"Almost royalty," Eleanor retorted. "Almost."

Was everyone expecting Madeline to be changed by her travels? Changed as much as Horatia? Because if that were the case, Eleanor might, just might, pull off this ruse.

A great many people hovered nearby, waiting for their chance to speak with her, and as soon as she looked up, the first gentleman rushed forward as if leading a charge. Short, bald, and dressed in an outlandish yellow-and-blue jacket, he bowed with a flourish. "Your Grace, how good to see you've returned to England. We've sorely missed your beauty."

She remembered him: a cit who had bought his way into society. Like a moth, he flitted from one wealthy, titled person to another without ever lighting, and she was sure he wouldn't notice she was an imposter, and if he did, he wouldn't dare say a word for fear he was wrong. "Thank you, Mr. Brackenridge." She let him take her gloved hand and bow over it with all the ardor of a beau enthralled.

"Careful, Brackenridge, I'd hate to have to call you out." Mr. Knight stood at her left, tall, straight, and unsmiling, like some dragon protecting the lady he had won. And in a way, perhaps he was. A good many people here in this ballroom must think this union between England's noblest of women and an American businessman to be a disgrace. Yet while he stood over her, none of them would have the audacity to dispute his steely-eyed claim.

Eleanor didn't have a chance to hear Brackenridge's nervous reply to Mr. Knight's challenge, for the next gentleman stepped up. Red-haired and freckled, he looked as if he were no more than eighteen, yet he said, "Your Grace, so good to meet you again."

Again? Eleanor didn't remember ever meeting him. Smiling politely, she tried desperately to remember his name.

"Stop teasing her, Owain, you know she scarcely noticed us when last we met." A girl who looked remarkably like Owain curtsied gracefully. "He's my twin, and when you met us, we were in the nursery. I'm Miss Joan Hanslip, and this is Owain."

"Ah, I recall now!" Madeline and Eleanor had visited the Hanslips five years before and found the family both large and jolly. "It is good to meet you again, Mr. Hanslip. Is this your first Season, Miss Hanslip?"

"Yes, and I'm having a marvelous time." She flashed a grin at the tall, thin man behind her.

He was about Mr. Knight's age, and Eleanor remembered him very well—as he would undoubtedly remember her. "Lord Martineau. How good to see you." She spoke softly and again braced herself to be revealed.

"A privilege to have you back, Your Grace," he said, but he didn't care whether she was here or in Hades. He had eyes only for Miss Hanslip.

Eleanor looked around at the people crowding around her and worked to recognize all the faces, to remember all the names, to be the duchess they expected. She had to pretend to be an aristocrat. And not just any aristocrat. One of the highest in the land, one who had created a scandal that had sent her flee-ing on an extended journey, one who had been wa-gered and lost and now, in the eyes of society, belonged to an upstart American. In short, one who excited the curiosity and interest of everyone in the ballroom.

"Your Grace, such a privilege to be present at your return after so long in exile." The gentleman's corset creaked as he bowed, while his bushy blond whis-kers formed an almost living entity on his florid cheeks. "You must be happy to be back in civiliza-tion. Such a savage expedition! So ill-fated!"

"I'm pleased to have returned in one piece." Peo-ple chuckled as if she were a wit, while around her, the number of faces continued to grow. Eleanor squinted as she stared at this gentleman and tried to recall his name. Then she did, and thrilled with her-self, she said, "But it wasn't all unpleasant . . . Mr. Stradling."

He reared back, thoroughly offended. "*Lord* Stradling."

Eleanor turned crimson. "Of course. Viscount Stradling. Forgive me, my memory temporarily de-serted me."

"Good to see you, Stradling." Mr. Knight sounded amused by her faux pas. "How did your horse do in that last race?"

As Mr. Knight drew Stradling aside, a lady stepped forward, and she rolled her eyes toward Lord Stradling and shrugged, as if indicating Eleanor shouldn't take his discontent seriously. "Your Grace, I'm sure your adventures have driven every name from your mind. I'm Lady Codell-Fitch, and like so many of us, I wish to offer congratulations on your betrothal."

"Yes, congratulations." "Congratulations!" "Amazing betrothal!"

The felicitations were insincere and accompanied by many an ogling stare, but Eleanor pretended, as Madeline would, to be pleased. Taking Mr. Knight's arm, she pressed it. "He is quite handsome." She found herself daring to defy them all with an up-tilted chin. "I wish you all could be so lucky."

The lushly garbed and overly perfumed people were obviously taken aback. They must have expected her to align herself with them, the English nobility, and with a wink and a sigh show how very much she hated this match. But she didn't even have to wonder how Madeline would react to this situation, for in this instance the two cousins thought as one. Neither of them would allow Mr. Knight to suffer the slights of society. They might not wish for this marriage, but the de Lacy pride wouldn't allow them to let anyone else know.

Close by her ear, Mr. Knight said quietly, "A pretty pretense, yet lest you imagine I'm impressed, let me assure you I remember this morning when you tried to escape. Tonight you defied me in the matter of your hair and your clothing, and lied to me to get your way. I take your words with a grain of salt." He chuckled deeply. "Smile as if I'm whispering words of love in your ear, and all these ladies will go to bed dissatisfied with their mates tonight."

Eleanor did better than that. She wished, for long, hopeless minutes, that she was somewhere else.

Anywhere else. Standing here with Mr. Knight while all eyes avidly observed them made confronting a French battalion or facing life in a Turkish harem seem like child's play. But at least so far no one had recognized her. At least no one had called her bluff. The people she'd met four years ago had changed, and they expected that she—or rather Madeline—had changed, too. More important, Eleanor had been Madeline's companion, a woman considered so unimportant by the ton that few had bothered to look at her closely. That, combined with her own re-tiring nature and the aristocracy's belief in their own omnipotence, made her safe from detection.

Eleanor had never thought she would be so lucky.

Then her luck ran out.

A mature beauty of perfect proportions elbowed her way forward. She had a fashionably narrow face and chin. She held her full lips in a perpetual, half-smiling moue of superiority. Her hair was a golden blond, and her eyes were brown and exotically tilted.

She was gorgeous. She was graceful.

She was Eleanor's oldest nightmare.

Chapter 11

Lady Shapster, Eleanor's stepmother, waited to betray Eleanor in the most public of places, in the most humiliating of ways.

Eleanor was the center of a circle with all attention on her, and she found herself backing up—into Mr. Knight's arms.

Placing his hand on her waist, he steadied her . . . and confined her.

Caught. Trapped between an old nightmare and a new.

Eleanor struggled to take a breath, to quell the rise of panic. She knew only too well how spiteful Lady Shapster could be. Time and again, from the moment Eleanor was eleven and her father had brought the elegant widow home as his new wife, Eleanor had suffered as her every fault had been reviled, her every failing exposed.

And she could only imagine what Mr. Knight's vengeance would be when his gullibility was revealed.

Peculiar, how as the hours had progressed she'd feared the crowd's ridicule less and Mr. Knight's disdain more.

"Your Grace." Bowing her head, Lady Shapster curtsied in a symphony of elegance, spreading her shimmering blue silk skirt like a peacock displays its feathers.

So she hadn't yet recognized Eleanor. But when she looked up and realized she had given obeisance to her humble stepdaughter, how Eleanor would pay!

In her deep, warm, and oh, so cultured voice, Lady Shapster said, "How good to see you home and safe. Your uncle has asked about you time and again."

It had been eight years since Eleanor had escaped Lady Shapster's domination, eight years since they'd last seen each other, but as always when facing her stepmother, Eleanor felt awkward and overgrown. "My . . . uncle?" *My father!*

"Your uncle, Lord Shapster. My *husband.*" Lady Shapster looked at Eleanor, commanding by sheer force of will that Eleanor acknowledge the relationship. She hadn't yet really looked at the face before her. Instead, she concentrated on imposing her will on the girl she thought was the future duchess. By forcing Madeline, who had no patience with Lady Shapster, to admit that they were related, Lady Shapster had some small claim on the loftiness of Madeline's nobility.

"I remember Lord Shapster. I remember . . . you." Eleanor wished she could forget, but she had been scarred by this woman, by her malice and her ruthlessness.

Imagining victory, Lady Shapster smiled, her lips stretching in a parody of graciousness. Her Roman nose tilted into the air. She planted her feet firmly apart so that no one could budge her, and her stance showed one part of her character: tenacious, haughty, and determined. But beneath the facade of nobility was a core of ice that never melted.

How well Eleanor knew that. How many times she had been frozen by a glance!

An icy wasteland stretched before her. At her back, Mr. Knight's warmth penetrated her gown, and the fires of hell burned. She had nowhere to go, so reluctantly, she stood her ground.

"Where is dear Eleanor?" Lady Shapster glanced about, as if anxious to see her stepdaughter, when Eleanor knew very well nothing could be further from the truth. "Do tell me she returned from the Continent with you. It would be dreadful if she had somehow . . . perished."

Dreadful? No, for Lady Shapster, Eleanor's demise would be a grand relief. Eleanor had never been more than an annoyance to be squashed into submission.

"Eleanor returned in good health. She didn't come to London, though. She'll be"—Eleanor almost choked on the words—"sorry to have missed you."

"The dear girl. Awkward, of course, and remarkably unhandsome. She resembles you not at all,

Your Grace." Lady Shapster simpered like a girl. "But her father and I are fond of her. We've quite missed her."

A large, warm hand landed on Eleanor's bare shoulder.

Mr. Knight. The press of his fingers should have felt like a goaler's, come to take her to Newgate.

Instead, for some reason, it felt like comfort.

"Introduce me," he commanded, and his voice held a rough edge. "I would know who this lovely lady is."

Did he find Lady Shapster attractive? So many men did. They never noticed the chill with which Lady Shapster watched them and weighed their value. Certainly Lord Shapster had never noticed, but then, he cared only for his own comfort, and Lady Shapster made sure he had that.

Reluctantly, Eleanor said, "Lady Shapster, this is my fiancé, Mr. Remington Knight." Then, silently, she cursed herself. Why had she laid claim to him? It was as if she were marking him as her own, when in fact nothing was further from the truth. She didn't want him. More important, *Madeline* didn't want him. He was betrothed to Madeline. Why did Eleanor keep forgetting?

"Mr. . . . Knight." Lady Shapster purred his name as she extended her hand to be kissed. "How good to know you'll soon be one of the family."

Why? Eleanor wanted to ask. Why would Lady Shapster want him in the family? She lived and breathed her social position. She was willing to claw and fight her way upward through the ton. Why would she welcome a commoner when so many of the aristocracy would consider the match a contamination?

Then Mr. Knight took her gloved fingers and bowed over them, and Eleanor knew why. Because he was handsome, and more than that, he had about him that indefinable air that told a woman he knew how to satisfy her.

And Lady Shapster loved to be worshipped, to provoke that kind of fawning attention that fed her conceit so nicely.

Eleanor wanted to tear them apart and stand between them with claws bared.

Releasing Lady Shapster, Mr. Knight stepped back. "How charming to meet a member of my betrothed's family." Taking Eleanor's hand, he kissed it with that kind of concentrated attention that flattered—and made her nervous. Smiling down into her face, he said, more to her than to Lady Shapster, "I hope to meet Lord Shapster, and all of the de Lacy family, soon."

Lady Shapster's darkened eyelashes fluttered, and she spoke only to him. "And I look forward to seeing you at another, more private time."

Eleanor flinched, feeling as if she'd been slapped.

"Bold as brass," Eleanor heard Lady Codell-Fitch murmur.

Lord Stradling harumphed. "Shameless!"

Ah, yes. For all that Lady Shapster had been born an aristocrat and was an acknowledged beauty, few liked her and more than a few scorned her.

Lady Shapster heard the comments and stiffened, her bared, smooth shoulders so straight and pale they looked as if they might break under the strain.

Indignant, she looked toward Eleanor—and her eyes narrowed. "Your . . . Grace?" She searched Eleanor's face, as if seeing her for the first time. "You've . . . changed."

Oh, dear. Oh, no. The moment had arrived. Lady Shapster had recognized her. At last she'd looked past the handsome clothing and stylish hair.

Eleanor forgot about bravery. She forgot Madeline's advice. And she cowered.

Yet Mr. Knight was still there, still held her hand and stood too close. In a voice so quiet it should never have reached the edges of the throng, but somehow did, he said, "Her Grace is happy to greet you all, but one at a time. She needs air—and I can no longer wait to claim a dance with her."

The sigh of approval from the ladies almost knocked Eleanor off her feet.

But Lady Shapster didn't sigh. She was still staring at Eleanor, searching her face, seeking confirmation. . . .

Gladly Eleanor turned into his arms. "Yes, let us dance."

The dance floor was small, crowded, and far away, and, taking her arm, he guided her away from the crowd of her admirers. When he'd put distance between them, he said, "You don't like that woman."

Eleanor struggled to be polite. "I find her less than pleasant."

"You don't like her," he repeated.

Eleanor couldn't say that. She'd been taught to be nice at all times. "Lady Shapster can be tactless, and occasionally she hurts people's feelings with her insensitivity."

"You don't like her," he insisted.

"All right! I don't like her." Eleanor held her breath and waited for lightning to strike.

Nothing happened. No one even noticed her admission. No one except Mr. Knight, and he had driven her to that grievous offense. "But I don't want you to think badly of her because of my disaffection."

"Why not?" he asked impatiently. "You're going to be my wife. Who else would I listen to?"

His blind faith took her breath away. Especially when the skin between her shoulder blades twitched, and she knew Lady Shapster was staring at her through narrowed eyes. Before the night was out, that woman would ruin Eleanor's life—again.

They reached the dance floor and paused, waiting for the next set to form. "She's your aunt," he said.

"My uncle's second wife, Eleanor's stepmother." And how Madeline had hated even that distant relationship!

Looking back on the encounter with Lady Shapster, Eleanor realized she should have done as Madeline would, and been harsh in her handling of that monster. Then Lady Shapster wouldn't now be circling the dance floor, peering over shoulders, trying to get another look at Eleanor.

"She's cold as ice," he said.

His acumen surprised Eleanor.

"Am I wrong?"

"No, you're right"—amazing how it got easier to

be impolite once one had taken the initial step—"but most men see only her beauty."

"Beauty's more than a hank of blond hair and a nice pair of—" He caught himself.

Eleanor looked inquiringly into his eyes.

He smiled, a frankly amused smile. "You act like an innocent. Didn't that fiancé of yours ever teach you anything?"

Madeline's fiancé had taught Madeline more than Eleanor wanted to imagine. Primming her lips, she said, "I don't know what you mean."

Mr. Knight searched her face. "Maybe you don't. How interesting. When I met Campion, I would have sworn red blood flowed in his veins." The music stopped. The couples left the dance floor. Taking her hand—an English gentleman would have allowed her to place her hand on his—he led her into the forming set. He asked, "What did Lady Shapster do to make you despise her so much?"

In a voice pitched to reach only his ears, Eleanor said, "She tried to force Eleanor to wed."

He didn't seem surprised. The music started. They separated, circled, then returned to each other. "Eleanor didn't like the choice?" He, too, kept his voice low.

"Eleanor was sixteen. Mr. Harniman was seventy. A quite disgusting, lecherous seventy, with that old man odor and those old man sores." Eleanor's stomach roiled as she remembered, and bitterly she added, "But he was wealthy, with one foot in the grave and the other on a patch of ice. That dowry would have been a fine addition to the family coffers."

The dance separated them again, and Eleanor glanced toward the crowd around the floor. A great many people watched her and Mr. Knight; they were obviously the subject of much speculation.

They came together for long measures of music. "You're loyal to your cousin," Mr. Knight said.

"Yes." Madeline had saved Eleanor from the match, and Eleanor had never forgotten. "Eleanor, who I swear is the most timid of women, sent me a plea through the housekeeper, and I came posthaste. I took her away, and she's never returned to her father's home."

He located Lady Shapster with his gaze, then looked back at Madeline. "How did that woman try to force your poor cousin?"

"She used that voice of hers, and Eleanor . . . Eleanor cringed." She cringed now in remembrance. How very much she'd hated those scenes when it had seemed hell's fire was raining down on her head. Only the memory of Mr. Harniman's groping hands had kept her from giving in. "Then, when that didn't work, she locked Eleanor in her room and fed her bread and water. Finally, when the duchess rescued Eleanor, Eleanor was disowned."

Eleanor had had no home. She'd had nothing except what Madeline had given her, and although Madeline had tried always to make Eleanor feel as if she was earning her way, Eleanor had known very well what she'd owed Madeline. That was why she'd agreed to come on this mad errand. And never had it seemed more insane than now, with her stepmother speaking to Horatia and gesturing in accusation.

"Why does Lady Shapster presume on her relationship to you? She must hate you."

"She despises everyone, but she longs to take her *proper place in society*," Eleanor enunciated, making it clear she was quoting Lady Shapster. "She didn't understand the relationship between us cousins when she tried to force Eleanor's hand, and now she regrets her actions, for she would trade on her relationship to the duke of Magnus and make much of the fact her husband is the duke's younger brother."

"When we're married, we'll make a place for your cousin in the household. Never fear, dear duchess. I will love her as you do."

Eleanor flushed. Mr. Knight had a way of saying the right thing and lighting a glow in her heart. He would hate her when he found out the truth. But she wouldn't let that dismal prospect ruin tonight. Tonight he belonged to her. As she moved with him, he filled her vision, soaked into her pores. Occasionally she would catch a whiff of his essence, like bracing cold air, spicy cinnamon bark . . . clean white sheets.

While around him, she must *not* think of things like pleasure and beds. It might lead to . . . pleasure and beds.

But of course that was impossible, for across the ballroom, Lady Shapster finished her speech to Horatia and pointed an accusing finger toward the dance floor.

The moment Eleanor had dreaded all evening long had arrived at last.

To her amazement, Horatia flung back her head and brayed with laughter. One of her friends leaned close and asked a question, and when Horatia spoke, her friend looked between Lady Shapster and Eleanor, and laughed, too. One by one, people heard. And they sniggered, staring at Lady Shapster as if she were a fool.

Lady Shapster had given voice to her suspicions and incited the mockery of the ton.

The rouge on Lady Shapster's cheeks burned like red coals as she tossed her head and swept away, and Eleanor was trapped between a sense of triumph, for she had won, and a fear of the future, for Lady Shapster never forgot, and never forgave. Someday, somehow, she would have her revenge.

But perhaps, tonight, Eleanor should do as Madeline would do—and live for the moment. Tonight, she would abandon her fears and behave as any young lady would who danced her first dance at her first ball with the most handsome man in the room.

Catching a glimpse of the dancers in one of the mirrors, she admired one young lady who moved with grace, who dressed with flare and whose hair looked dashing and sophisticated. As Eleanor watched, the lady imitated Eleanor's movements. She wore Eleanor's clothing. And Eleanor realized . . . the dashing female was herself.

She was the one who danced like a dream. Her haircut had transformed her face. She appeared younger, joyful, strikingly modish. She looked less like Madeline and more like . . . like Eleanor might have looked if her stepmother had never made her appearance in Eleanor's life.

Eleanor laughed at herself. Foolish to think a simple cut could change her, but spying herself unaware made her realize that looks were deceiving.

No matter how frightened she felt inside, no one could see past the fashionable facade.

No one except Mr. Knight. He took her hand for the promenade and looked into her eyes. He had a way of dancing that was almost like . . . making love. With him, she felt like the finest dancer in the world. They moved together, and when the music ended, she couldn't restrain her smile.

She was happy. Tonight, for this moment, she was happy.

From the top of the stairs, the majordomo smacked his cane on the floor and shouted, "His Royal Highness, George, the Prince of Wales."

The ballroom turned to see a large figure of a man poised above them, smiling graciously. His light brown hair waved across his forehead, his belly rolled before him as he descended the stairs. He'd been handsome in his youth; now in his forties, he was not so handsome, but he loved a party, and it showed as he called out names in recognition. As he made his way across the floor, the men bowed and the ladies curtsied. Eleanor did the same, and as she rose, she realized he had stopped directly in front of her.

With a beaming smile, he pinched her cheek. "Lady Sherbourne—or should I call you the duchess of Magnus." He chuckled, so she did, too. "So good to see that you've returned to our shores after so extended an absence. We have heartily missed you!"

She was bewildered. He had paid Madeline little heed during her debut. Indeed, Eleanor had thought him a bit afraid of her frank and vivacious cousin. So why was he singling her out now? "Thank you, Your Highness. I'm pleased to be home."

"You must come to Carleton House and pay me a visit." He turned to Mr. Knight. "And bring your American gentleman! He is a pleasure to know. A pleasure to game with."

Mr. Knight bowed. "Your Highness is too good. We look for your presence at our ball two nights hence."

"You shall have it. Indeed, you shall!" Prince George beamed. Lady Picard caught his eye, and he swerved toward her. "Capital party, as usual, my lady!"

As the crowd's interest moved on, Eleanor turned to Mr. Knight. "What was that all about?"

"He owes me money." Mr. Knight smiled with chilly satisfaction. "So I believe, my dear, our union has received the royal blessing."

Chapter 12

*A*t three o'clock in the morning, Eleanor sat on a sofa near the back of the Picards' ballroom and fluttered her fan to create a breeze. It had grown hot, and she was very tired. What with worrying about Mr. Knight and his nocturnal intentions, she hadn't slept well the night before, and the day had been spent in apprehension and anguish. Now her first public appearance as the future duchess was almost over, everything had gone well, better than well, and she was almost faint with relief and exhaustion. Soon she would ask Mr. Knight to take her home . . . but such a request held dangers, too. Mr. Knight could misinterpret it, and the consequences would be dire.

She watched his upright figure as he strode toward the refreshment table to fetch her a lemonade.

He was such a harsh man, trusting no one and

nothing. She had no doubt that he had ruthlessly arranged for the prince to recognize them and give them his blessing. He had imagined that made their relationship inviolate in the eyes of the ton; but more important, the prince's acknowledgment had made Lady Shapster's suspicions look even more like the ravings of a madwoman. Lady Shapster had retreated to her home as soon as the prince had left. For tonight, at least, Eleanor was safe from her.

But not from Mr. Knight. He was unwavering in his pursuit of his goal, and Eleanor pitied the woman he eventually would marry. Pitied her . . . and envied her.

From behind her, a deep, creaking voice said, "They tell me you're to be the new duchess of Magnus."

Turning in her chair, she saw an old man standing there, leaning on an ivory cane. Like so many of the elderly, he wore the clothes of his youth: a white-powdered wig, high-heeled, buckled shoes, moss green satin breeches and a lace-edged silver satin vest with stiffened skirts. He was tall, very tall, and thin, so thin his silk stockings hung loosely on his legs. "If I could be so bold." He bowed, low and graceful, like a courtier of old. "I'm Lord Fanthorpe."

In the far reaches of her mind, memory stirred. She knew the name, although why she didn't know. She only knew it wasn't a pleasant memory, like biting into an apple and finding a worm.

But Lord Fanthorpe was an elder, and trembling a

little from standing, so she gestured to the seat beside her. "My lord, how good to meet you. Won't you take a seat?"

Taking her hand, he lifted it to his lips and looked down into her eyes. His narrow face looked like a gravestone, hard and angular, with a thin nose that drooped at the end. He wore pale powder and rouge on his cheeks, and a velvet heart-shaped beauty mark had been affixed above his upper lip. His rheumy eyes were kindly. "I had to come over and tell you how much I admire your pretty fan."

"Thank you." She opened it wider to show him the scene etched in needlepoint upon the spokes. "I worked it myself."

His voice was faraway and reminiscent. "Yes, you are very like her. Very like her indeed."

She recoiled. "Her?" *Madeline?*

"Lady Pricilla. She also was very talented with her needle."

"Ohh." Now Eleanor remembered where she had heard of Lord Fanthorpe. It was in conjunction with an old family tragedy. Lady Pricilla had been her aunt, her father's sister, and Lady Pricilla had been murdered in a heinous crime.

Using his cane and the arm of the sofa, Lord Fanthorpe inched himself down beside her. "You're aware of me. I wondered. It was so long ago. It's hard to believe more than forty years have passed. Yes, I was Lady Pricilla's betrothed." His old voice quavered yet more, and his black-rimmed eyes filled with tears. "The man she left brokenhearted with her passing."

"I'm so sorry." Inadequate consolation, for after so many years the man still mourned.

"If she had lived, I would be your uncle."

"Yes."

Lord Fanthorpe looked out into the ballroom, but he seemed to gaze on a different scene. "I'll never forget seeing her body lying there on the grass, her poor face battered beyond recognition, the blood welling from the wounds in her breast. It was a horror from which I have never recovered."

"I'm so sorry," she said again. This was not party conversation, but Lord Fanthorpe was lost to his memories, and she . . . she had never heard the whole story. It was as if Lady Pricilla had never existed, and Eleanor hesitated to stir up hurtful memories by asking about the dreadful incident.

Lord Fanthorpe's hand twisted on the head of his cane. "That bastard, that commoner who had killed her, held her body. He was covered in her blood, and he cried as if he had had nothing to do with the tragedy." He almost spit as he said, "As if he were innocent."

His virulence took Eleanor aback. "He was deported, was he not?"

"To Australia. Mr. George Marchant had an *alibi.*" Lord Fanthorpe said the word as if it were an abomination. "Three noblemen swore he had been with *them.* Men of good character. Pah! So the authorities wouldn't hang Marchant. Myself, I would have drawn and quartered him, for daring to imagine he was worthy to soil Lady Pricilla with himself."

"I don't know what you mean."

"Don't you?" Lord Fanthorpe looked at her, and his brown eyes were bleak. "He had fallen in love with her, and he wanted her to run away and wed him."

Eleanor covered her mouth with her hand. "And when she refused, he killed her?"

"The lower classes have all those emotions—love, hate, happiness, melancholy—roiling inside them, and when it all becomes too much, it explodes into violence. Do you remember when the peasants in France stormed the Bastille, my dear?"

She shook her head. "I was just a child."

"You look so much like your aunt, I forget how young you are. But the Bastille proved the peasants' bestiality, and why we rightfully hold the power."

"We?"

"The aristocracy." He waved his long, narrow hands. The fingers were bent sideways, as if he'd been tortured by some terrible disease. The knuckles were swollen, but his fingernails were manicured and shaped. "We have the whip hand. Thank God someone does, or this country would be in the same shambles that afflict France. The Little Colonel, indeed." His voice rose. "Napoleon's nothing but a Sicilian thug."

Eleanor held a lurking regard for Napoleon; she might not agree that he should control the world, but she admired his confidence. Yet she had too much respect for the old lord to say so. Instead, she nodded and smiled.

"I never thought to see Lady Pricilla again, but you're the living image of her." Lord Fanthorpe's shaking fingers reached out and tilted her chin up.

"So beautiful, with your black hair"—his gaze scanned the shaggy cut as if it bewildered him—"and your big blue eyes. Do you know, I still dream about her eyes, looking at me in adoration? As I age, I think about her more and more, and to see you sitting there makes my silly old heart leap."

"Well . . . I'm glad." Eleanor had never felt so ill-equipped to make conversation, yet at the same time, she felt sorry for him—and horrified by his revelations. The vague tragedy of long ago had acquired a face, and that face was her own.

"Here comes your young man." Lord Fanthorpe's sharp eyes picked out Mr. Knight and watched him make his way through the crowd, holding her glass and smoothly evading collision with dancers and drunks. "Handsome enough. Yet a mongrel, too."

Lord Fanthorpe echoed the conviction of almost everyone in English society, but as much as Eleanor disliked Mr. Knight's high-handed ambitions, she couldn't mock him behind his back. "He's very determined."

Lord Fanthorpe turned his chilly gaze on her. "You are like Pricilla. Softhearted. Foolish. Who is he? Who are his people? Where did they come from?" His wrinkled lips curled in a sneer. "From America, the land of mongrels. All mongrels."

"But Mr. Knight's feelings are quite refined." Her jaw dropped when she heard her own voice spouting nonsense. Mr. Knight? Refined? She couldn't believe she had said such a thing.

But neither did she want this old aristocrat, with

his blind prejudices and his casual insults, to malign
Mr. Knight. Mr. Knight might lash back, and the old
man would suffer an embarrassing loss at the hands
of the younger, ruthless American.

For no other reason did she defend Mr. Knight.

"I doubt that. I believe your father lost you in a
card game. I admire your filial duty—and your loyalty. All women should be so proper." Rising, Lord
Fanthorpe bowed to her, then hobbled away without acknowledging Mr. Knight in any way.

Mr. Knight took the seat Lord Fanthorpe had
abandoned. "Who was that?"

She watched the old man depart and wondered at
the strange encounter. Lord Fanthorpe had suffered
a dreadful tragedy, and she felt sorry for him. So
sorry for him. "His name is Lord Fanthorpe. He was
once betrothed to my aunt Pricilla."

Mr. Knight watched Lord Fanthorpe with the
same intensity Lord Fanthorpe had used to ignore
Mr. Knight. "Why didn't he marry her?"

"She died."

He looked down at the glass he held, then up at
her. "That won't happen to you." Putting it down,
he stood and extended his hand. "Let's go home."

"There's our carriage." Mr. Knight assisted Eleanor
and Lady Gertrude down the porch steps while the
London fog swirled around in an endless, mad-
dened dance that the lanterns scarcely pierced. A
long line of carriages snaked away from the Picards'
door as the tired guests at last headed home.

The footman handed Eleanor and Lady Gertrude

into the dark interior, and Mr. Knight followed. They settled into their seats, the ladies facing the front, and with a jolt the wheels turned.

Lady Gertrude patted her hand over her mouth as she yawned. "It's very late."

"Yes." Eleanor stared into the darkness and fog. She could see nothing, yet her every sense was alert to Mr. Knight, seated across from her. In the tiny interior, his knees jostled hers, and she knew he was staring toward her, watching with brooding intensity. Her conversation with Lord Fanthorpe had swept through him like a strong wind, removing all softness and compassion and leaving only the harsh bedrock of his character. She didn't understand it, but the shadows that encircled him made her uneasy, and she glanced out the window as if anticipating danger.

She could see nothing out there. The lanterns on the carriage barely penetrated the fog, isolating them within the shelter of the carriage.

Insensible to the atmosphere, Lady Gertrude spoke again, her voice slurred with weariness. "The perfect ball to introduce you two as betrothed! Everyone was there. Even that dreadful Lady Shapster. I tell you, children, the day Lord Shapster married her was a sad day for the family."

"Most assuredly." Eleanor knew Mr. Knight was as aware of her as she was aware of him. It was odd, to feel close to a man who threatened her and everything that she was. Yet irresistibly, he drew her.

The carriage rolled on, separating from the other carriages, moving deeper into London.

Lady Gertrude fell silent, and a soft snore sounded from her corner of the carriage.

With a sigh, Eleanor tried to relax. It had been such a long day, and tomorrow would be just as difficult. She needed to sleep . . . she must have drifted off, for she roused at a roar from the street. The coachman shouted and pounded on the roof.

Lady Gertrude snorted and woke. "What . . . what is it?"

Mr. Knight said nothing, but Eleanor heard him pick up his cane. Her heart beat faster, her breath caught. Outside, the commotion grew louder. She recognized these sounds.

The carriage lurched to a halt.

"We're being robbed," Eleanor said to them quietly.

"Robbed?" Lady Gertrude sounded panicked and indignant at the same time. "I've never been robbed in my life."

"I have." Sliding her hand along the wall of the carriage, Eleanor sought the pistol she'd seen on the ride to the ball.

"Really?" Mr. Knight sounded interested and not at all worried by their situation. "Where?"

"In the Alps. The bandits there are fierce." The pistol had disappeared. Did he have it? "I can fight if I have a weapon." She never had had to, but she would if it was necessary.

"I think not." Mr. Knight placed his hand on her shoulder. "Stay in the carriage." Before she could reply, he kicked at the door, knocking it violently open. Outside, someone yelped as he went flying, and Mr. Knight launched himself into the street.

At once Eleanor peered out the window. In the dim light of the carriage lanterns, she saw two burly thieves leap at Mr. Knight.

She came half off her seat. "Lady Gertrude, do you have a hat pin? An umbrella?"

Mr. Knight lifted the pistol and shot one man in the chest. At the same time, he used the tip of his long cane to jab the second man in the stomach.

Eleanor blinked in shock and relief. Mr. Knight knew how to fight. Fight like a street brawler.

"I don't have anything!" Lady Gertrude said.

The footman leaped off his perch and into the fray.

Sinking down, Eleanor said, "I think Mr. Knight will be fine."

Three more men hurled themselves out of the fog. Before she could scream a warning, the broad side of Mr. Knight's cane snapped around and smacked one in the throat.

The thief went down, choking and gagging.

Eleanor clenched her fists at her waist and made small, jabbing motions, as if that would somehow help.

The footman smashed his fist into one robber's face.

The robber's head snapped back. His hand came up and gave the footman a clout, and the two went down in a brawl.

The carriage rocked as the horses pranced in alarm. The coachman held them and shouted encouragement.

The last bandit rushed Mr. Knight, knife held low.

Mr. Knight caught his wrist and pulled him toward

him, stepped aside, and slammed the thief into the side of the carriage hard enough to rattle Eleanor's teeth.

Lady Gertrude whimpered softly. "Is Mr. Knight hurt?"

"Not yet." Eleanor removed her cloak and, with a swirl, tossed it out the door onto the staggering villain. Giving a yell, he tried to fight his way out.

With one foot, Mr. Knight kicked the muffled form into the darkness.

Another ruffian charged Mr. Knight—no, it was the second man again. He landed a clout on Mr. Knight's shoulder.

Mr. Knight staggered sideways. He brought his cane around behind his back.

The thug went down with a blow behind his knees.

Mr. Knight finished him off with a crack to the head.

The footman came up, dusting off his hands.

Abruptly, the street was silent. It was over.

The footman climbed up on his perch.

Mr. Knight leaped into the carriage and called to the coachman, "John, let's go!" and the vehicle was moving before he finished closing the door.

Before she could ask if he was hurt, or run her hands over him—or, what was more likely, move to her place on the forward facing seat, he crowded her into the corner. "That was amusing."

"Amusing?" She didn't like his snarl, or the way he held his arm across her chest like an iron bar. "Terrifying would be a better word."

"I wonder who sent them." He sat too close. The aggressive heat from his body scorched her.

"Sent them?" Eleanor didn't understand, but her hackles rose.

"What do you mean, Mr. Knight?" Lady Gertrude asked. "Do you think this was done deliberately?"

"I don't believe in coincidence." He smelled of sweat and violence.

To her distress, Eleanor breathed it in as if it were perfume. On some primal level, she *liked* that he'd fought for her.

"Of all the carriages leaving the Picards' ball, ours was the one stopped." He spoke right at Eleanor, as if he were accusing her of something. "I throw Dickie Driscoll off my property this morning," he said, "and thieves attack my carriage tonight. Thieves who didn't want to rob you but only wanted to hurt me."

Shocked, Eleanor asked, "Are you saying Dickie Driscoll tried to kill you?"

He didn't answer, but she heard—and felt—the heaving of his breath.

"You are!" Eleanor couldn't believe Mr. Knight's effrontery. "I'll have you know that my servant is a good, kind man who would never hurt a flea."

"Unless that flea bit his duchess."

"Well, of course he's totally dedicated to the duchess, but—" Abruptly, she realized how she had incriminated Madeline's groom, and she couldn't allow Mr. Knight to be Dickie's enemy. She knew all too well how very deadly Mr. Knight could be. "I've known Dickie Driscoll my whole life, and I swear to you, Mr. Knight, he did not arrange to have you hurt."

"Hm." Mr. Knight slowly sat back.

Eleanor released a long-held breath.

He said, "Then I wonder who did."

Chapter 13

The stable was warm and quiet. The morning sun slipped through the cracks and knots in the gray boards, and dust motes rode on the bright rays. Holding the bridle of the staid old mare, Remington said gently, "Your Grace, this mount would suit you. She's sober and quiet. She won't run with you, and when we ride, I'll stay by your side every moment." He was trying not to alarm the duchess, who had taken a tumble as a child and broken her arm. Fearless in every other manner, she'd ridden nothing but miserable hacks since, and those with trepidation—or so he'd been told.

Yet the duchess paid him so little heed that he might not have spoken, for in the next stall stood a magnificent gray gelding, and she and the gray appeared to be having some kind of communion. Slowly, carefully, she extended her hand. The horse stepped forward and snuffed at her fingers, like a dog that wanted petting. "Ah, you are a beauty," she breathed. "I wish I had a carrot to give you."

Remington had been disappointed to hear of his duchess's timidity. He loved to ride and had plans to parade his ducal acquisition all over London on a fine piece of horseflesh. Now she was behaving like a woman who loved riding. "That horse is called Diriday," Remington said, "and he's spirited. He requires a firm hand and a good gallop every day."

"Of course he does." The duchess stroked the gelding's nose and used the kind of slow, gentle voice experienced grooms used to tame a stallion. "Diriday. What a beautiful name. Diriday needs to be groomed and admired and guided. He needs to be"—her voice dropped into a croon—"loved."

Remington believed the same about the future duchess.

When he thought about the attack last night, that someone had deliberately stopped them, *them*, and no others, he wanted to beat those men all over again. If he'd been alone, he'd have questioned them, found out who was behind the assault. But with the duchess and Lady Gertrude in the carriage, he'd had to get them away.

Who had it been? Madeline had sworn over and over that it wasn't Dickie Driscoll. Remington doubted that. Dickie served the duchess faithfully, and he might have feared for her safety. Certainly he feared for her virtue—and in that matter, he was right.

Her long form was clad in a thin white calico morning gown, a fashionable garment that looked to Remington's eyes to be nothing more than a sheer nightgown that clung to her bare legs. Her half-boots were soft brown leather, her brown velvet pelisse matched, and frivolous blue ribbons decorated her straw bonnet. She stood with her shoulders back, her arms graceful curves, her fingers long and slender.

She was the daughter of his most dire enemy, and it didn't matter. He wanted her as he had never wanted another woman.

Perhaps the duke of Magnus had arranged last night's attack. He'd lost his daughter to Remington. Remington detained her in his house. Both good reasons to arrange Remington's death, and Remington knew only too well how lethal Magnus could be.

And although it was unlikely, Magnus might have uncovered Remington's true identity. If he had, then he most certainly had ordered Remington's death.

Of course, there were other enemies. Men with whom Remington had had business dealings. Men who despised Remington for trying to become one of the English aristocracy. Remington didn't discount anyone. That was why he carried at least one weapon with him everywhere—a knife, his gold-headed cane—and watched and weighed every situation. He was not going to die now. Not when he was so close to retribution.

Leaving the mare, he slowly advanced on the duchess, observing how intensely she stroked the horse before her. "Diriday is a handful unless he has an experienced hand on the reins."

"I can ride him," she whispered.

"My informants said—"

"I can ride him!"

Was his duchess always going to surprise him? This boded ill for his control of the situation, and he liked to maintain control. That was why he had investigated her. That was why he had had her watched.

Was she testing the limits of her fear in hope of having access to a swift mount? Did she imagine she could escape him?

He would quash those pretensions now. He glanced around. The grooms had vanished as soon as he and Madeline had entered the stable. Only the restless movements of the horses disturbed the silence of the stable. It was time to find out what the duchess was made of. It was time to see if her blue blood was chilly, or if she had warm, red blood flowing in her veins. Moving with the stealth of an army scout, he paced toward her.

Unaware of the danger that stalked her, Eleanor caressed Diriday. She was enthralled by the gelding. She loved to ride; loved the communion with an animal who enjoyed wind and speed. Because of Madeline's childhood accident, she seldom rode, which had left Eleanor sitting in coaches and sedan chairs, keeping Madeline company while others had galloped past on mounts Eleanor had longed to try.

"You've made me very happy," Mr. Knight said.

He was, she realized, suddenly close. And as always, he was taking up too much space, breathing too much air, crowding her far too much. "Why is that?" She wanted to edge away from him, yet she didn't want to abandon Diriday.

"Because this horse was my first choice for you."

Mr. Knight rubbed the gelding's nose too. The fickle animal recognized a master and responded with an adoring snort.

Withdrawing her hand, Eleanor grasped the top rail of the stall. Very well. Diriday liked Mr. Knight. That wasn't surprising. If she weren't in this awkward situation, she would adore Mr. Knight, too. As it was, she pretended to stare at the horse so she wouldn't gape at Mr. Knight. She'd already noted with one glance his dark blue riding costume, cut precisely to display his broad shoulders, his narrow waist, the broad muscles of his thighs. His black boots shone, and his blond hair had a ruffled appearance, as if he'd discarded his hat and shoved his fingers through the strands.

Nothing in his face betrayed the strain of last night's attack, while the memories still haunted her. She hated that her heart had pounded as he'd fought, hated that she'd wanted to spring out of the carriage and help him—when, obviously, he had needed no help. He was a strong, capable man, a man with a background she knew nothing about. Lord Fanthorpe had pointed that out all too vividly, and her own response mortified her even now. She had called Mr. Knight *refined*.

And why? The question haunted her. She told herself it was because she didn't want a fight between the two men. Because she was timid, and couldn't bear to be the cause of a scene. It couldn't be that she worried about Mr. Knight's feelings. He had proved time and again he had no feelings to worry about.

He was still caressing the gelding, but he was

watching her. The silence stretched between them, a silence he obviously didn't fear.

But she did. Every time words faded between them, she said something stupid. Something revealing. But not this time. In a clipped tone, she said, "Diriday is the perfect mount for me."

In that low, deep, beastly growl, he replied, "It's good to know you'll . . . ride . . . as I wish."

She flushed. Her toes curled, and her nipples tightened into firm beads that ached to be touched.

How had he done it? She'd said the most obvious thing, and he'd made it clear he wasn't talking about the horse.

He pried her bare fingers from the rail of the stall and kissed them.

"I find Lady Gertrude is a good chaperon," he said.

Eleanor nodded, stricken dumb by the brief brush of his lips that had sent goose bumps racing up her arms.

He placed her hand on his shoulder. "So good, you and I haven't had a moment alone together."

"We're alone now." Unwise to remind him!

He crooned with satisfaction, "So we are."

"So we should go now." She tried to step away, to obey her instincts and flee.

Mr. Knight maneuvered her so that her back was to the post. "Fortunately, Lady Gertrude doesn't ride, and doesn't see that our being together now is a cause of concern."

"It's not." Eleanor tried to speak firmly, yet she ended on a questioning note.

"Lady Gertrude has no imagination." In the dim

light, his eyes watched her relentlessly, like a falcon watches a fleeing morsel. In slow increments, he extended his free hand and wrapped it around her waist. "I find myself wondering about you."

When had the situation turned dangerous? "I'm easily understood."

"You're a mystery, one I find myself compelled to solve. I want to know whether you like to kiss with your mouth closed . . . or open."

Her eyes widened.

"If you enjoy being embraced so closely that your breasts press against a man's chest."

She gasped in shock.

"Where you find most pleasure when a man's mouth, *my* mouth, roams your body."

She wanted to gasp once more, but the gratification she saw in his face stopped her. Yes, he shocked her. He enjoyed shocking her. But she *hated* being so craven. She yearned to take him aback, and out of the depths of that need, she found the nerve to reply, "You may ask me those questions, and mayhap, if I wish, I'll reply. But don't imagine you yourself can discover the answers."

"*Ask.* What a novel idea." A small smile played across his velvet lips. "Yes, you could *tell* me, of course, but I find I like to make discoveries on my own." Pulling her close against his body, he sealed them together.

Discoveries? She could tell him about discoveries. She *did* like being embraced so tightly that her breasts pressed against his chest; and that, and the amusement in his gaze, were reasons enough to leave—at once.

With a twist, she freed herself and ran.

He sprang after her. Two stalls down, he caught her by the waist. He swung her against the gate and held her hard against him.

She stared into his pale blue eyes and with all her heart wished she had some experience in these matters, for she had never felt so helpless in her life.

"I'm not going to hurt you." His voice was deep and heated. "I'm not going to ravish you. I'm just going to kiss you."

Just? Just? She had never been kissed in her whole life, and if he laid his perfectly sculptured lips against hers, she would be marked as surely as if he had branded her. "Not here." She glanced toward the end of the stable, toward the open door. Surely if she reminded him of the proprieties, he would respond correctly.

Instead, he opened the gate, and with the same finesse he'd used on the dance floor the night before, he whirled her inside the stall. "The straw is clean, and the stall is private. You needn't worry about the grooms. No one will interrupt us."

She had had nothing in her mind but putting him off. Now he acted as if she had very properly asked for privacy. "I don't . . . we can't . . ."

His white teeth flashed in his tanned face, and he pulled her up against him so that she stood on her toes, so that her balance depended on him. "I can't believe I've managed to wait so long."

What did he mean, so long? They'd met only two days ago.

Then she saw his expression as he lowered his

head to hers, and she realized that for this man, two days of restraint were an eternity. The man saw what he wanted and he went after it—and he wanted her.

Her eyes closed as his lips touched hers. Her first kiss. Close-mouthed, gentle, seeking.

She tried to pretend this wasn't happening. Madeline didn't want him and wouldn't wed him, yet it wasn't right for Eleanor to kiss her cousin's fiancé.

But the crackle of hay beneath her feet and the scent of the horses gave this moment an unrelenting reality. The buttons on Mr. Knight's jacket dug into her sternum. His arms handled her with an expertise that bespoke familiarity in handling an unwilling woman, and he kissed . . . like a beast of sensual powers.

His lips were silky soft, skilled in the art of love, giving pleasure with the lightest touch. He barely brushed her lips, yet she found herself lifting her face, seeking his touch like a flower follows the sun.

For a first kiss, it was very pleasant—and ultimately unsatisfying.

Which surprised her. She had thought Mr. Knight would kiss very well.

Well, not that she allowed herself to think about it, but sometimes the stray wicked idea crossed her mind before she could quash it. Yet it was true; she had expected better of Mr. Knight. She hadn't expected him to leave her wanting more than these light touches.

So when he drew back, she pressed her lips more firmly against his and coaxed him with soft mur-

murs and the pressure of her body on his, the pressure of her lips on his. He hesitated as if unsure, then deepened the kiss.

His lips parted slightly, and it seemed that he urged her . . . challenged her . . . to do the same. She opened her lips and found herself breathing into his mouth—and he breathing into hers.

It felt as if they were exchanging pieces of their beings, of those essential parts that made them human. She could almost taste him in his breath, and that frightened her—and intrigued her. She wanted to know his flavors, his odors, his touches. She needed to know everything about him . . . at least at this moment.

For this moment would never come again. She must never kiss him again. She would never kiss any man again. And she wanted him so earnestly . . .

She wanted him.

The words echoed in her mind, and with a snap, her good sense returned. She pulled away from him. She backed against the wall and held her hand over her heart. "You must think I'm . . . unchaste."

He didn't laugh at her, or even look amused. "No, I think you're lonely."

"What?" *Lonely?* "I'm not lonely." She had her duties. She had her relatives. She lived a productive life.

"You kiss like a woman who stands on the outside, always peering in the window of life and wishing she were there, yet never having the guts to demand entrance."

"That's not true." Curse him, it was exactly true.

He paid her no heed. "Those days are over. Whatever you're afraid of, you should be more afraid of me."

He didn't have to insist. She was.

His brows were lowered, his jaw firm, his eyes flinty. "Listen to me. From now on, you're going to be at my side every minute. No matter what happens, no matter how objectionable the events, no matter how unhappy you make yourself, at the end of the day you're going to go home with me. And at night . . . I'll show you all the wonders of desire. Our nights will be passionate and grand beyond your wildest dreams, and I'll take you to the edge of passion again and again. You'll squirm beneath me and atop of me, you'll touch every inch of my skin, you'll live for my kisses. Until one day you'll wake up and all you can think of is me. Of the pleasure I bring you. Of how it feels when I'm inside you. All the sorrow will fall away, and you'll be mine forever."

As she stared at him, wide-eyed, her body throbbed from his touch—and worse, from his words.

She was in such trouble.

She had to tell him the truth. She couldn't let this go on. Blast Madeline and her clever plot and all the things Eleanor owed to her. If he knew who Eleanor was, he would stop talking to her this way. He would stop parading her around as his fiancée. She could go home—wherever that was now—and huddle in her bed and thank her lucky stars for her escape. And think of him and dream of him and touch her own body and pretend he touched her.

In a furious tone, he said, "You're not who they say you are."

She caught her breath on a sharp shard of horror. He already knew! "No." Her voice squeaked. "I'm not."

Again he reached for her. Again he brought her up against him. But this time he showed her how very much he'd restrained himself before.

Sliding his hand along the base of her neck, he thrust his fingers in her shorn hair and cradled her skull. He put his open mouth on hers, demanding response at once with the thrust of his tongue, and when she didn't open to him, he nipped at her lower lip.

She cried out, an incoherent, startled sound.

He was inside.

Their first kisses had been exploration, a chance for him to taste her, a chance for her to grow used to him.

His tongue thrust rhythmically into the cavity of her mouth. Her lips grew tender under his assault. She hardly knew what to think, what to do . . . but it didn't matter. He had taken control. The care he'd used the first times he'd kissed her was absent now. This time he sought satisfaction, and he sought it angrily, passionately.

Keeping a tight hold on her, he glared down at her. "You're different than everyone says. Everything I know about you is wrong."

She tried to answer, to explain, but he swung her off her feet. She was a tall woman, and he picked her up as if she were light as a feather. Kneeling, he rested her on a pile of straw. He covered her with his body, and it was hard and hot, weighing her down. The stall was warm and dim. The straw crackled beneath them, enveloping them in the dry, golden scent. He ground his hips against hers and against her belly she felt the length of him.

He kissed her again, using his lips to caress hers, using his tongue as an incitement. He buffeted her with passion so strong she tossed beneath him. She didn't understand how this man of icy composure had so unexpectedly become wild and perilous. She had glimpsed the beast that lurked beneath his civilized exterior, but never had she imagined he would release it to feed on her.

But feed on her he did, without a care for her inexperience. He slid his hands down her arms, lifted her wrists and placed them around his neck. Nothing remained between them but their clothes, insignificant when compared to his obsession, which burned and spread from his flesh to hers.

To her surprise, her own passion rose to meet him. She wanted to claw at him, to tear his shirt from his throat and bury her mouth there, to wrap her legs around him. He had gone mad with passion, and he carried her with him.

And she swore she felt the ground move beneath her.

Or maybe it was something inside her that shifted. Something profound. Something significant.

His palms stroked down her sides, finding the shape of her waist and hips, lingering as if tempted to learn more. His knee slipped between hers; it pressed between her thighs and created a throbbing that spread up her belly to her breasts. Her skin felt feverish. His heart thundered against her breasts, and they ached as if they were swollen. Her body hurt with need, and she wanted the kiss to go on forever.

No. She wanted the kiss to become something more. Everything more.

He threw himself sideways so suddenly that she moaned in shock.

Savagely, he pitched himself onto the straw beside her. "God damn it." He sounded livid. "I want to mate with you, and I can't. Not here. Not now."

And she wanted to mate with him. "Certainly not here and now."

"I can't take my future wife in a stable," he said furiously. "You're a gently bred young woman, not some trollop."

"No, definitely not a trollop." She touched her tender lips. Nothing had changed. She ought to tell him who she really was. She ought to tell him now.

But she didn't want to. She liked his kisses. She wanted more of them. "You're angry with me."

He took deep, harsh breaths. "Not with you. With myself, for taking this too far too soon. I was going to . . ." He wouldn't tell her what he was going to do, so he repeated, "You're a gently bred young woman."

Eleanor would accept every kiss he pressed on her. More than that, she would seek them out, and come what may, she would accept the consequences of her actions.

She could be foolish. She was, after all, just as much of a de Lacy as anyone else in the family.

Chapter 14

*H*is duchess rode like a woman born to the saddle, moving gracefully with the horse. Here, on the riding path in Green Park, her smooth mask of serenity slipped, and she became a woman saturated in bliss. It was as if the wind in her face and the great beast beneath her made her forget who she wished to be—and instead made her who she was.

Remington wanted her to look like that for him, too. He wanted her to rise and fall above him, her face absorbed in pleasure, as she took him inside her again and again . . .

And it was damned difficult to ride with a cock-stand. He needed to keep his attention on his fiancée in case she fled, not appreciate the jiggle of her breasts as she rode. For given the chance, she *did* ride well enough to escape him.

Green Park was close to Berkley Square, a pleasant piece of ground. A pavilion was set in a wooded grove, and there cows grazed in bucolic splendor. Here aristocratic Londoners came to pretend they were in the country, to watch the cows being milked and the chickens fed, and perhaps turn their hand to the tasks themselves. The riding paths provided Remington some security. Here his stallion could outpace her, and Remington would ride posthaste when the stakes were high. But on the streets of London, with its turns and its traffic, she might well be able to slip away into an alley and disappear.

In the future, he would drive them to the park to ride and have his groom lead the horses.

Of course, once he had attached her to him with the bonds of flesh, he would have control of her—and that thought made him realize his cockstand hadn't subsided at all. If he could just concentrate on Madeline's whereabouts and not on Madeline's person . . . but she drew him like a single candle flame in a world of darkness.

Drawing up, she patted her horse's neck, then lavished a smile on Remington. "That was wonderful. Thank you so much."

That was another thing. She didn't act like a duchess. Each thing he did for her, gave her, seemed to surprise and dismay her. The horse was the first present she'd accepted without reservation. Most aristocrats lived in a world of privilege where their every whim was indulged. Why was this lady surprised when he catered to her? And when had his previous determination to bring a duchess to her knees changed to the desire to indulge this waif's every wish?

Her smile faltered. "Is something wrong?"

"No. Why?" If only he hadn't tasted the loneliness on her lips and recognized the same loneliness that pervaded his soul.

"Because you're staring at me so grimly." She glanced down at Diriday, and she patted him more firmly. "He hasn't been hurt by the exercise, has he? I didn't notice anything wrong with him, but it's been long since I've ridden so fine a mount, perhaps—"

"The horse is fine." It annoyed Remington that she so easily transferred her worry from him to her gelding.

The kisses in the stable had shaken him to his core. Before he'd met her, he'd mapped out his seduction. An aggressive pursuit for the first three days, filled with desirous glances and lingering caresses to accustom her to his touch. A first kiss at their ball, and another, deeper kiss after the guests left. From that moment until their wedding night, a barrage of caresses to soften her animosity and prepare her for his ultimate possession. It didn't matter that he didn't personally know her; he foresaw no problem wanting her. Impeccable sources had told him that she was pretty and personable, and he enjoyed women: their smiles, their bodies, their chatter, their little furies.

Then the duchess had appeared and upset his plans. How the hell was he supposed to keep his hands off her when she defied him at every turn? She wouldn't wear the clothes he'd provided. She'd cut her hair. She answered his kisses. And it seemed that with each defiance, she blossomed a little more.

Worse, he liked it. He liked seeing her chin lift and hearing cheeky remarks burble from her lips. He encouraged her to face the world with the haughtiness that so set his teeth on edge from the other aristocrats. With artless guile, she was destroying his plans.

Gesturing to the groom, Remington brought the man forward. "The lady and I will stroll."

"Aye, sir." The groom took the bridles.

Remington dismounted, then walked to Diriday's side and held up his hands to Madeline.

Something of his lustful thoughts must have shown in his face, or perhaps Madeline recalled the events in the stable, for she hesitated, then slid slowly out of the saddle. He caught her, allowed himself a shameless moment when their bodies rested briefly against each other, then set her on her feet.

The groom walked the horses toward a patch of trees near a stream.

Today the sun shone, but the sky had a gray cast to it, and again Remington thought a tempest must be brewing. The air held a scent of iron, as if the hammer of a storm waited to smash through London's streets and prove its mastery of mankind.

Yet the air was warm, the day rife with opportunities, and he gestured toward the pavilion. "Shall we go and see the sights?"

She sauntered ahead of him, a fine figure of a woman in a misty gray riding costume that clung to every curve. Her hat sported a cardinal red feather, and the fringe of her matching red scarf fluttered around her neck. Her hips rolled with each long stride. "I have milked a cow, you know," she said. "We were in Italy, traveling a mountain road. A freak snowstorm came up and drove us to the first shelter, which was a barn with five cows and no owner in sight. We were hungry, and the cows became increasingly more miserable when no one showed up to milk them, so Dickie showed us how. We had warm milk for supper." She chuckled, lost in reminiscences of her European tour.

As he was lost in the memory of what had happened in his stable.

She shouldn't have run from him. With all the good sense of his own stallion responding to a mare, he'd chased her. Chased her and would have mounted her but for some lingering good sense.

"I had a great many adventures on my trip." She glanced back at him, her eyelashes fluttering in womanly enticement. "You'd be astonished to hear them all."

How did she do that? Beckon him with a glance, ensuring that he would trail after her like a lovesick swain? Two days ago she'd scarcely had the courage to look him in the eyes. A few kisses—a few very good kisses—and she was flirting.

She added, "Someday I'll tell you . . . if you ask nicely." A cascade of climbing roses blossomed on trellises they passed, and she stopped and, with tender fingers, lifted a blossom. She smiled down at the furling petals, then, closing her eyes, she sniffed it deeply. "I love roses, especially yellow roses. They're not cherished like red roses, but they're invariably cheerful. Add them to a bouquet of lavender, and they make a heavenly smell and a beautiful display. Put them in a vase by themselves, and they nod and smile at everyone who passes."

It was one thing to leap a few steps in the courtship, to kiss Madeline ahead of schedule. It was quite another to jump the girl like a soldier on a rampage. But when Remington had made his plan to seduce his duchess, he'd failed to consider two contingencies. He'd not expected her to respond as if he were the man she'd waited for all her life . . . and he'd not anticipated his own undisciplined passion for this one woman.

Without changing her tone, she asked, "Mr. Knight, are you going to speak, or are you going to continue to maintain that enigmatic silence which tells me nothing and our onlookers everything?"

Startled out of his reverie, he asked, "Our onlookers?"

"People are wandering the paths. Riding, walking, exchanging greetings—and we're of interest to them. If you appear to be not speaking to me, they'll put an unfavorable explanation on your truculence, and the rumor will sweep London that we're quarrelling. From there, it's a short journey to a broken betrothal and a cancelled wedding."

Was she hinting at insubordination? Taking her arm, he pulled her to a halt. "There will be no broken betrothal. There will be no cancelled wedding. We shall be wed, and once wed, you'll wear my ring and my clothes, and accept my possession and my authority." He waited for her to complain, to challenge his decree.

Instead she stared intently over his shoulder at the riding path.

He couldn't believe her. He was talking to her, telling her what their life would be, and she ignored him.

Her eyes grew bigger and bigger.

Swinging around, he saw a black, scrawny, medium-sized dog skulking across the path in front of a spirited stallion. The fashionable youth on the stallion paid no heed. The dog was going to be hit.

With a scream, Madeline pulled free of Remington and dashed into the path.

The driver shrieked and sharply pulled up the horse.

In terror, Remington shouted a warning and raced after her.

She caught the dog around the belly.

In a smooth movement, she jumped off the track and rolled in the grass, the dog clasped in her arms.

The rider fought with his rearing mount.

The dog yipped in an ever increasing crescendo. Struggling out of Eleanor's grasp, it limped away to huddle on the ground not far away.

Skidding on his knees at Madeline's side, Remington demanded, "Are you hurt?" His heart pounded, and he wanted to shake her. Or embrace her. He didn't know which.

"I'm fine." She struggled to sit up.

Afraid she was injured and didn't realize it, or wouldn't admit it, he tried to keep her down.

Slapping his hands away, she crawled toward the cowering dog. "Are you hurt, my beauty?" she crooned.

Beauty? The dog was nothing but a mutt. At two stone or a little more, it looked like an elkhound who'd been washed in hot water and shrunk to half size. Its black-and-tan fur was matted, its belly was sunken, and the creature gave off an odor of ripe garbage, probably from foraging for scraps.

As the duchess neared, it bared its teeth and growled.

She extended her fist, fingers down. "You poor little thing."

"Be careful," Remington said sharply. Damn the woman, she ran from one danger to another.

"I am." The growl subsided to a whimper, and Madeline scratched its chin. "It won't bite me."

Apparently she was right, for the mutt fixed its brown eyes on the duchess, and when she stroked its head, it responded by burying its head in her chest.

She ran her fingers over its left rear leg. The dog whimpered, and she said softly, "It's hurt."

Remington badly wanted to say that he didn't care, but he couldn't quite. He liked animals, but damn it to hell! She'd almost gotten herself killed for this one.

From behind them, Remington heard the stomp of boots. The youth stalked toward them, slapping his gloved hand with his whip. "Lady!" He was white and shaking. "What in Hades were you doing, lady? I almost hit you."

Remington rose to confront him, but before he could say a word, Madeline came up like an infuriated wasp. "What was I doing? What were you doing? You almost hit this dog." Her cheeks and the tip of her nose glowed scarlet with fury. Her eyes sparked with brilliant blue. She had a smudge on one cheek and her hat was askew, but that didn't matter, for all the passion she had revealed in the morning's kiss she put into the defense of a mutt she had never before seen.

Surly with guilt, the youth said, "It was just a flea-ridden stray." Then her loveliness registered. He jerked to attention, back straight, shoulders back. He stared with avid fascination into her face. "I believe we may have met, although I can't quite remember—"

She rampaged on, "Is that the way you were taught? To run over defenseless animals?"

Stepping back, Remington folded his arms. This youth didn't stand a chance.

Her eyes narrowed. "Wait a minute. I recognize you. You're Lord Mauger!"

"Yes, I . . . I am. Viscount Mauger, humbly at your service." Whipping his hat from his head, the youth bowed, eager to make a belated good impression on the beauty before him. "And you are. . . ?"

She wasn't impressed or interested. "I know your mother, and she would box your ears for this."

Dull red rose in Mauger's cheeks. "You won't tell her."

"Not if you promise to be more careful in the future. I won't be around to rescue the next dog, and I remember what a fine lad you were. You love animals, and you'd feel guilty if you killed one."

"You're . . . you're right." Mauger's pleading eyes

looked much like the dog's. "I just bought the chestnut, and came into town, and I wanted to show him off, but that's no excuse . . ."

As Mauger dug his toe into the dirt, Remington realized he was observing a master at work. She had taken the young man from fury, to infatuation, to guilt in one smooth journey, and Mauger adored her for it.

In a comforting tone, she said, "I know you won't do anything like this ever again."

"I swear I won't." Mauger smiled winsomely.

With an unpleasant start, Remington realized the young man was quite handsome.

"Please, ma'am, won't you tell me the name of my goddess of justice?" Mauger implored.

She blinked at him.

"He means you," Remington said dryly, and did the honors. "Mauger, this is the marchioness of Sherbourne and the future duchess of Magnus. Your Grace, the Viscount Mauger."

"*You're* the duchess of Magnus?" Mauger's eyebrows raised. "You visited us one summer eight years ago, but I didn't remember you being so beautiful."

It didn't sound like a compliment; it was too sincere for that. And Madeline cringed as if she'd been slapped.

Remington picked up her hand and conveyed it to his lips. "She grows more beautiful every day."

"Yes. Obviously!" Mauger bowed again, as if eager to make amends for his less than tactful comment. "Her Grace is as fair as the sun in all its brilliance."

If possible, Madeline looked even more dismayed.

Infatuation. The youth was infatuated with Remington's duchess. That would never do. She was Remington's, and other men could envy him, but they were not to want her. So Remington bowed and introduced himself. "I'm Mr. Remington Knight." He waited, but nothing registered on Mauger's face. The lad hadn't heard the gossip. "Tomorrow night, the duchess and I are having a ball to celebrate our betrothal." He watched Mauger deflate as he realized his sun-goddess was already out of his reach. "I hope you'll do us the honor of attending."

"Thank you. Yes. Of course. I'd be delighted. A pleasure to meet you both. Sir. Ma'am." Mauger's gaze lingered on Madeline as he tipped his hat, but he manfully made his way back to his groom and his horse, and with shaky care rode away.

Madeline didn't bother to watch him leave, which gave Remington comfort. Instead, she again knelt beside the dog—which filled Remington with trepidation. He squatted at her side and with his finger under her chin, brought her to face him. "Never mind the mutt. Are you all right?"

"Yes," she said brightly. "Of course."

Taking her hand, Remington removed her shredded glove. Her palm was skinned, one fingernail broken. He hadn't a doubt that she'd banged her knee or wrenched her wrist or some other injury to which she wouldn't confess. But now that the incident was over, he wanted to shake her. "For a mongrel? You risked your life for a mongrel?"

The dog raised its hackles and bared its teeth at Remington's tone.

"Down!" Remington snapped, and the dog settled back. But it kept its gaze warily on him, and Remington knew the damned dog had attached itself to Madeline.

"Some people might call you a mongrel." She wore an odd expression, as if some people already had.

Had she defended him as she'd defended this strange dog? Was he a stray she'd taken under her wing—or had she laughed and agreed that, because of his birth, he was less than her? It shouldn't be a matter of interest to him—but it was. Everything about her was of interest to him, and why?

Because he was infatuated with her. Infatuated . . . and obsessed with the one woman he should never love.

Chapter 15

Eleanor shifted uncomfortably beneath Mr. Knight's gaze. He looked at her as if he wanted to pry open her head and peer inside.

Well. He could scarcely have stumbled on the truth here in the middle of Green Park, could he? That was impossible . . . wasn't it?

She moved from foot to foot, trying to ease her aches and pains. Now that the excitement of the rescue had ended, she was aware that her palms hurt where she'd scraped them and she'd landed on her knee wrong. She wouldn't complain, of course. Mr. Knight would tell her it was her own fault, and right now his eyes looked cold and thoughtful, and his broad, delicious mouth grew thin.

Then his lids swept over his eyes, and when he looked at her again, she could see no censure—and no interest. "You don't know what this dog is or where it came from, except that Lord Mauger is no doubt right—it is flea-bitten."

Her ire rose again. "So I should only care about creatures with the proper pedigree and the proper hygiene? Thank you, sir, but no. I abhor cruelty, especially to poor beasts who can't do anything to help themselves, and if you can't see the value of caring for the lost and the forlorn, then I'm sorry for you."

In a cool, flat tone, he said, "Not at the cost of your life."

Bitterly aware that her life was only valuable to him because he believed her to be the duchess, Eleanor shrugged. "My life is not so important." Then some errant resentment made her taunt, "Oh, but I forgot—I'm your passport into the ton."

He apparently didn't appreciate cynicism, at least not from her, for his voice held a warning. "Madeline . . ."

Madeline. She wasn't Madeline, she was Eleanor— but this was no time for confessions. She gestured behind him. "We have attracted an audience." An audience comprised of a number of guests from the Picards' ball, and a few others, unknown to her, but costumed in the finest garb and obviously noble. All ogled her in openly expressed amazement, and two of the ladies released a series of high-pitched giggles.

To her astonishment, she wasn't so much embarrassed as annoyed. She hated scenes, yes, but these people needed an occupation if their best entertainment was tittering about a dog rescue.

"Poor Mr. Knight," she murmured. "Your plan to

impress the ton with your sophistication and your fiancée has taken a downward turn." Sinking back down beside the dog, she left him to deal with the situation.

But he surprised her. With a smile that looked genuinely amused, he faced the crowd.

One gentleman in particular seemed to hold his attention. The gentleman was perfectly groomed, with a crisp cravat, a snowy white shirt, and boots so shiny and black that the sun gleamed on the leather. He looked thoroughly shocked by the proceedings, and Eleanor idly reflected that Madeline would have a dreadful time clearing up her reputation when she finally arrived in London. Yet Eleanor wasn't nearly as sorry as she might have been, and growing more impatient.

Where was Madeline? This situation was disintegrating by the minute.

"Brummel," Remington said. "Good to see you."

Brummel. Eleanor knew that name. Beau Brummel was the arbiter of English society, the man who spent hours tying his cravat, the man who cared little for aristocratic prestige, and everything for an ideal appearance.

Eleanor was aware she failed to present an ideal appearance. In fact, she was a mess, and without a bit of contrition, she reflected that Mr. Knight was in trouble now.

"Mr. Knight." Beau Brummel stepped forward and bowed to Eleanor. "I don't believe I've had the pleasure of meeting the lady."

With a last scratch under the dog's chin, Eleanor rose as Remington made introductions.

Beau Brummel's gaze flicked over the scene. "You . . . like dogs, Your Grace?"

With innate honesty, Eleanor answered, "I find them more trustworthy than most humans."

"I don't know any trustworthy dogs," Beau Brummel said.

"Do you know any trustworthy humans?" She was speaking of the little crowd gathered behind him, the people who last night had thronged about her and after this escapade would shun her.

To her astonishment, Beau Brummel comprehended—and smiled. "Your Grace, you're all too right." In a solicitous tone that revealed his true concern, he said, "But I fear that you've ruined your riding costume."

With an audacity that surprised even her, she said, "I'm the duchess of Magnus. I set the fashion. Tomorrow you'll see ladies riding with torn gloves and their hats askew."

Brummel was startled into a chuckle. "I would be most honored if you would walk with me."

"Toward the horses. I suppose I should go and repair my appearance." And her injuries were hurting her more and more.

"Of course, to the horses," Beau Brummel agreed.

They strolled side by side toward the wood where the groom waited; Mr. Knight and the dog walked a step behind.

When they had moved away from the mob, Beau Brummel said, "I understand that you've been away from London for quite some time, Your Grace. If I might be so bold as to offer advice . . . you have a style all your own and, I suspect, a prediliction for trouble."

"She does, indeed," Mr. Knight offered.

Eleanor shot him a glare—and checked on the limping dog. It was keeping up, but it couldn't go far. She switched her attention back to Beau Brummel and pretended it had never wavered.

With a weary gesture, Beau Brummel asked, "Is the multitude still watching?"

"Of course," Mr. Knight answered. "They always watch you, Brummel."

His blatant flattery startled Eleanor, but Beau Brummel's answer startled her more.

"My popularity is a cross I must bear." He looked serious, leaving Eleanor in awe of his conceit. "Your Grace, I wouldn't suggest anything quite so outrageous as this escapade again—"

If he only knew the scandal that would erupt when Madeline arrived!

"—but you should continue as you've begun. You *are* the future duchess. You *will* set the fashion. You *are* a belle—I have decreed it. You have a marvelous manner. Never apologize for your eccentricities." He swept her tattered riding costume with a glance. "Although, do remember—a well-gowned traveler is a happy traveler."

Eleanor maintained a straight face with difficulty, and she suspected Mr. Knight shared her amusement. Yet she wasn't like him. He wasn't like her. So to think that the two of them were of like mind on any matter disturbed and distressed her.

Beau Brummel had finished making his pronouncements to her, and asked, "Mr. Knight, may I assume I've been sent an invitation to your ball?"

"You have," Mr. Knight assured him.

"I'll be there." Beau Brummel placed the back of his hand against his forehead in an affected faint. "Now I have walked too far for my delicate constitution. Farewell, Your Grace. Farewell, Mr. Knight."

Together, they watched him mince away.

"Well." Mr. Knight's mouth had a suspicious pucker. "That went well."

Her heart sank. She was right. He *was* amused by Beau Brummel. They *did* share a sentiment—a disturbing thought and one she put away to contemplate later, in the dark of night, a time when she unfortunately woke and thought of Mr. Knight. "*Obviously* it went well. Because I *am* the future duchess and I *will* set the fashion." Leaning down, she gently stroked the dog.

"What are you doing with this . . . animal?"

She hadn't known what she was doing with it, but now she did. "I'm befriending it." Gently, she picked it up, taking care not to touch its hurt leg. It was just light enough that she could carry it, just heavy enough to drag her down. Tucking it under her arm, she trudged toward Diriday. The dog's gangly legs stuck out, its weight pulled at her arms. Her hands hurt, her knee ached, and it seemed the distance to the horse grew as she walked.

Remington walked beside her, his gait effortless, and he made no attempt to help her. "Are you doing this as some sort of revenge on me? Because I will force you to become my wife?"

They reached the horses and stepped into the

wood, out of the sun and the sight of any curiosity-seekers who waited for further scandalous exhibitions. The groom tugged his forelock and discreetly stepped away.

Panting, she put the dog down. It huddled at her feet, while she put her hands on her hips. "Mr. Knight, I know this is a difficult concept for you to grasp, but not everything I do or say is related to you. In fact, the world does not revolve around you. The moon lights in the night sky without you. And my existence does not depend upon you. Now." She again bent down to pick up the dog. "I will take my dog home and give it a bath—without thinking of you in any way."

"Wait." Taking her arm, Mr. Knight pulled her erect once more. "I would not have you continue in this reckless behavior."

Once again, he confused her. "What reckless behavior?"

"Of not thinking of me." Sliding his arm around her waist, he kissed her.

Their first kiss had been gentle and enticing, their second demanding . . . and enticing. This one was once again different. With a gentle nip on her lower lip, he insisted she think of him, and when she opened her mouth to scold, he kissed her with wicked intent. He wanted all of her attention, and with his experience, he knew how to get it. He seduced her with teeth and tongue. His lips moved on hers until she was insensible to the dappled sunshine, to the scent of roses on the breeze, the dog and Beau Brummel and the dilemma she faced being with him. Every thought, every feeling was absorbed in the press of his body on hers and the appetizer of pleasure he fed her.

Then he let her go. He steadied her with one hand on her elbow while she tried to gather her dignity and her prudence.

The longer she knew him, the less she knew herself.

Helping her into the saddle, he handed her the dog.

She adjusted the creature under her arm, murmured comfortingly to it, and started toward Mr. Knight's town house.

It was frightening, to change so radically in so short a time and for so simple a reason as a kiss. Would Madeline even recognize Eleanor when she came to London? Would Eleanor recognize herself when the time came to concede her rights to Mr. Knight?

Would she surrender him? Or would she fight for him?

Chapter 16

*R*emington strode along the gallery above the foyer. "This damned dog has got to go."

His duchess hung over the stair rail, watching the servants scurry back and forth in last-minute preparations, setting up tables, icing bottles of champagne, filling vases with masses of yellow roses. Turning her head, she looked at him and at the dog trotting at his side. Although her face remained solemn, she glowed with an inner delight. "*Damn* is not a word one uses in mixed company in England."

But *damn*, she looked good in a sweep of turquoise silk that turned her eyes a startling blue. A turquoise ribbon was threaded through her hair, and diamonds sparkled like stars in the short, dark strands.

Her own clothing, of course. Her own ribbon. Her own diamonds. She still wouldn't wear what he had bought her, but although she didn't yet know it, soon she would have no choice.

In the meantime, he had a dog following on his heels. Stopping by Madeline's side, he pointed at the animal. "Look at it. It's shedding black hair on my white stockings and tan hair on my black breeches."

"It's not as bad as all that." She smiled at him and the dog, that charmed, secure smile that eased his tension. The smile she allowed herself so infrequently. "You have to admit, Mr. Knight, that Lizzie is much more appealing now that she's had a bath."

"Lizzie? Who's Lizzie?" He was afraid he knew.

"Your dog."

"It's not my dog, and who ever heard of a dog named Lizzie?" He snapped his fingers at the frolicking animal. "Sit!"

At once, the mutt obeyed, adoring him with its eyes, its tongue lolling out of its mouth. Washed and dried, it did present a better appearance and heaven knew a better smell, but rather than be grateful to Madeline, its rescuer, it had attached itself to *him*. It followed him up and down stairs, it lounged on the Persian rug in his bedchamber, it barked at his valet.

His duchess didn't seem hurt by the mutt's defection. Instead, Remington's exasperation amused her. "Mr. Knight, you look very handsome, hairy breeches or not."

"Hm. Thank you." He straightened his formal black jacket. "I suppose. Although I don't know if that is truly a compliment."

She glanced at him, then away, as if that would hide the sensual awareness in her eyes. "It is."

He smiled, wondered how she would cope with

the dramatic announcement he had planned for the end of the evening.

Lady Gertrude bustled past in her party finery and clapped her hands. "Children, children, hurry up! The guests will be arriving soon." Casting a stern glance at Lizzie, she said, "And put the doggie away. You know Lady Fendsworth is terrified of dogs."

Lizzie barked reproachfully at Lady Gertrude.

"I'm sorry, but we can't have you frightening the guests." Lady Gertrude spoke to the dog as if the creature understood her.

Worse, Lizzie sighed as if she did understand.

"Off you go, then." Lady Gertrude hurried down the corridor.

"All right. *Lizzie* is going in her crate." He started for his room and felt a nip on the heel of his boot.

Swiveling, he glared at the dog, who pranced in joy at having obtained his attention. "Do you know what my valet is going to say about this?" Remington pointed at the scuff on his boot. "He's going to . . . to give you another bath!"

At once the dog's black tail wagged hard enough to thump the railing. Furthermore, Remington could have sworn the stupid thing smiled up at him.

Madeline burbled briefly, a choked half-laugh that seemed unpracticed in the art of joy. Then, as if she couldn't resist, she went off into peals of pure merriment.

The duchess seldom smiled, and when she did, it was only politely. She seldom smiled with happiness, and Remington had never, never heard her laugh. Now this stupid dog with its sloppy tongue and its bizarre devotion to him—and his boots—had made her chuckle, and he liked the rare, sweet sound. Her joy sent a thrill up his spine like no other, and if this dog was what it took to entertain her, then this dog was his favorite animal, ever. Squatting beside it, he petted its head. "Good girl. Good . . . Lizzie."

Lizzie's frantic attempt to lick his face made the duchess laugh again.

As he listened and fended off the dog, he realized a new purpose. He would make Madeline laugh more often.

The candles cast a golden glow about the ballroom. Clad in their colorful garments, the guests stood or danced or drank. This party celebrating Remington's betrothal to the future duchess of Magnus was a resounding success, except . . . catching the butler, Remington asked, "Has the duke of Magnus arrived?"

"No, sir." Bridgeport leaned closer and whispered, "He is not in London."

Magnus wasn't here. "The bastard didn't even come to his daughter's betrothal party."

"Perhaps, sir, he is embarrassed to face the ton after the loss of his daughter."

"Perhaps." Remington doubted that. Magnus was a bluff English bulldog of a man who drank deep and gambled without compunction. And beneath that jovial facade lurked a cruel man, one who didn't quibble at murder to get his way. Had he learned Remington's true identity? Was he even now hiding on one of his estates, concocting another pitiless scheme?

Tomorrow Remington would send out his men to discover the duke's whereabouts. Then Remington himself would go and beat a confession from the damnable duke, and find out what further mischief he had planned. For Remington wasn't entirely sure that the duke wouldn't annihilate his own daughter before allowing her to marry a commoner.

But for tonight, the evening was a success, and midnight was fast approaching. Midnight . . .

Bridgeport asked, "Sir, shall we prepare for the toast?"

"At once." As the fresh glasses of chilled champagne made their way across the ballroom on silver trays, Remington conversed with his guests, nibbled on the salmon, and always, always positioned himself to watch Madeline.

She stood still, allowing the guests to approach her. She listened to every comment, she considered each person gravely, she touched their arm or their hand, and it seemed that more and more, the women came to her to converse. Not to flatter or to gossip, but to tell her about themselves. The men came, too, in droves, and one and all they fell deeply in love.

How could they help it? What was it that fool Viscount Mauger had said? *She is as fair as the sun in all its brilliance.* Preposterous sentiment, except that it was true.

Madeline's beauty was a complication Remington hadn't planned on. He understood, of course, that with Brummel's endorsement and her own exquisite style, it had become all the rage to suffer for love of her. He also knew that the infatuations of the gentlemen were shallow, and when Madeline became a matron, she would no longer hold the allure she held as a single girl. He looked forward to that day for, to his own incredulity, he suffered little stabs of jealousy with every alluring glance sent winging her way. He found himself wanting to take her aside and explain that the other men were superficial and untrue, while he . . . but no. He wouldn't admit his fascination to her. Her female hands could take his heart and wring it dry. Besides, if his own infatuation was not shallow, then it was based on . . . on what?

Big blue eyes, an uncertain manner, a smile she almost never used, a lush body, a strong belief in doing what was right, a gentle kindness, a sharp intelligence she kept carefully hidden . . .

Excusing herself from the little crowd around her, she circulated throughout the ballroom. Stopping in the corner where the chaperons, governesses and companions were seated, she spoke to them. The chaperons and companions stirred and answered, but uneasily. She ordered drinks and trays of food for them, and left them feasting and sipping their drinks—and uncertainly eyeing their mistresses, as if waiting for retribution.

With a word to Bridgeport, Remington ordered that the chaperon corner be served throughout the rest of the evening. Again Remington moved into a position where, from across the ballroom, he could watch Madeline. He wanted to reach into his mind and claw away his absorption in her. He couldn't afford this insanity. Not now. Not with his plans coming to fruition. For this maneuver, he needed a cool, clear mind. He did not need to be distracted by a woman.

A gorgeous woman, yes, but just a woman.

He didn't understand her. That was the problem. She was beautiful but unaware of her beauty. She was rich but not grasping. She was timid, yet she rode fearlessly, and for a scroungy dog she roared like a lion.

Because of her, he'd had his best boots nipped by a mutt's sharp teeth. Because of her, he'd ordered all flower arrangements changed from red to yellow roses. Because of her, he spent far too little time plotting the next step of his revenge, and far too much time plotting their wedding night. A night full of silk sheets, fine foods, and a gloriously gentle seduction.

So now, at last . . . with a nod to Bridgeport, Remington sought out his duchess. She watched him gravely as he crossed the floor toward her. "You're beautiful tonight," he said.

"Thank you, sir. Is there something you require?"

"Come with me."

As if she knew his plans, she placed her palms together in a prayerful attitude. "Must I?"

The woman before him had changed so much in the last few days. She'd cut her hair short. She no longer feared to appear in public. Her fair skin seemed to glow, as if lit from within. She was growing more gorgeous every day, and he would never let her go. "It's too late to turn back now."

She gave a shaky sigh. "I'm beginning to fear that is the truth."

Offering his arm, he led her toward the platform

where the orchestra played. Recognizing their cue, the musicians played a fanfare.

The guests turned and smiled. They thought they knew what he would announce—the betrothal.

But they didn't know everything. No one knew except Bridgeport, who had helped him arrange matters, and Remington himself. Remington assisted Madeline up the stairs to the stage. She cast him an agonized, beseeching glance, but he paid no heed to her last-minute nerves. Joining her, he pulled a small box from his pocket. The last of the conversations died. Projecting his voice to the very edges of the ballroom, he said with theatrical flare, "I thank you for coming tonight to help me celebrate my betrothal to Madeline de Lacy, the marchioness of Sherbourne and the future duchess of Magnus. It's a great honor to put my ring on her finger"— opening the box, he showed her the magnificent sapphire, set in a swirl of gold—"which I chose as a compliment to the beauty of her eyes."

As he eased her glove from her left hand, most of the guests clapped.

A few did not. Despite the fact she had no invitation, Lady Shapster had arrived early and had spent an inordinate amount of time observing his duchess. Remington didn't like the malevolent, narrow slit of her catlike eyes, and he had made sure Madeline was never alone with her for one moment.

Lord Fanthorpe did not applaud, either.

That didn't surprise Remington. At Remington's club, and at the Picards' ball, the old man had ignored him with meticulous iciness. Fanthorpe was like the others, men and women who were willing to drink Remington's champagne and dine at his board but who were not willing to welcome him into society.

Yet with the approval of the prince and the hand of the duchess, Remington would become one of the ton . . . and at last his sister's suffering would be avenged, and his father's ghost would rest in peace.

As Remington lifted Madeline's bare hand to place the ring on her third finger, he felt the muscles spasm as she tried, for one second, to reject his brand of possession.

Lifting his gaze to hers, he saw panic there. Reality had at last overwhelmed her. In a dark, intimate whisper, he said, "Don't try and resist me. I *will* put my ring on your finger."

Her defiance collapsed. Her gaze fell. She waited docilely for him to complete the deed . . . but to his amazement, he, too, suffered a moment of hesitation.

The ring should be his mother's. The girl should be his true love.

But those dreams had died twenty years ago in a fiery tragedy, and nothing could bring those dreams—or his family—back to life. He could only hope that marrying the daughter of the duke of Magnus would ease his pain—or at least give him someone with whom to share it.

His duchess watched as he slid the ring, fitted exactly to her hand, over her slender knuckle and settled it tightly against her palm. Lifting her hand, he held it so the ring sparkled in the blaze of candlelight. "Thank you, my friends, for helping us celebrate this moment, and celebrate with us again! Lift your glasses and toast our happiness!"

The guests drank with good cheer.

Remington wasn't done. Still holding Madeline's hand, he looked into her eyes, and announced, "This moment is especially precious to me. The archbishop of Canterbury has granted us a special license, and we will be married at St. James's Piccadilly on . . . the day after tomorrow."

Chapter 17

As Eleanor absorbed Mr. Knight's announcement, the crowd, the ballroom and all its lights faded. She thought she was going to faint right here on the stage, but strangely, she could still hear his voice clearly proclaiming, "With the blessing of God on our union, we will live among you for the rest of our days."

That didn't sound like a promise to Eleanor; it sounded like a threat. Everything about Mr. Knight's face and figure looked like a threat. He was going to force the ton to accept him on his own terms, and she was the instrument of his determination.

"Breathe," he commanded softly.

She took a gasping breath and realized she'd been holding her breath.

"Smile," he said.

She did smile, a tremulous smile, and from the answering beams around her, everyone found her apprehension completely normal and the whole affair *so* romantic. Apparently, few cared that the betrothal had come about through a despicable card game. With his pale blond hair shining like a halo, her fallen angel had mesmerized the whole of the ton.

He offered his hand to help her descend the stairs.

Well, not the whole of the ton. Lady Shapster stood twirling her full champagne glass, watching Eleanor as if trying to decide how best to expose the truth. Her malevolence made Eleanor shiver, yet it was Mr. Knight who occupied Eleanor's mind. Anything Lady Shapster could do paled in comparison to Mr. Knight and his schemes.

As soon as her feet touched the dance floor, the orchestra struck up a minuet. Other couples rapidly joined them. The proceedings had been coordinated by Mr. Knight to achieve maximum impact, and on the surface, everything looked like every maiden's fantasy.

But Eleanor was still reeling from his coup d'etat. She couldn't marry him in two days. She had to tell him so. But although he danced with inexpressible grace, always less than three feet away, he might as well be on the moon. He wore a mask, one comprised of a charming smile and opaque eyes that hid the secrets of his soul. The softening she had thought he'd had toward her was a chimera. The common sentiments she had imagined between them did not exist. The blue-eyed devil had forced a ring on her and now threatened her with immediate marriage.

And why? Eleanor didn't understand why he wished to marry the future duchess of Magnus. He said it was because he wanted her fortune and her status, but Eleanor didn't believe him. There was something more, something lurking beneath the surface of his smile, some deeper plan that frightened her in its enmity.

The dance ended. The gentlemen closed in on Mr. Knight, slapping him on the back and congratulating him.

Eleanor backed away, wanting desperately to flee, but escape was impossible.

Horatia caught up with her first. "You sly puss. You never gave us a hint of your imminent wedding!"

"I didn't, did I?" Eleanor hadn't been cagey, she had been ignorant.

Lady Picard hurried forward with all the bustle of a confirmed and exalted gossip. "Congratulations, Your Grace. You must be so pleased!"

"Words cannot express my feelings." Eleanor's stomach twisted. What was she supposed to do now?

Madeline's advice chased across Eleanor's mind. *Whenever you are in doubt, think, What would Madeline do in this situation? And do it.*

Without a doubt, that was the silliest counsel Eleanor had ever heard. It helped her not at all. Not at *all*.

Mr. Clark Oxnard hurried over, his petite wife in tow, and Clark beamed jovially, his round cheeks cherry red with pleasure. "When you asked me to stand as your best man, Remington, I had no idea it would be so soon. Congratulations, Your Grace, congratulations indeed!"

"Yes, you're right." Did Eleanor make sense? She didn't think so. She didn't care.

"My felicitations, Your Grace." Mrs. Oxnard's voice was surprisingly low for so small a woman, and her eyes scrutinized Eleanor shrewdly. "A marriage is always exciting, but somewhat overwhelming, also. Perhaps, when you're settled, we could meet for tea?"

She sounded so normal, so absolutely calm, that Eleanor wanted to put her head on Mrs. Oxnard's shoulder and weep. "That would be delightful," Eleanor said. "Thank you."

Beau Brummel strolled up, flicking his handkerchief to clear himself a path. "Your Grace, what excellent news! You're to be married at once. Trust Mr. Knight to charge in where others fear to tread and sweep you off your feet as you deserve."

"I deserve this? I suppose I must." *For lying about who she was.*

Young Lord Byron lifted his soulful gaze to hers. "Such a romantic gesture inspires me to write a poem. An epic poem. Or perhaps a sonnet."

Eleanor took a small step back, then another. "Mr. Knight will be pleased, I'm sure." She was sure of the exact opposite.

"Dear girl." Lady Gertrude stood on tiptoe and kissed Eleanor's cheeks. "I'm so excited!" In Eleanor's ear, she added, "This will halt rumors about where you're staying before they get started. A relief, I will tell you. Servants gossip, and a few more days could be fatal to your reputation."

In that she was wrong, for Lady Shapster pointedly examined Eleanor's belly. In that smooth, warm, assured tone that used to drive Eleanor to tears, she said, "You aren't wasting any time getting to the altar. Is there a reason for the hurry?"

Every jaw within hearing dropped.

Mr. Knight twisted around like a vengeful whirlwind.

In unison, the guests stepped back.

But for the first time, Lady Shapster hadn't the power to shame or terrify Eleanor. Maybe Eleanor had matured. Maybe the last four years, the last few days, the last few minutes, had shown her real adversity. For whatever reason, a rush of fury chased anxiety out of her mind. She didn't need Mr. Knight to defend her. She could stand up for herself.

With a smile that was more tooth than benevolence, she said, "Lady Shapster, I arrived in England less than a week ago. If you wish to spread rumors, that isn't one that will take."

Lady Shapster blinked, as if a kitten had attacked her ankles and drawn blood. Then that terrifying smile spread across her lips, and she stepped closer to Eleanor.

Before she could speak, Lady Gertrude said in an insufferably outraged tone, "What an ill-bred observation. Don't you agree, Lady Picard?"

"I do, indeed." Lady Picard looked sincerely shocked, like a woman not adverse to gossiping in private but horrified by public scenes.

"Lady Shapster." Mr. Knight took her by the arm. "I don't remember including you on the guest list."

Lady Shapster turned on him like a cornered tiger, all teeth and claws. Then she caught a glimpse of his face, and something there made her soften into the guise of a lady. "I realized it was an oversight, so I—"

"Not an oversight at all." Mr. Knight clipped off his words. "I do not like coarse, vicious women. I most certainly don't want them at my betrothal ball."

Lady Gertrude patted Eleanor's hand and murmured incoherent comfort.

"But that's what I have to tell you." Lady Shapster pointed a long finger at Eleanor. "You don't aspire to marry *her*."

Eleanor wanted to leap at her, to stifle her and that dreadful, smooth, accusatory tone.

Mr. Knight's lips drew back from his teeth, and his voice was scarcely audible when he said, "Do not tell me what I aspire to do. You know nothing about me or my aspirations. Now—*you* want to leave. I'll escort you to the door."

"Such a scene," Beau Brummel murmured. "So sad when a noted beauty fades to infamy."

Mr. Knight didn't hear him, but Lady Shapster did. She cast a venomous glance at Eleanor, and as Mr. Knight marched her away, she said, "I promise you, you'll be sorry you humiliated me this way."

Mr. Knight answered, "For your own safety, my lady, don't say another word."

Eleanor drew a quivering breath. She had confronted her stepmother and escaped unscathed. She wouldn't truly win until she faced her as Eleanor, but now she was grateful to Lady Shapster. Lady Shapster had distracted Mr. Knight and given Eleanor a chance to escape, for just a moment, the suffocating blanket of interest. "Excuse me. I see a friend I must greet."

"Of course you do, dear." Lady Gertrude patted her hand. "Go and freshen up."

"Thank you. I will." Eleanor tried hard not to rush away, for she well knew everyone was watching her. And she tried very hard to walk a straight line, since she hadn't the foggiest idea where she was headed. She only knew she needed to get away. Away, before she suffered her first ever attack of the vapors.

The open door leading to the garden promised fresh air and the veil of darkness, so she steered toward it—and heard a hiss emanating from the plant by the French doors.

"Psst."

She looked around but saw no one.

"Psst, miss!"

Walking around the pot, she saw a red-haired man crouching almost on the floor. In an instant, the anguish that filled her turned to hope. Dickie Driscoll had never failed to help her. He wouldn't fail her now. "Dickie! What are you doing here?"

"Rescuing ye." Dickie peered over the plant at the dance floor, where couples dipped and rose in the minuet. " 'Tis the first chance I've had to get to ye without that Mr. Knight or one of his henchmen intercepting me. Come on." Catching her hand, he stood and slid furtively toward the doors. "Let's go."

"Oh, yes! Let's go!" She followed him onto the terrace, rejoicing in her freedom. "I want to get away from here. I need to get away from him, before . . . I need to get away."

"Sh." Dickie's voice was hushed as he led her down the stairs. "Knight's men are everywhere. I had a fair difficult time getting in here, and I dunna relish being tossed out again."

"You mean—like the other day when they caught us coming out of the stables?"

The garden path was not lit, but she heard the gloom in Dickie's voice. " 'Twasna fun, Miss Eleanor."

She tensed. "His men didn't hurt you, did they?"

"Nay, Mr. Knight instructed them to keep it clean, and they did—for the most part."

She slowed. "So Mr. Knight kept his promise." *He* had promised not to hurt Dickie.

She had promised not to run away.

But Mr. Knight hadn't told her that they should wed immediately!

"Hurry, Miss Eleanor!" Dickie urged.

So what if Mr. Knight hadn't told her the whole truth? She hadn't demanded it. She had simply promised him she wouldn't run away. She had set no restrictions on her vow. "Dickie." Reluctantly, she set her heels. "I can't go."

"What do ye mean, ye canna go?" Dickie tugged harder. "This is na a game, miss. I heard him. He's announced yer wedding for the day after tomorrow, and Her Grace is nowhere in sight. I dunna know where she is, but I do know we've got a bit of a crisis here."

"I understand. Believe me, Dickie, I understand. But the fact is—I promised Mr. Knight I wouldn't flee again." Eleanor had to stay. She'd given her word.

Dickie knew it, for he sputtered, "P . . . promised? Nay, Miss Eleanor, ye wouldna be so foolish. Tell me ye wouldna be so foolish."

She laid her hand on his arm. "Dickie, when his men were taking you away, they were going to hurt you. I couldn't let them do that. So I promised to stay with him until he told me to go."

"If I were na a guid Protestant, miss, I would curse down the Tower of Babel." Dickie stood still, head down. "Miss, what are ye going to do? Are ye going to tell him?"

"Who I am? No!" No. When he discovered who she was, she wanted to be far, far away.

"Ye can't marry the man with him thinking ye're the duchess. When the truth comes oot, he would kill ye."

"Of course I won't. I can't." Because that wouldn't be the right thing to do. She would not dare think about how very much she was enjoying herself: being the toast of London, having a fine horse to ride, being bold enough to occasionally, very occasionally, speak her mind. She would not remember how her heart tripped when Mr. Knight looked at her with his pale blue eyes hot as banked coals. To imagine herself as his wife was asking for pain and heartache, and she had plenty of that coming anyway. "Dickie, here's my idea. I'll write a note. You'll take it to Madeline. I'll tell her about the wedding, and she'll come to my rescue."

"And if she canna?"

Eleanor stood in the dark garden. Her new ring was cold on her finger. The breeze flirted with the leaves above her. The fresh air filled her lungs. In her soul, a struggle took place. A struggle between the old, meek Eleanor and the new Eleanor trying to be born. The old Eleanor was timid and took what life handed out without a whimper. The new Eleanor fought for herself and her happiness and didn't care about consequences.

Madeline didn't want Mr. Knight. The new Eleanor did. She wanted him desperately in her heart and in her loins, and if Madeline didn't arrive in time to stop the wedding . . .

The new Eleanor spoke. "If Madeline doesn't arrive in time to stop the wedding, then fate has made its decree. And now I believe I shall go have a small libation or two." Anything to quiet the old Eleanor shrieking warnings in her head.

In a voice thick with dread, Dickie Driscoll asked, "What do ye mean, miss, that fate has made its decree?"

"I mean—if Madeline doesn't arrive in time to stop me, I mean to wed Mr. Knight."

Chapter 18

Alone, Remington bade farewell to the last guest. The duchess was nowhere in sight. He'd seen her disappear up the stairs half an hour ago, but he hadn't seen her return. He hoped the guests had believed that she'd left to go to her own home. It wouldn't do to have them think she was staying with him, for they would make the assumption he had already breached her maidenhead.

He extinguished a few of the sputtering candles.

Nothing could be further from the truth. Blast it. A few kisses, albeit glorious kisses, could scarcely be called significant. He only wished his rampant body would settle down into a dignified acceptance of what was really a very short wait.

"Will there be anything else, sir?" Bridgeport looked as fresh as he had this morning, proving once again that English butlers had the most remarkable stamina.

"That will be all, Bridgeport. Tell the staff they've done very well, and there'll be a suitable reward come Sunday."

Bridgeport bowed and went to supervise the cleanup.

As Remington unhooked his cuffs, he idly wondered if his duchess had recovered from the shock of hearing she would wed him in thirty-six hours.

She had taken it well. She hadn't screamed or fainted, or repudiated him or railed at her father, and Remington had been prepared for all of those reactions. Instead she had stared at him in wide-eyed and mute bewilderment, reminiscent of a raccoon facing a speeding carriage. He'd almost felt embarrassed for springing it on her in such a fashion.

But she had connections. If she had known earlier, she would have somehow worked out a way to disrupt their wedding, and he couldn't take that chance.

Then one of his men reported that Dickie Driscoll was on the grounds, and Remington had watched to see if she would run. She hadn't, and for no good reason whatsoever, that pleased him. Her restraint could be, and was, probably, a result of having given him her word. The de Lacy family had a reputation for making promises and keeping them; that was why she'd stayed, not that she wanted to wed him.

But even that unflattering assumption shook him down to the bedrock of his beliefs. The aristocrat who slept under his roof kept her word.

Tugging off his jacket, he wondered, did she have other virtues, too?

As he passed the library on his way to the stairs, he heard a voice, convivial and slightly slurred. "Mr. Knight, what a pleasure to see you again."

Halting, he stared into the pocket of darkness inside the room. "Your Grace?"

She stepped into the light. Her silk gown draped her figure with the same glorious detail to attention as it had earlier, but one glove was gone, her hair ribbon was wrapped around one ear, and her cropped hair stood up wildly. She looked beautiful, she incited his lust, and she was listing like a ship about to sink.

With a smile that looked mellow and far too cheerful, she said, "Mr. Knight, you are to be congratulated. You give quite a good party for a single gentleman."

"Have you had too much wine?" It seemed a safe deduction.

"Wine? Wine?" She used every incredulous intonation, and shook her head in an exaggerated gesture. "No. That would be so inappropriate at my own betrothal party." She stopped and tapped his chest. "Don't you think so?"

He looked down at that slender finger as it stopped tapping and instead twitched his cravat askew. She was foxed—and when had that happened? He'd not seen a sign of it an hour ago. "Not at all. If you can't have a drink at your betrothal party, when can you?"

She squinted at his chest. "Your cravat is crooked.

You're an American. I should warn you—Brummel says a mushed cravat is not allowed." She smashed her palm on the cravat, flattening the last of the graceful curves. "And yours is a mess." She staggered.

He caught her arm. "So I see. But the party's over, so it doesn't matter." Was this intoxication her reaction to knowing she would marry him so soon? He supposed it must be, and how unflattering for him.

But she was so charming, and the wedding date had been a shock. He would excuse her this once. "Would you like me to help you up to bed?"

Her smile tilted up on one corner and not on the other. "You are a very naughty boy."

Under normal conditions, he would agree, but he couldn't take advantage of a souse, especially one who seldom indulged in more than a sip at a time. "How much did you drink?"

"A little tiny glass." She showed him a miniature size with her fingers.

"Of what?" He led her toward the stairs.

"Brandy." The word rolled richly off her tongue.

"A little tiny glass, or several little tiny glasses?"

"There might have been two," she allowed as she ascended the stairs, leaning hard on him all the way. "Or seven. It was some derivative of five. Do you know I'm actually very good at math?"

"I had no idea." He knew the way to her bedchamber, of course. He'd stood outside it every night since she'd arrived in his house, fingering the key, weighing the odds . . . enjoying the anticipation.

"Very good. Math and languages—which came in

handy in our travels, I can tell you that. And riding. I'm a magnificent horsewoman. Everyone says so." Her voice deepened and grew husky. "And swiving. I'm good at swiving."

He stopped so short that she almost fell backward.

"Whoa," she said. "Raise a flag before you change course like that, sailor."

In a falsely gentle tone, he asked, "Who taught you about swiving?"

"Those women."

He stared at her hard, half-convinced she was pulling his leg, yet sure that, in her condition, she couldn't manage comedy.

Solemnly, she stared back at him. Lifting her hand, she patted his cheek. "Do you know how handsome you are? Oh, yes. It's a fact! Tonight, when Horatia was pouring me a glass, she told me the ladies giggle about wanting to unbutton your breeches and unwrap what's inside like an early Twelfth Night present. Or late, I can't remember."

"Flattering." He had to discover what she meant by *I'm good at swiving*. He didn't believe it. He couldn't. For God's sake, she lacked the most elementary skills of kissing. Sliding his arm around her waist, he steered her into an alcove and pushed her down on the cushioned window seat. Snatching a single candle from a wall sconce, he placed it in a glass bowl. "What women?"

"The ones at the party tonight."

"No. What women taught you about swiving?" His heart had developed a funny rhythm, quite unlike its usual, leisurely beat. With vicious motions, he freed the velvet drapes from their ties and twitched them over the opening, enclosing the two of them in a dim, small, private recess ideal for an interrogation.

"I wish you'd pay attention. I already told you. The ones in the harem."

A harem? Had she lived in a harem?

Had she slept with a man?

Standing directly in front of her, he used his strongest tone to get her attention. "What harem?"

She seemed not at all impressed by his severity. "Haven't you heard that story?" She tilted her head back to see him and tumbled back to the cushions propped against the wall. Curtains covered the windows, shutting out the draft that made its way through the frame, but the wind groaned as it made its way around London street corners. "It's really quite amusing, now that it's over."

Amusing? He doubted that. Anxiety rose in him. Anxiety for her. "Tell me."

"We wanted to go to see Constantinople, my cousin and I—that was my idea, actually, and it turned out so badly it was the last idea I suggested— but when we got there, there was this man. A lot of men, actually, and almost no women. Odd place. This man, he was all black-haired and black-eyed, and he was rich. Powerful!" She lowered her voice to a whisper. "A bey. He thought we were twins— you know, sisters born at the same time—"

A vase of roses sat on the small table in the corner. Their fragrance reminded Remington of yesterday in Green Park: of her riding, of her valiance, of her splendor in the sunshine. . . . In Constantinople, had she been hurt, in fear? He grew furious at the thought, but he kept his voice low and coaxing. "I know what twins are. Tell me about the harem."

"You would know, wouldn't you?" She petted his waistcoat, her fingers lingering on the embroidered silk. "You're a very smart man."

Not a smart man. A stupid man, to be flattered by the praise of an owly-eyed drunk. "I'm glad you think so."

"I don't understand why you haven't figured this whole thing out. I'd be so relieved if you did."

What whole thing? What did she mean? "I'm doing my best."

"I suppose you are, and I can hardly tell you the truth, can I?" She gestured extravagantly.

"You could." Catching her fingers, he stroked them and coaxed, "I'm going to be your husband. You can trust me."

"I think I can." She sounded as if she marveled. Then she added, "But that would be a betrayal of everything I believe in. No. Can't tell you all about me, but you can guess."

She stared at him, as if expecting him to know her secrets, when in fact he didn't care. Not right now. Not when she'd told him she knew about copulation. "Why did the bey care if you'd been twins?"

"He fancied our pale skin, thought he'd like to tousle us both together, so he stuck us in his harem. Just like that." She tried to snap her fingers. Nothing happened. She stared at her fingers and tried again. Nothing.

Trapped in a nightmare of fury and compassion, Remington demanded, "What did you do?"

She smacked the wooden windowsill, and the impact seemed to satisfy her. "We tried to complain to the authorities, but there're no laws against that sort of thing there. Such barbarity!"

"Tell me what happened to you." *Tell me if you've been violated. Tell me what I'm going to have to do to soothe your fears.*

"We didn't want to be in the harem. The other females there thought we were funny, because they liked it. Sweets all the time and baths with no modesty whatsoever, all these women bathing together, washing each other, if you can imagine—"

He could imagine only too well.

"—All they talked about was taking a man inside of them, and how it felt, and what a woman could do to prolong the pleasure. It was quite outrageous when the concubines practiced on each other." She sat straight up, her eyes wide with remembered disbelief. "I hadn't known such a thing was possible."

"My God." He would have said nothing could shock him, but this did. She'd been imprisoned with women who lived to please a man, and that man himself had . . . had wanted her. Of course. No man alive could resist her. After all, she'd been in a harem.

She *wasn't* a virgin. And *he* wasn't angry that she was experienced, only that she'd been forced.

He'd lost his mind.

"Yes!" She waggled her head. "Of course, we listened and we watched. We couldn't not. We were aghast!" Her horrified expression collapsed, and she giggled. "And curious."

He wanted to smash something. The wall. The vase. Instead, with gentle fingers, he smoothed a lock of hair from her cheek. "Did the bey hurt you?"

"The things those concubines said men and women perform on each other! Did you know that men like to have their private parts bathed in a woman's mouth?"

"I did know that." He liked that. He couldn't think about it now.

"You knew?" She looked straight at his privates as if she could see through the cloth. "Really? Have you had it done? Is it true that your parts grow and swell? What makes them do that?"

Grasping her by the shoulders, he crouched down and looked into her eyes. "What did the bey do to you?"

"The bey?" She sounded incredulous. "He placed us in his harem, and then left town."

Leaning his palm against the wall, Remington closed his eyes in relief.

"I wish you'd pay attention," she complained. "If you paid attention, you'd know that."

He stared up at her. "So you're still a virgin."

"Sir! Yes, of course I am!" Her disarrayed hair looked as it might after a good tumble. Her bosom fit into her bodice, but with a creamy show of cleavage that made him want to kiss each breast. Her eyes were heavy with weariness and drink, and for the first time since he'd met her, she smiled without moderation. She lavished smiles on him, her soft, red lips slightly open, her white teeth glistening. She had been taunting him all evening—hell, ever since he'd met her—with her long limbs and her strong arms and those big, blue eyes.

She was an innocent, but an innocent with the knowledge of a courtesan. She knew he wanted her, he'd made sure of that, but more important—she wanted him, and she didn't know how to deal with her desire. He had woven a very satisfactory web around his affianced wife, and now he found she had woven an equally strong web around him. He could think of nothing but possessing her. He could think of nothing but their wedding night. Even his plans for revenge took second place to the need for her that clawed at his gut.

She was still talking, and all of a sudden, his attention snapped back to her.

"If I took your manhood out and bathed it in my mouth, I wouldn't really be compromising my purity." Spreading her arms across the cushions in an attitude of abandon, she stared up at him speculatively. "Would I?"

It took all of his considerable strength of will not to agree with her, for the male part involved grew and pressed so hard against the flap in his breeches he feared the buttons would pop. Slowly, he stood to ease the pressure. "You would."

With the pugnaciousness of a drunk, she argued, "But it doesn't involve you putting any male parts *into* my body."

He didn't know what to say to that, but if she didn't soon stop talking about the act she would find out the truth.

Then her face fell. "But . . . I suppose it does. You would put your—"

"Yes!" He suffered a disreputable agony.

Her hand lifted, and with his lust-impaired vision he saw her reaching toward him to once again twitch his clothing out of place. Instead, she brushed her fingers against the bulge in his breeches. "Is this it?" She giggled. "I suppose it is, or else you've got a nightstick in your pocket."

He wanted to tell her it wasn't appropriate to laugh when she was holding his genitals, but he relished her touch so much he found he didn't care. She could laugh all she wanted, as long as her fingers searched out the length and breadth of him.

She grew appropriately solemn as she explored him. "It's very long and thick. It seems as if the act between a man and a woman is impossible. I don't understand the mechanics. The positions seem so awkward, and the sizes don't match at all."

"It works." If she didn't stop caressing him, he was going to show her how well it worked.

He had to remember his strategy. He planned to do this with appropriate ceremony. To bring his duchess to the church, and that night sacrifice her virginity on the altar of his revenge.

Her family owed his family, and she was going to pay. Or at least—she would make the first payment.

Yet she fiddled with his buttons, and each accidental touch sent jolts of bliss—or was it agony?—through his body. "Can I take it out?" she asked. "Can I see it?"

Her eagerness was the greatest aphrodisiac he'd ever imagined. "On our wedding night."

Pausing, she pouted, her lower lip charmingly full. "No. Not then. Now." She began to unbutton him.

He stopped her with his hand on hers. "If you do that, more would happen than is . . . proper."

She wasn't so tipsy, after all, for she giggled. "I can't believe any of this is proper. Not even in America." Her fingers wiggled beneath his as she tried to reach for him again. "We shouldn't be here alone. I shouldn't be living in your house. So why not—"

"Because I wouldn't be in—" *Control.* No, he couldn't admit that to her.

But he could turn the tables. In a knowledgeable, coaxing tone, he said, "A man can also bathe a woman's private parts with his mouth."

Her eyes widened and lost a little of their clarity. "Really?"

"Really."

"Are you sure?" she asked suspiciously. "The concubines never mentioned that."

"It's something a man does for a woman when he wants to teach her desire." More than desire. It was what a man did for a woman when he wanted to give her satisfaction, but his duchess didn't need to know *everything*. Some things were better performed as a surprise.

"But such a practice seems very . . ."

"Very?"

She chose her words cautiously. "Letting a man do that would involve a great deal of trust on the woman's part."

"It would. But when the man does it right, it feels wonderful . . . so I'm told. A man's mouth explores and kisses each part, tastes and licks, sucks ever so gently . . ."

She pressed her knees together, and the faint sound she made was not a rebuttal but a moan.

Tossing one of the cushions on the floor, he knelt on it. He stretched his face toward her lips. "I'm going to kiss you. We've kissed before, remember?" Pitching his tone to be low and seductive, he asked, "You liked it, didn't you?"

Her voice wobbled. "Very much."

She was so trusting. So damnably, beautifully honest. "I put my tongue in your mouth, explored and tasted. Like this." He brushed her lips, his mind anticipating the shy blossom of her mouth beneath his. He loved the little catch of breath she gave as he slid his tongue inside, loved the flavor of brandy, loved that she couldn't resist putting her arms around his shoulders and twining her fingers in his hair. The liquor had loosened her inhibitions; she touched his tongue with hers, then when his tongue fell back, she followed, delving into his mouth, touching his teeth, ringing his lips. Her diffident exterior hid a siren of uncommon power and boldness, and he would show her everything her instincts only suspected. Gently, he sucked at her tongue, rasping the end with his own. When she fell back, out of breath, he slid her one glove down her arm. "Can you imagine me doing that to you . . . down there?" Ever-so-gently, he kissed the soft, pale skin at her elbow. "Can you imagine that?"

"Yes," she said faintly.

Removing the glove completely, he kissed each of her fingers, then nuzzled her palm with open mouth. "This marriage wasn't your choice. I can allay only a few of your fears, but I do promise your every womanly yearning will be fulfilled—even before you know what it is. Do you trust me?"

Without taking a moment to think, she said, "No."

Looking up at her, he saw her wide-eyed dismay, her trembling mouth, the flush on her cheeks. "To pleasure you with my mouth?"

Her indrawn breath betrayed how very tempted she was. If she wasn't intoxicated, she would have been screaming and running, but her hidden, hesitant desires made her malleable as clay in his hands.

Stretching out her arms, he placed her hands on the cushions. "I'm the man you've been waiting for all your life." He put his hands on her thighs.

She started.

Moving his palms gently up and down, he warmed her flesh with his touch . . . and stealthily moved between her knees. "Trust me to pleasure you." Grasping her hem, he lifted the slippery silk up to her waist.

In a panic, she shoved at his shoulders. She tried to close her legs.

He was between them, on his knees before her, and even in this dim light, he was privileged to see . . . everything. Her legs were long and well formed, her calves clad in white silk stockings with a garter at her knee. Her thighs were pale and strong, the kind that could ride a horse, or a man, and control every movement. The thatch of hair between her legs was black and curly, and beneath that he could see her slit, pink and beckoning. "Perfect." He looked up at her. "Beautiful."

She watched him with a scandalized gaze, and yet . . . he saw fragments of hope and excitement sparkling in her eyes. She wanted him. She sought knowledge. She wanted to experience this iniquitous bliss.

And he wanted to give it to her. When he was done with her, she wouldn't remember anything except him and what he had taught her.

He saw a mark on the pale skin of her knee, and gently slid his thumb over it. "Poor knee! How did this happen?"

"When I . . . rescued Lizzie, I fell."

"You must promise never to do something so madcap again." He kissed her bruise, his lips lingering. "Poor knee. Do you promise?"

"Can't." Her toes curled. "Not even for you."

"You're a stubborn woman."

"I didn't used to be. I used to be . . . pliable."

He chuckled. "You're changing before my very eyes. But if you would be pliable one more time, and put your hands back on the cushions, I would be most grateful."

She swallowed. "I don't think . . ."

"You can't push me away. You don't even want to. Put your hands back, and relax."

Gradually, she stretched her arms out across the pillows and settled back. "But I wanted to . . . to pleasure *you*."

She was totally open to him. She had no defenses. She did trust him or, virgin that she was, she would never have allowed herself to yield herself so thoroughly.

He smiled at her, lavishing charm while trailing

his fingers up her inner thighs. "Not tonight. Tonight is yours." He held her gaze with his, calming her while he neared his goal. The closer he got, the warmer she was, her body a stove to wrap him in heat. As the moments progressed, as his heart beat harder, he grew as intoxicated as she, but he was intoxicated with passion . . . and power. "On our wedding night, when I finally put myself inside you, we're going to burn into cinders."

She sat up straight. "Please . . . we shouldn't . . ."

He was so randy, his cock knocked at his buttons. At the same time, the wickedness of hiding in a darkened alcove, of holding his affianced wife captive with dissipation, drove him on to ignore his own condition and concentrate on hers. He smoothed his palm over the tips of her hair. "Sit back. I won't take you tonight, I promise."

"It's not that. We shouldn't be doing this at all."

"That is one of the charms." He slid one finger down her folds, scarcely touching skin, yet he saw the way her eyes blurred. "Sit back. I am going to do what I want, and you are going to like it."

"I shouldn't."

He chuckled, and in his most agreeable tone, said, "If you resist me, I'll use the curtain ties to tie you up and do whatever I like with you." On her dismayed gasp, he thrust his finger inside her.

She was hot and wet from desire, and she went rigid, not in rejection, but with passion woven of words and deeds.

"Would you like me to tie you up?" he asked in his most coaxing tone. "You wouldn't have to blame yourself for anything then. You could say you had no choice, and I forced you to my will."

She didn't appear to be listening, but he knew she could hear him. Her eyes were closed, her head was thrown back as his finger probed her depths. She'd pulled a cushion into her chest and hugged it with both her arms, as she would him when the time came.

As he slid his thumb up to seek out her nub, he said, "We have all the time in the world to try every position, everything you heard in your harem, everything I know, and everything we can make up."

Her legs were clutching at him now, twining around him. She was trying to draw him in, and she didn't even know what she was doing. She was drowning in instinct, and he loved it. Loved knowing that this woman, so soft and tender, could blaze to passion with a single touch. And he was going to give her . . . more than a touch.

Leaning his head down, he breathed in her fragrance. "My darling girl, tonight is the first of a thousand nights. Remember this—I'm going to possess you in every way a man can possess a woman, and you're going to beg me for more."

Her eyes opened as if she wanted to retort.

But before she could form the words, he placed his mouth between her legs and enticed her into heaven.

Chapter 19

At two in the afternoon, a crack of thunder shook the house.

Eleanor's eyes snapped open. She stared at the ceiling of her dim bedroom. She listened to the rain pounding at the window. Blinked as the flash of lightning blinded her. And remembered . . .

Last night, she had been drunk. Some people, when they drank, remembered nothing. But she was not so lucky.

Covering her face with her hands, she cringed with embarrassment.

She remembered . . . everything.

Oh, God, she remembered every last embarrassing, wonderful moment.

Mr. Knight had done things to her she had never, ever, imagined. Just because she had refused to accompany Dickie Driscoll and had lost her last chance to escape Mr. Knight, just because she'd been sunk in guilt at her decision to let fate decide if she should marry Mr. Knight, she had taken refuge in drink. And as every woman she had ever met had warned her a man would do, he had taken advantage of her.

But just because she had taken refuge in drink didn't mean Mr. Knight should have used her inebriation to seduce her.

If only she hadn't told him about being in the harem . . . she groaned with mortification. What an idiot she was! Now Mr. Knight knew that she was familiar with acts most Englishwomen never imagined . . . and he'd given her her first lesson in passion.

She pulled the sheets over her head as if somehow she could shut out last night's memories.

But putting her head under the covers showed her the dim outline of her bare body, and that reminded her of how she'd got to bed last night, and that reminded her . . .

The concubines had said that a man's touch on one's inner tissues was ecstasy. They hadn't told her how a single finger, sliding inside her, would shock her. Mark her. Even now, lying among her crumpled sheets in her bedchamber, she could feel his touch inside her. She pressed her fingers to her temples, as if she could squeeze the memory from her brain.

At the same time, she slid her heels along the mattress to raise her knees, tenting the sheet and, as if he were here, now, making a place for him between her legs. Because no matter how mortified she was by the way she had acted the night before, no matter how often she told herself he had taken advantage of her inebriated state . . . she still wanted him. He was all she could think about.

Already, he had filled her with wickedness, for her fingers glided under the covers, across her belly, into the hair between her legs. Her hand halted, quivered, but her willpower proved no match for her memories. Her fingers slid down between her slit to carefully touch herself. Everything seemed the same, yet everything was different.

Nothing the concubines had said had prepared her for the rough sensation of his tongue against the tenderest tissues between her legs. She had thought she would faint from the pleasure of his warmth, his breath. The dim, close world of the window seat receded to a pinpoint of consciousness. All of her senses were concentrated between her thighs and deep inside her womb.

Even now, the memory of his attentions made her fingers grow damp and her folds swell.

The memory of his mouth, his lips, his tongue . . . the way he used them, skillfully creating passion where nothing but skepticism had existed before. Gradually, sensation built from lavish pleasure to unbearable sensation. Her skin, all of her skin, flushed with desire. Her nipples grew tight and rasped against her chemise. Deep inside her, she'd tensed, as if her whole body had been waiting for one defining moment.

When he'd tenderly sucked on that most sensitive nub, she'd moaned in anguish. In ecstasy. She'd lifted herself, spasming against his mouth. As if he had known what would happen, he continued to suck, pulling her from one peak of ecstasy to another. And when at last she would have stopped, overwhelmed, trembling with exhaustion, he'd slid his finger inside her again, and sent her into another spasm, greater than the first.

Finally, she'd finished. Not because she could no longer continue, but because he'd allowed her respite. She'd melted onto the cushions, almost numb with satiation, and with a chuckle that had sounded both diabolical and satisfied, he'd picked her up and carried her to her bedchamber.

There Beth had been waiting up to help her to bed.

But Mr. Knight was having none of that. He'd sent Beth away, laid Eleanor on the bed and undressed her himself.

If only she could forget his expression as he'd eased her gown off of her! If only she could stop being pleased that he had looked absolutely rampant with desire!

His eyes had grown hot as he'd stared at her, sprawled on the bed clad only in her light silk chemise and her stockings. His chest rose and fell like a great bellows, and she knew, with every feminine instinct, that he'd wanted her. The woman on the bed had relished his desire. Had wanted him at that moment.

The brandy had made everything crystal clear. The marriage would probably never happen. This was probably her only chance to know his possession.

So she had let him look his fill. When he'd made no move to join her on the bed, she had loosened the tie at her neckline. With a hand on each side, she'd slid the chemise off her shoulders and freed her breasts.

Only his harsh breathing had broken the silence in her bedchamber. He'd stared with intense concentration, and his attention had stoked her confidence. She'd slithered out of the chemise completely, wiggling on the bed in a prone and erotic dance.

His lips had parted. Color had ridden high in his cheeks.

Lifting her knee, she'd untied her garter.

His gaze had skittered down her body to look between her legs. He'd already seen everything, but that didn't seem to make a difference. As she'd lifted her other knee, he'd caught and held her ankle. With definite motions, he'd untied the garter and tossed it aside. He'd pushed the stocking off her foot and tossed it, too, leaving her completely nude.

Bracing himself on either side of her head, he'd kissed her briefly and hard. Taking her cheeks between his hands, he'd looked into her eyes. "Not until after the wedding."

It hadn't been a rejection. It had been more like menace, for his gaze had seared her from head to toe and his hands beside her head had curled into fists. He hadn't touched her because if he had, he wouldn't stop, and he knew it, and she knew it.

It had been a triumph of sorts, and after he'd let himself out, she had gone to sleep hugging her victory to her heart.

Even now, mortified and unable to consider facing him ever, ever again, she wanted nothing more than to lie in his arms and mate with him.

She scarcely recognized herself. The old, prim

Eleanor was almost vanquished, defeated by so many things: her exposure to Madeline and the confidence she'd learned from her, the experiences during the years abroad, and, most important, meeting Mr. Knight. By wanting Mr. Knight. Fool that she was, she loved him. Loved him . . . the new Eleanor thrived on that emotion.

Love. It changed everything, made the world a rainbow, sent fear scurrying away. Last night, Eleanor had even confronted Lady Shapster—and won. Her life was changing.

Eleanor was changing.

Eleanor was in love.

Rolling off the bed, Eleanor found her robe and donned it, then rang for Beth. The maid came at once, bustling in with a beaming smile.

Lady Gertrude was on her heels. "At last! Mr. Knight commanded that we let you sleep, but we have so much to do to get you ready for the wedding tomorrow I don't know how we're going to get everything accomplished. Just like a man! Never thinking of the logistics, just commanding that all be done." She chuckled. "And we ladies do it for them, too. Aren't we foolish?"

Firmly, Eleanor tied the tie on her robe. "What do we have to do?"

"Your wedding gown, my dear." Lady Gertrude clasped her hands in glorious anticipation. "Mr. Knight has chosen a lovely dress for you, and the seamstress is here to fit it to you exactly."

Eleanor lifted her chin. "It isn't appropriate that Mr. Knight provide my wedding gown." Abruptly,

Eleanor realized how ludicrous she was being. If she married the man, she would marry him under false pretenses. To cavil about her wedding costume was ridiculous.

"It is appropriate that he provide everything for you from the moment you take your vows until death do you part," Lady Gertrude said with severity.

A tight knot formed in Eleanor's belly.

Lady Gertrude seemed not to recall anything about Eleanor not really being Madeline. Had Eleanor misunderstood her? Did she not know the truth? Eleanor's tension translated to her rigid voice. "But is it appropriate for me to wed him?"

Lady Gertrude looked at her from rumpled head to bare toes, assessing her with sharp eyes. "You're beautiful, you're aristocratic, and you're intelligent. Mr. Knight could search the world over, but he will never find a finer woman to take to wife."

Eleanor stared back at Lady Gertrude in astonishment. "You *do* think I should wed him."

"Indeed I do. All marriages suffer through a little difficulty at the beginning, and yours, I'm sure, will be no different." Lady Gertrude picked at a piece of lint on her sleeve. "A little difficulty, a lot of difficulty, who can say? But the two of you make a beautiful couple, and—pardon my frank speaking—you want each other desperately. If he hadn't announced the wedding for tomorrow, I fear your chastity would be at risk."

If only Lady Gertrude knew.

"Besides, who do you think will rescue you?" Lady Gertrude looked pointedly at the storm lashing the windows. "If this keeps up, we'll be lucky to make it to the church tomorrow. Roads are flooded all over London, and all over England, I'm sure. Beth says the wind has knocked over a church steeple in Cheapside."

"Aye, mum, dreadful out there," Beth agreed.

"So you see, dear niece, you have no choice in the matter. No choice at all." Lady Gertrude shrugged philosophically. "And isn't that always the case with weddings? The girl has no choice but to do as she's forced to, and the male bitterly complains until she sweetens him in bed."

Lady Gertrude *did* know Eleanor's true identity, and still she thought Eleanor should marry Mr. Knight.

Well. Fine. Eleanor thought so, too.

"Mr. Knight has gone to the bank to attend to business," Lady Gertrude said, "but he says he'll see you at the church at ten o'clock tomorrow morning."

"Won't I see him today?"

"Absolutely not! It's bad luck to see the groom before the wedding." Lady Gertrude smiled ruefully. "And this wedding is courting bad luck enough."

Eleanor battled disappointment and relief. Disappointment, because she had developed a need to see Mr. Knight every day. Relief because she didn't have to face him yet . . . after last night.

As she stood on a stool in her bedchamber, allowing the seamstress to alter the beautiful gown Mr. Knight had chosen, she watched the rain sluice down the windows and wondered, could Madeline arrive in time to stop the wedding?

Chapter 20

The next morning, Remington stood on the steps of St. James's and listened to the bells ring ten o'clock. They were late. His duchess was late.

"Just like a woman, eh?" Clark asked. "Late to her own wedding."

Usually Remington enjoyed Clark's cheerfulness, but right now the man's jovial voice grated on his nerves. "She'll be here soon." He stared down the street, straining to hear the rumble of carriage wheels.

She couldn't have discovered a way to escape him now. After the night of the betrothal ball, she wouldn't even have tried. In a frenzy of passion, she had been willing to give herself to him—and he, fool that he was, hadn't taken advantage of her. He had wanted her to know what she was doing when they made love. He had bound himself to his self-imposed schedule. He had told himself she would be glad for his restraint.

But the schedule didn't matter when compared to his own desire. Furthermore, she might not have appreciated his honorable intentions and counted his refusal as rejection. And in the thirty hours since, his body had given him hell every minute for his honorable intentions. He'd spent the hours in semi-arousal—except for those minutes when he was fully aroused. Nothing had given him relief, not even discussing his shipping profits, and the day a woman distracted him from business was a black day indeed.

But this wasn't just a woman. She was his duchess, and she had tasted like heaven and responded with an untutored ardor. When he finally got her under him, he wasn't going to let her up for hours, days . . .

When he finally got her under him. They had the wedding to get through, then the wedding breakfast, then supper, then . . . my God, what had he been thinking? He couldn't survive five minutes without wanting to swive her senseless. Now he had to wait hours?

Clark rocked back and forth on his heels, uneasy with Remington's silence and Madeline's tardiness. "The weather could have been worse. It could still be storming, and that, my friend, would be a disaster."

"So it would."

Puddles filled the streets. Clouds hid the sun. The wind was dashing down the streets and around corners with a moan—and Remington's duchess still had not arrived.

"Rained half the night." Clark looked up at the scuttling clouds. "I thought it would never stop. I thought we'd be here, holding a canopy over your fiancée to get her into the . . . what's that?"

Remington heard it, too. The rumble of carriage wheels. Remington's barouche took the corner at a dignified pace and pulled to a stop in front of the church steps.

"There they are," Clark said heartily. "Your duchess is here. She's going to wed you, after all. You lucky dog, you don't deserve such a beauty."

"Yes, I do." Remington watched relentlessly as she gave her hand to the footman and descended the carriage—and deep inside him, a knot of disquiet loosened. "I most certainly do."

She was wearing the clothes he had provided. At last, she dressed as he demanded.

The gown was white velvet, holding to her elegantly slender body with the care of a lover. Her spencer was Madonna blue silk, encasing her bosom so perfectly that his mouth grew dry with desire. She wore white leather boots and a hat that framed her sweet face in the same blue as the spencer. Of course, her bouquet was yellow roses. He had planned on white roses, for then she would have been, in his mind, the perfect bride. But his old ideal of perfection had wavered and changed, and he could see no one but his duchess. Nothing but his duchess. And whatever his duchess wanted, she should get.

She looked like an angel—and only he knew how very earthy she was. Only he knew how she tasted, warm and womanly. Only he knew the way she looked without her clothes. Bare and smooth, with high, firm breasts and pale rose nipples. The indent of her waist, the flare of her hips, the notch between her thighs . . . he had wanted nothing more than to see her in her wedding gown.

Now he couldn't wait to strip that gown off her and look on the lacy chemise she wore . . . she had worn it, hadn't she? He had picked it out especially for their wedding day. She wouldn't niggle at that, would she?

It wasn't as if he would ask Lady Gertrude. Her aunt might object at discussing Madeline's undergarments with him. Yet he needed to know, and a light perspiration sprung up on his forehead as he considered how long it would be before he could find out.

But while he could look nowhere but at his duchess, she looked everywhere except at him. A blush tinted her cheeks, and she looked uneasy, as if he would accuse her of something—immodesty, perhaps, or lasciviousness. He would speak to her. He would explain that a man like him did not think less of a woman for enjoying what he taught her.

But as he started toward her, his coachman heaved himself out of his seat and planted himself in Remington's path. Reluctantly, Remington halted. "Yes, John?"

John pulled his forelock, and in a loud voice, said, "Sir, I beg yer pardon that we're late. We 'ad a bit o' a problem at Old Bond Street. Some fool fired a shot and spooked the 'orses."

Remington halted in his tracks, his mind racing. "Fired a shot?"

Clark joined them, and echoed, "Fired a shot?"

In a quieter tone, John added, "I don't know, sirs, but I would 'ave sworn the shot was fired right at the 'orses."

Fury roared through Remington, an old fury, directed at the duke of Magnus, and all the more dangerous for being long thwarted. "Damn it!" Remington cut a glance toward Lady Gertrude and Madeline. Lady Gertrude was fussing with Madeline's gown. Madeline was pulling her bonnet forward, as if she could hide behind its concealing brim.

"The ladies appear to be all right," Clark observed.

"Aye, sir," John said. "Lady Gertrude screamed a bit, but 'Er Grace is plucky t' the backbone!"

"That's a blessing." Clark shook his head. "But if I were superstitious, I would call this a bad omen."

"Omen? Hell, this wasn't an omen. This was deliberate." Remington clipped his words.

Clark goggled at him. "What do you mean?"

"Second time in less than a week that my carriage has been attacked," Remington informed him.

Taken aback, Clark asked, "Do you suppose? . . . That is, is this associated with the incidents you related to me?"

"Without a doubt," Remington answered. "There may be others who want me dead, but few who can marshal such lethal forces." He asked John, "Did you see the man with the gun?"

"Nay, sir, nary a soul, but I couldn't look fer a time. Poor Roderick—he's the left gray, sir—the bullet cut a notch in his ear. He kicked up a fuss, o' course, and the ladies was jostled around before I got the team under control." Pulling a handkerchief from his pocket, John wiped sweat from his heavy brow. His complexion was gray, and his hands were shaking. "I don't like t' brag on meself, sir, but a lesser coachman wouldn't 'ave pulled it out."

One of the footmen had crept close, and he cradled his own arm as if it were hurt. "Aye, sir, Mr. Knight, sir, 'e's right. Went flying off, I did, and I thought the carriage was going t' topple, but John Coachman fought the grays t' a standstill. Best bit o' driving I've ever seen!"

Remington had hired every one of his servants with an eye to their skills, their loyalty, and their fighting ability. Now he'd been proved right in his choices on two separate occasions in the last week. He would have reflected with satisfaction on his shrewd choices, but he could not. Not in good faith.

Looking down at his hands, he saw they were clenching and unclenching. He had provided his duchess shelter, food, and now clothing. With this ceremony, she would be utterly dependent on him—and he had put her in danger. Yes, he was the target of these attacks, but she could be hurt, could even be killed.

He, who had planned every step of his revenge with such care, hadn't thought of that.

Or perhaps it was simply that, before he'd met her, he hadn't cared.

" 'As someone got a grievance against 'Er Grace?" John asked.

"Unlikely," Clark answered. "Most brides don't go to the church in the groom's carriage, so I suspect that Remington was the target."

The men uneasily looked around at the surrounding buildings.

"Yes, I know," Remington said. "It's not a pleasant idea, to know you're working for someone with people who shoot at him. Nevertheless, I must ask that you remain to take us home. On our return, we'll not be going elsewhere."

John was an older man, well-trained, and he nodded solemnly. The footman couldn't manage such discretion and fought a grin.

"When we're back at Berkley Square, go to the tavern on my largesse. In fact, go to several taverns. Express your dissatisfaction with my employ. See if you can hear any gossip about me. Someone is trying to make trouble." Remington knew very well who it was, but he needed to know what further peril he could expect. "Disgruntled servants are a fertile ground for gossip, and perhaps someone will seek you out."

John nodded, but the footman had been chosen for his fighting ability, not his brains, and he said, "But sir, we're not disgruntled. We're very gruntled."

John cuffed him and led him away. "Come on. I'll explain it t' ye."

Clark touched Remington's sleeve. "Lady Gertrude thinks it odd that you've not come to welcome your bride."

A chill swept down Remington's spine. Was his duchess in peril now, standing on the church steps? He started toward her. "Come on," he tossed back to Clark. "Escort Lady Gertrude." Who was also in peril.

His duchess looked alarmed as Remington approached, but he didn't care. He wanted her off the street.

In a breathless voice, she said, "Mr. Knight, I have something I need to tell you."

Catching her by the hand, he said, "Tell me after the ceremony."

"But sir, you'll be angry when you hear it."

Leading her through the heavy open doors, he turned on her. "I'm already angry."

"I'm sorry for that, sir." She clutched her bouquet in both of her trembling hands. "Could you tell me the reason?"

It was pure politeness that made her ask; she didn't sound as if she cared at all, and in the relative safety of the narthex, he relaxed. "I trust you weren't hurt on the way here."

"What? No, I thank you, I'm well, although Lady Gertrude said riding in your carriages is most eventful." Eleanor glanced down at the bouquet she held, out the open doors toward the clouds, as if seeking an answer. Then, craning her neck, she looked down the street as if expecting to see someone riding to her rescue. "I truly do need to tell you something."

Pulling her further away from the doors, he said, "I know you're embarrassed to look me in the eyes."

Her gaze snapped up.

At the sight of that sweet, anxious face, his resolve

strengthened. He needed to carry out his plan. He needed to keep her safe.

Regardless of the danger, the circumstances, or the environs, the need to mark her as his drove him ever more fiercely. He needed to put his ring on her finger so every man would know she was claimed. So that she knew she was claimed. He wanted every breath she took, every movement she made, to remind her of him. Of his possession.

He had never been as unsure of a woman as he was of her, and it wasn't that she had aristocratic connections or that he'd won her in a card game. The woman herself was elusive, fey. She seemed always about to slip away from him, as if no claim he could make would keep her in his world.

In a quiet voice, pitched to reach only her ears, he said, "Don't you dare imagine that I think less of you because you showed me the sweetest passion I've ever been privileged to witness." He was so close to owning her. To having her.

She made an incoherent sound of objection and glanced frantically at Lady Gertrude and Clark.

"They can't hear us. They deliberately aren't listening." That much was true. They'd moved away to give Remington and his duchess privacy. "I promise I'm going to show you the same madness of passion . . . although not so sweet. But don't fear me. I've never hurt a woman, and you . . . you're special. You're going to be my wife." Tenderly, he brushed his finger across her lips. "I promise I'll make you happy. Do you believe me?"

To his surprise, his speech didn't seem to lessen her fears. If anything, she looked less embarrassed and more wretched. She glanced longingly at the door as if expecting to see someone come through. "Yes, I believe you. It's just that . . . Mr. Knight, I pray you listen—"

He placed his gloved hand across her lips. "Tell me after the ceremony."

She stared at him, but she didn't seem to see him. She seemed to be looking inside herself, seeking escape.

"No one's going to save you," he said softly. "It's far too late for that."

Her eyes grew determined, her chin lifted, and with a firm nod, she said, "I know. I'm going to have to do as I've resolved."

"What is that?"

"To wed you."

Triumph roared through him. Her declaration was what he'd been waiting for. There would be no last-minute balking at the altar. She would speak her vows, and nothing could go wrong now.

Chapter 21

"Then come." Mr. Knight offered his arm and led Eleanor into the nave. "It's time—past time—to get married."

Eleanor blinked as her eyes adjusted to the dim light. The church's ceiling soared out of sight. A few people sat in the back pews, their faces hidden by shadows. Curiosity-seekers, probably, and perhaps a well-wisher or two who had heard Mr. Knight's announcement of their wedding. Certainly no one stood and called her name, or Madeline's, either. And thank God, for she wanted this wedding to happen. Sin or not, she wanted to marry Mr. Knight.

And there. Straight ahead. The altar. Candles burned in the great gold candelabras, the flames mere pinpricks of light. The clergyman waited in all his raiment, the parish clerk stood off to the side.

The church was enormous and echoing, but the walk down the aisle seemed all too brief. Her last moments as a free woman were fleeting.

They stepped up to the altar. She smelled the beeswax on the wood, the faint odor of dust, age and holiness. Clark and Lady Gertrude standing beside them as their witnesses.

The clergyman was elderly, with glasses that rested on the tip of his nose and a worn, brown leather Bible that trembled in his veined and palsied hands. He smiled at her kindly, his face breaking up into a network of wrinkles. "I'm Mr. Gilbert, my dear, and I'm to have the privilege of performing your marriage." He shot Mr. Knight a reproving glance. "I like to know the young people I marry, and I asked that you two come in for counseling, but your swain didn't want to take the time. So busy, these young men—"

"Yes, exactly," Lady Gertrude said. "One never knows what might happen if matters aren't handled correctly."

Gracelessly, Eleanor blurted, "Mr. Gilbert, could I see the information you've been given?"

Someone out in the pews coughed, as if in a great seizure.

"What?" Mr. Knight stared at her forbiddingly. "Do you think I would make a mistake? About *this*?"

Eleanor cleared her throat nervously. "I . . . um . . . would like to make sure that everything is correct before we proceed."

"If you're planning to make trouble—" Mr. Knight warned.

Mr. Gilbert's white, bushy eyebrows shot up at Mr. Knight's tone. Putting his arm around Eleanor's shoulders, he said, "If you would come this way, my dear, we'll talk in my office."

"I'll come, too," Lady Gertrude announced, and reassured Mr. Knight, "we want this marriage to be completely legal."

The skin between Eleanor's shoulder blades twitched as they made their way into Mr. Gilbert's office, and she knew Mr. Knight was glaring at her, trying to discern her purpose. The man was suspicious and distrustful, and she was a fool for doing this. But she had let fate make her decision. Unless something occurred to stop the ceremony—unless Madeline or Dickie or the duke arrived—Eleanor was going to marry Mr. Knight.

Pulling the door shut behind them, Eleanor tersely said, "Let me see the personal information." Seeing Mr. Gilbert's surprise, she added, "Please, sir, the personal information." Vaguely surprised, she realized she sounded like Madeline when the ducal mood was upon her, but then, that voice always produced results.

As it did now. Mr. Gilbert opened his book of prayers and extracted a small sheet of paper with the names scribbled on it. "I've never seen anyone so anxious about so simple a matter." Taking Eleanor's hand, he asked, "Are you sure you don't truly want to discuss something else? Advice on how to handle your husband? He appears to be very domineering, and sometimes that's frightening to a new bride."

"He is domineering." Eleanor wasn't really paying attention to what she said. "But I'm not frightened." Realizing that Mr. Gilbert looked shocked, she added hastily, "Lady Gertrude has given me many lectures on how to be a good wife."

Lady Gertrude folded her hands and nodded piously.

"Ah." He peered over his glasses at Lady Gertrude. "Very well. It's good to know you have a mother figure to guide you through these turbulent new waters."

Eleanor looked at the paper, and with a *tsk*, she told Mr. Gilbert, "This is what I feared. This says Madeline Elizabeth Eleanor Jane de Lacy. I'm Eleanor Madeline Anne Elizabeth de Lacy. Madeline and Eleanor are both de Lacy family names, and my dear Mr. Knight confused mine with my cousin's."

"Oh, dear." Mr. Gilbert almost wheezed with distress.

"It wouldn't do to make my vows incorrectly, would it?" Eleanor inquired.

"No, indeed." Mr. Gilbert went to his desk, uncorked his ink, and made the change, his fingers shaking. "That would be quite irregular."

"We can't have that." Eleanor indicated the door. "Now that everything is in order, shall we proceed?"

"Yes, but—are you sure you don't have another concern?" the elderly clergyman asked.

Can you go to hell for pretending to be someone you aren't? But there was no way to phrase the question, and no good answer to be had, so Eleanor shook her head and sailed through the door. As she returned to her place beside Mr. Knight, he placed her hand back on his arm and covered it with his, holding onto her as if, even now, he feared she might flee.

She stole a sideways glance at him. He looked irate at the delay, and . . . she hadn't seen him at all yesterday, and even in that brief time apart, she had forgotten how handsome he was. He was tall, with broad shoulders that filled out his black jacket, and long, muscular legs that made her think blasphemous thoughts right here in the church. His blond hair glinted like polished gold. His austere face made her want to trace his cheekbones and his strong jaw. His lips . . . all she wanted from his lips was to feel them on her somewhere, anywhere. His eyes were pale blue and distant—except when he looked at her. Then they held the heat and beauty of the hottest coals, and she knew they could burn her just as surely as warm her.

If he had set his mind to courtship, he could have had any woman in the ton. He might not have followed the prescribed methods, but Eleanor knew he could have cajoled his way into the marriage mart, and when he'd decided on a girl for his wife, she would have defied her parents and all of society to have him.

Look at Eleanor. She was taking him under false pretenses, and with the promise of anguish in the not-too-distant future. But she wanted him badly enough to betray her own ethics to have him, and she swore she would face the consequences, no matter what they were.

"Holy matrimony is an honorable estate . . ." The clergyman began the ceremony, his sonorous voice carrying across the pews.

Eleanor's teeth clenched as she listened to him exhort them to enter into matrimony "reverently, discreetly, advisedly, soberly, and in the fear of God." She wondered if lightning would strike her through the roof for bastardizing such a solemn occasion. She waited for the moment that she knew would come.

"Face each other," Mr. Gilbert commanded.

Eleanor's heart thumped against her breastbone as she turned to find Mr. Knight staring down at her, his eyes brooding as he observed her.

"Repeat after me," the clergyman intoned. "I, Eleanor Madeline Anne Elizabeth de Lacy, do solemnly swear to obey and serve . . ."

Mr. Knight frowned, but Eleanor gave him no chance to think about the change.

In a clear voice, she said, "I, Eleanor Madeline Anne Elizabeth de Lacy, do solemnly swear to obey and serve . . ." Dimly, she was aware of a small commotion in the depths of the church, a burst of mad laughter that made Mr. Gilbert frown.

Eleanor paid no heed.

Nor did Mr. Knight. All of his attention was focused on her. She almost thought he was compelling her to give herself into his keeping, and she had committed herself beyond hope of redemption.

He repeated his vows in a deep tone, each word resounding through the church. No one could say they didn't hear or didn't understand.

Finally Mr. Gilbert proclaimed, "I now pronounce you man and wife."

Eleanor was stunned.

She had done it. She had taken what she wanted—who she wanted—without regard to what was right, and she would have to face the consequences. But not now. Not yet. Tomorrow, perhaps, or next week. Some time when she'd tamed Mr. Knight, shown him her love and perhaps, just perhaps, taught him to love in return.

Right now, she faced a man with a predatory smile. He viewed her as a starving man would look at a hearty pub meal. Taking her hands in his, he leaned down and pressed his lips to hers in a chaste kiss, but in that kiss was the promise of so much more.

Clark broke in. "Eh, eh, there's time enough for that later. Congratulations to both of you!" To Eleanor, he said, "You've got a good man, there."

"I know." She did know. She was depending on his goodness.

Mr. Knight looked sharply at her.

Lady Gertrude dabbed at her eyes. "Weddings always make me cry. Mr. Knight, be good to my niece. She deserves better than she's had."

Now a cynical twist tugged at Mr. Knight's mouth, but he nodded. "I intend to take care of her."

Mr. Gilbert herded them into the vestry, where they signed the register, Eleanor carefully etching her name below her husband's. Then with thanks to Mr. Gilbert, they descended the stairs and started down the aisle.

Mr. Gilbert followed them, his robes flapping. "Look out the door," he said. "The sun has come out. What a good omen for your marriage! A very good omen indeed!"

"Clouds first, then sunshine," Lady Gertrude added.

At the back of the church, in front of the door, they could see a woman silhouetted by the watery sunlight. A single glance told Eleanor it wasn't Madeline, but she did appear to be waiting for them. Something about the way she stood looked familiar. . . .

As her face became clear, Eleanor stopped breathing. Stumbled to a halt. Lady Shapster. Dear Lord. It was Lady Shapster. Eleanor knew that sneer, that satisfied, catlike slant of the eyes. Lady Shapster had come to make mischief.

All Eleanor's bravado shriveled away. How could she ever have imagined she wouldn't be found out?

"Mr. Knight," Lady Shapster purred as she blocked their way out the doors. "You look so handsome in your finery."

"Madam." He bowed and tried to lead Eleanor outside.

Lady Shapster moved in front of them again. "I came especially to see you wed, and you should be glad. So few guests. No friends." She gestured at an ill-dressed fellow who scribbled on a slate. "Just a few newspapermen . . ."

A newspaperman. This got more and more dreadful.

"I wish you wouldn't," Eleanor said.

But that was too much to ask. Lady Shapster smiled in purse-lipped amusement and slowly shook her head.

Mr. Knight looked from one to the other. He didn't understand what was happening, but he didn't like it, for he stepped in front of Eleanor as if to protect her from the malevolence of the cruelest woman in the world.

In a cold, clear voice that made Eleanor shiver, he said, "Lady Shapster, I didn't invite you, and in case I haven't made myself clear, I intend never to invite you to anything ever again. That you decided to attend my wedding is an act of unparalleled brazenness, and in the future, I demand that you leave my wife and me alone." Placing a protective hand on Eleanor's back, he pushed around Lady Shapster and onto the church porch.

"Mr. Knight! You're so rude, and to one of the family. It's a sign of ill-breeding, and you don't want to suffer that reputation. After all"—Lady Shapster cast Eleanor a gloating smile—"I am now your step-mama-in-law."

Mr. Knight observed Lady Shapster casually, as if her ravings only slightly interested him. Turning to Eleanor, he asked, "What does she mean?"

Eleanor wanted to run, but she knew it would do her no good. Lady Shapster would trip her. Shout the truth up and down the street. There was no escaping justice now. It had hunted her down, and she would pay the penalty. Her lungs wouldn't expand, and she used the last of her breath to say, "She means . . . she means I'm not Madeline. I'm not the future duchess of Magnus. I'm Madeline's cousin and companion." Painstakingly, she told him the truth. "I'm Eleanor."

He stared at her, and slow comprehension overtook him. It was as if he had been trying to solve a puzzle, and this was the piece that had been missing.

"I could have interrupted the ceremony, Mr. Knight," Lady Shapster said. "I could have saved you from this dreadful blunder. But you thought you were better than me. You didn't invite me to your party. You didn't invite me to your wedding breakfast. And now you're bound to stupid little Eleanor forever."

"Shut up," Lady Gertrude said.

"How dare you?" Lady Shapster drew herself up in outrage. "You knew. You can't tell me you didn't. You—"

"Shut up." Like a small goat, Lady Gertrude lowered her head and ran at Lady Shapster, butting her off her feet.

Mr. Gilbert wrung his hands.

Clark exclaimed and reproved.

But although their mouths moved, Eleanor heard them only faintly. Although their arms waved, she saw them dimly. They were on the periphery of her attention. All of her being was concentrated on Mr. Knight.

His pale blue eyes grew bitterly cold. He looked at her as if she weren't worth grinding beneath his heel. Slowly, his hand rose and touched her cheek. "I thought you were the one." His whisper vibrated with feeling. "I thought you were real. I should have known." His fingers slipped around her throat. "No one in your family can be trusted."

She felt the faintest of pressure. A threat, not realized, but there nevertheless.

Leaning into her face, he said, for her ears only, "I won't make the same mistake again."

Chapter 22

"*S*it down, dear." Lady Gertrude relaxed on the fainting couch, sipped her brandy and watched as Eleanor paced across the library, Lizzie at her heels. "Mr. Knight will come home when he's ready, and you'll want to be the same dear, serene self you always are."

Parting the curtains, Eleanor looked out into the dark. No fog or rain softened the black of this night, but the wind rattled the panes and sent a chill up her arms. This morning at the church, after Mr. Knight had handed her and Lady Gertrude into the carriage, he had mounted his horse and escorted them to his town house. She'd been scared, planning an explanation of her misdeeds. But he'd waited until they'd entered the front door, then, without a backward glance, he'd ridden away.

Although Eleanor had faithfully watched, there'd

been no sign of him since. "What good does it do to be my usual serene self, when Mr. Knight wants another?"

Lady Gertrude smoothed the burgundy cashmere shawl draped over her feet. "I've watched the two of you together. He might want to *own* a duchess, but he wants to *bed* you."

Whirling around, Eleanor faced Lady Gertrude. "I've been abandoned by my husband on my wedding day. I must point out, that doesn't bode well for the marriage." Vaguely, she was aware she was acting a Cheltenham tragedy. But if, after the events of today, she couldn't be dramatic, when could she?

"Pish tosh." Lady Gertrude dismissed Eleanor's apprehension with an airy wave of the hand. "He'll be back."

Again Eleanor prowled across the room. She had changed for her wedding breakfast, which she'd miserably shared with Clark and Lady Gertrude. They had chatted amiably about many topics, and the only time they'd faltered was when Clark had mentioned how disappointed his wife would be to have missed the occasion. He'd escaped immediately after, and all through the long afternoon, Eleanor had paced and waited—and remembered. When the time had come, she'd dressed for dinner, hoping against hope Mr. Knight would return.

He hadn't, and now her hopes faded. She watched as Bridgeport entered with another glass of brandy for Lady Gertrude and a cold rag, which Lady Gertrude placed on her head.

As Eleanor observed the odd ritual, memory

stirred. Vaguely she recalled seeing Lady Gertrude standing over the prone Lady Shapster. "Ma'am, do I remember correctly? Did you knock down Lady Shapster?"

Bridgeport fought a smile.

"I gave her a blow with my head—when one is my size, one uses the tools one has." Lady Gertrude rubbed the top of her head. "Glad I am I did it, too. Dreadful, spiteful woman."

"Yes. Thank you. That was possibly the bravest thing anyone has ever done." In her mind's eye, Eleanor saw Mr. Gilbert and Clark assisting Lady Shapster to her feet. Lady Shapster had shaken off their solicitousness and dusted off her skirt, but she hadn't been browbeaten. She was angry and she was ruthless. Eleanor had no doubt Lady Shapster blamed Eleanor for her humiliation. Lady Shapster would get revenge.

"Would madam like a refreshing cup of tea?" Bridgeport asked.

With a start, Eleanor realized he spoke to her. She was the mistress of this house, and every servant knew the circumstances of her wedding. The gossip must be flying around the servants' quarters— indeed, all of London—tonight. "Thank you, Bridge-port, but no. I think I shall do my needlework."

Bridgeport cast an unfavorable eye on Lizzie, now lolling at Eleanor's feet. "Would madam like me to remove the canine?"

"No." Leaning down, Eleanor rubbed Lizzie's ears. "She makes me happy."

Bridgeport stifled a sigh. "Very well, madam, but I

want to assure you that, should Mr. Knight return, I will keep the animal with me until morning. You don't need to worry about the creature."

"Thank you, Bridgeport, that's very kind," Eleanor said.

Still Bridgeport hovered. "Your needlework is here, madam, on this table. I'll send a footman in with an extra branch of candles."

Eleanor surmised he, like Lady Gertrude, wished her to become her usual serene self. Even the dog stared at her, its brow wrinkled expressively. The trouble with composure was that people, and creatures, came to expect it of one. Surrendering to the inevitable, Eleanor seated herself. Lizzie at once came and lay on her feet. The footman brought the candles. Bridgeport handed her the needlework, bowed and discreetly disappeared.

Eleanor stared at the work in her hands. It was a chair cover for Magnus Hall in Suffolk. She had done four of them. She had twelve more to do, and right now she didn't care if she ever finished another.

For no matter how much she tried, she couldn't shut out the picture of Remington that relentlessly played across her mind. His triumph when he'd kissed her at the end of their vows. His incredulity when her stepmother had told him of Eleanor's trick. And his disdain when he'd realized the truth. He hadn't married a duchess. He'd married a nobody, and all his words of wanting her, only her, were shown to be flagrant lies.

Yes, he had lied, too. He was as guilty as she was.

But then, she had known he lied. Only in a small,

hidden corner of her mind had she dared to dream that he might really want her.

Not love her. She wasn't so confident. But want her.

"You must stop worrying," Lady Gertrude said. "You'll make yourself ill, and that will never do. Mr. Knight is a man. They're simple creatures, and when he arrives, if you welcome him without reproach and smile and flirt, he'll soon come around."

Eleanor plunged her needle into the canvas. "Pardon me, my lady, I don't mean to be cruel, but did you not do that with your husband?"

Surprisingly, Lady Gertrude appeared not at all offended. Rather, she was thoughtful. "The difference is in the man. Some of them are rotten to the core, disgusting asses no woman can appease or satisfy. My husband, for one. Mr. Knight is different. He's not *kind*. Mind you, I would never tell you he is kind. But there's a core of honor in him. I don't know why he wanted to wed Madeline so much, but I still say that, after this rough patch, this union between you and him will work out."

The dog came to her feet and stared ferociously at the door.

Gesturing grandly toward the door, Lady Gertrude said, "I hear someone now. Could it be Mr. Knight?"

"No, it bloody well couldn't." The duke of Magnus stomped in the room, an exorbitant frown on his whiskered face.

Bridgeport followed on his heels, looking helpless and affronted. Sidling over to Eleanor, he muttered,

"Sorry, ma'am. He brushed past me before I could announce him."

She patted his arm, then petted the bristling dog. "Don't concern yourself. Magnus does as he pleases." Even when he should know better.

"Greetings, Magnus," Lady Gertrude said. "About time you got here."

Brow lowered in irritation, Magnus answered, "I came as fast as I could, as soon as I heard Knight and Madeline would wed today."

Eleanor stared in confusion. "But . . . but . . ."

"Where is that bastard? Where is he?" Magnus stopped and glanced about him. "Eleanor, Gertrude, good to see you and all that rot, but where's Maddie and where's that blackguard who would marry my daughter in such an unseemly hurry?"

Eleanor frowned. "You should know where Madeline is. She's at Mr. Rumbelow's."

"What's she doing there?" Magnus demanded. "Ramshackle fellow, not to be trusted."

"Oh, dear." Eleanor's heart sank. "When she heard about his gambling party, she resolved to go there and stop you from losing the queen's tiara."

"I didn't know that," Lady Gertrude said.

"Because it's not true." Magnus shook his head, as if he hadn't heard correctly. "I didn't go to his gambling party. The whole setup stunk to high heaven, and even if it hadn't—the queen's tiara is not mine to gamble."

How could a man who wagered his daughter have scruples about gambling away the historical de Lacy tiara? It seemed illogical, yet Eleanor didn't doubt him. He was every inch a duke; sure of his welcome, loud and bluff, with rosy cheeks, and a hearty voice he never regulated. Tall and broad, his belly jiggled when he walked, and right now he walked over to Lady Gertrude and peered at her glass. "Brandy. Good. I'll have one." He lowered himself into a chair, which creaked beneath his weight. Snapping his fingers at Lizzie, he said, "Silly-looking dog you've got there, Eleanor." Cautiously, Lizzie came over and sniffed his fingers, then allowed him to pet her. "Good for anything? Hunting? Birding?"

Eleanor smiled. "I doubt that, but she's very sweet and she adores Mr. Knight."

"Not too bright, then," Magnus said.

As if affronted, Lizzie returned to Eleanor.

"Bright enough." Eleanor rubbed the dog's ears.

Bridgeport gave a brandy to Magnus, then apparently decided Eleanor should have one, too, for he presented her with a cut glass goblet half full of amber liquid.

Eleanor wondered if she appeared so beleaguered and accepted it. With a gesture, she dismissed Bridgeport, who closed the door behind him.

After a hearty swallow, Magnus demanded, *"Did* Madeline marry today?"

Before she answered, Eleanor also took a drink. She coughed, cleared her throat, and answered, "Not exactly, Uncle."

"Not exactly? There's no such thing as a little bit married. She's either married or she isn't."

Lady Gertrude cackled. "When you're right, you're right, Magnus."

"To the best of my knowledge, Madeline is not

married." Eleanor wet her lips. "I've married Mr. Knight in her stead."

Magnus stared. A smile spread across his broad lips. He said, "Jolly good of you, dear girl! I knew you would always care for your cousin, but I had no idea you had the courage to take on a man like Knight."

Dryly, Eleanor said, "I'm as surprised as you, Uncle."

"How did you convince him?" He winked. "Or should I ask?"

Disgusted, Lady Gertrude proclaimed, "Magnus, you're as crass as ever."

To Eleanor's surprise, he flushed. "'Tain't crass. Eleanor's a handsome thing, and Knight isn't blind."

Eleanor interrupted before the discussion embarrassed her yet more. "I'm innocent of entrapping Mr. Knight in the manner you're suggesting, Uncle. He didn't know it was me."

Magnus stared blankly.

Eleanor added, "He thought I was Madeline."

It took a few moments, but when Magnus comprehended the state of affairs, he slapped his knee and roared with laughter. "Good jest! Didn't know, eh? Married the wrong gel, did he? How I shall love spreading this tale about!"

"Magnus, no!" Lady Gertrude sat straight up. "Mr. Knight is very angry with Eleanor. It's bad enough knowing the story shall be in one of those dreadful newspapers. Let us not stir his wrath yet more by having *you* mock him, too."

"Mad at Eleanor, is he? Yes, I can see he would

be." Magnus slurped up his brandy and placed the glass on the table. "Ah, well, even if I were tempted, I'm out of London on a mission to restore the family's fortunes. That's why it took me so long to get here." He frowned. "Although thanks to our little Eleanor, I suppose the family fortune is still intact." Cheering up again, he said, "Still, negotiations are ongoing, and I'll not abandon them now."

Although Magnus hadn't confided in them, Eleanor had known Magnus had a scheme to save Madeline. Convinced that he would gamble away a precious family heirloom, the cousins had decided that Madeline should follow him incognito into a den of gambling and iniquity. To the best of Eleanor's knowledge, Magnus had never succeeded at anything in his whole life, so Eleanor asked, "What are you doing, Uncle?"

"Old business. Sad business, in its way." He stirred restively in his seat and looked thoughtful. "Time enough to tell you if the prospect succeeds. Nothing to fret about if it doesn't."

Eleanor doubted that, but she had enough worries without assuming his.

"In the meantime, tell me all about the high jinks you gels have gotten yourselves into," Magnus commanded.

When Eleanor had finished the tale, Magnus sat with his hands on his knees. "Well, I'll be damned. Beg pardon, ladies." He shook his head as if bewildered, then asked Eleanor, "So you wed Knight in Maddie's place?"

"Yes, Uncle."

"And that blasted Lady Shapster spoiled your story?"

"Yes, Uncle."

"I never understood what my brother saw in her. A more petty and comprehensive harridan I have never met." He rubbed his face with his hand, and in a lower tone, said, "But I didn't expect any better from him. A more thorough scoundrel . . ." Straightening, he asked, "Eh, Eleanor, do you know why I made no objection when Madeline took you into our home?"

"I . . . never have wondered." Because when Madeline had decided to help, Eleanor hadn't thought Magnus had had a choice. But he *was* the duke. He could have made Eleanor's life miserable. Instead he'd pinched her cheek and treated her with the same indifference he showed his own daughter.

"I feared you would die if left there. Waste away—or take a fall."

Lady Gertrude took a breath. "So you think Lady Shapster is deadly?"

He bent a hard look on her. "I think both my brother and his wife are best avoided when possible."

Both sets of eyes turned to survey Eleanor, and she stirred restively.

"I'm back to my hotel, then on the morrow I'll return to Sussex." Magnus heaved himself out of his chair. "Gertrude, you keep an eye on Eleanor."

"I intend to," Lady Gertrude said.

The dog barked.

Magnus caught Lizzie under the chin and looked into her eyes. "Yes, and you, too." He pressed a kiss on Eleanor's forehead. "Congratulations on your marriage, my dear. Don't let Knight bully you, and remember—you're bigger than Lady Shapster, a good bare-knuckled blow to the nose will take her down."

Touched by his sign of concern, Eleanor replied, "Thank you, Uncle. I will remember."

Chapter 23

*E*leanor woke with a start and lay staring into the darkness of midnight and loneliness. Only the orange glow of the embers in the fireplace gave illumination to Remington's big bedchamber she shared . . . with no one.

No matter what she dreamed or what she wished, Remington had not returned to the house on Berkley Square.

Impatient with her wistful, old-maid illusions, she sat up. The bed was tall, its posts looming out of sight. Velvet bedcurtains hung at the corners, and the mattress was soft and luxurious. A silk-and-lace gown had been draped across the foot of the bed. She had donned it in hopes he would return, and now it slithered across her cool skin in a sensuous flow of luxury.

Well. She wasn't going to wear this forever. Cotton was much more comfortable, and when winter came, flannel was the only thing that kept her warm. Of course, if Mr. Knight shared her bed, she would wear nothing but desire.

Foolish dreams. When had she lost her firm grip on reality and fallen into wistfulness?

Sliding out of bed, she padded on bare feet toward the fireplace. If she had to be awake, she wanted the cheer and warmth of a crackling fire.

Kneeling on the hearth, she tossed on a few sticks of kindling, then placed enough logs to last her through the rest of this interminable night. Staring into the red and yellow flames, she wondered if Mr. Knight would ever return. Perhaps she would live her life alone, a virgin, married and abandoned.

If the look on his face today was any indication, she would be lucky to live long at all. She didn't know him. No one did. The questions Lord Fanthorpe had asked returned to haunt her. Who was Mr. Knight? Who were his people?

She thought she detected traces of kindness in Mr. Knight . . . but that was before. Before she had betrayed him.

The merest drift of air brought the scent of tobacco, of cards, of old leather. The skin on her neck prickled in warning. Lifting her head, she looked to the chair on her right.

There, darkness outlined by darkness, lounged Mr. Knight. He still wore the suit he'd worn to be married, but he'd discarded his jacket, and his satin waistcoat was unbuttoned. His shirt was open at the throat, and the slice of skin was tanned and dusted with hair. His features were the same, austere and still, but his chin was unshaven. The careful image he had cultivated, of a gentleman of leisure, disintegrated into a more honest and less civilized image—that of a master of the streets and alleys.

He was silence personified. As he observed her, his eyes reflected the fire's golden flame.

Rising, she faced him.

Still indolently sprawled in the chair, he said, "I used to think you did those things in all innocence."

He was here. He was speaking to her. The tightness of her throat eased. "What things?"

He gestured up and down her figure, using his long, blunt fingers in emphasis. "Like that. Standing in front of the fire so I can see the outline of your body through your clothes."

At once she started to walk away.

His voice halted her in her tracks. "No. Stay where you are. I didn't say I didn't like it."

"I won't stand here while you ogle and insult me."

"Yes. You will. I'm your husband, and I will see that for which I paid so dearly." His pale eyes glowed and seemed almost feral in their intensity. "You should be proud of your body. Your breasts are perfect, rounded and firm." His gaze feasted on her. "And I love to watch you from the back."

Her hands itched to cover herself, but which part? The fire heated the silk over her back, and his gaze heated the silk at her front.

"Your thighs . . . I love your thighs the best. They're slender, yet strong, and when you ride, so smoothly, so gracefully, all I can think is how you would move beneath me."

"Mr. . . . Knight!" Such an inadequate response. So ineffectual.

Taking a glass half-full of golden liquid from the table beside him, he lifted it to his lips, sipped, and put it back. "There's a quaint American custom in which I'd like you to indulge me. I'm your husband. For the rest of your life, we're going to share the same bed. Call me Remington."

She could do that easily enough. "There's no need to be sarcastic . . . Remington." To her surprise, the sound of his name on her lips made her shiver, as if she allowed him an intimacy so great she would never recover the pieces of herself.

As the logs caught fire, she could see his face more clearly. His brows were black and straight. Flames were reflected in the frozen blue of his eyes. Deep grooves were etched into his skin between his nose and his mouth. He looked diabolical, and he looked hungry.

Again she started to step away.

In a tone so deep he sounded like the voice of darkness, he said, "Stay. I insist. I like the way the material clings to your hips and the little puckers your nipples make in the silk."

He spoke softly, as if he were talking to himself, but each word seduced her as surely as a touch. It didn't matter who he was or who his people were. It wasn't hostility that gripped him tonight, but lust. Ladies should not respond to anything quite so vulgar as lust. Certainly they shouldn't lust in return. But the place between Eleanor's legs grew damp, and her nipples ached. *She* ached. She wanted to move. Not away, but toward, and with.

She found herself standing like a wanton: hip out, shoulders back, her spine a graceful curve. He still wanted her, and instinct told her that making him her mate would bind him as nothing else could. "Please, let me explain why I did what I did."

"What you did? What do you mean? Married me?" He laughed without humor. "No need to explain. I do understand. I've been married for my money."

Shocked that anyone could think that of her, she protested, "I didn't marry you for your money!"

"Please. Don't tell me Banbury tales in addition to your other sins. What other reason could there be for marrying me? It certainly wasn't for love. Love wouldn't have made a sacrifice of my needs."

At his scorn, she shriveled a little inside. But the habit of frankness had been easy to adopt, and she answered, "No one *needs* to marry a duchess, and I didn't *need* to marry a wealthy man. You've heard my story. Had I chosen, I could have married an old and moneyed man when I was sixteen. I would even now be a rich and merry widow."

"At sixteen, one always expects another man will come along. How old are you, my dear?"

Abominable man! "Twenty-four."

"Firmly on the shelf with the other old maids. You were more desperate now, and what an opportunity you had with me! Well, my darling"—taking her hand, he stroked it—"if you have plans to kill me for my fortune, be warned. I've escaped death at the hands of your family before, and now I'm warned. I shall watch my back."

"Kill you?" She yanked her hand free. "Are you mad?"

"Perhaps. A little, tonight." His fingers twitched, as if he wanted to pounce, to grip her and hold her still for his possession. "I sent for my man who had been watching you two, you and your cousin, the future duchess."

"Spying on us, you mean."

"Spying on you," Remington concurred amiably. "We agreed you must have made the switch at Mr. Rumbelow's house party. That is where the duchess remains, is it not?"

"I think so, but she was supposed to be here by now. I'm actually very worried about her."

"So worried you married her fiancé."

Eleanor could be cruel, too. "She didn't want you."

"Now that, I believe." He tensed like a beast about to spring. "You're saying she would approve of your ingenuity. I imagine she would. I imagine any woman would. I suppose you were supposed to give me a message telling me she'd be late."

"No. This is her scheme that I should portray her!" Eleanor drew a frustrated breath. "You commanded with such vigor that she appear promptly, we feared you would take some terrible vengeance if she didn't obey."

"I'm not so spiteful."

"A man who seeks a wife at the piquet table is likely to be quite insane."

"Hm." He stroked his chin. "Yes. Perhaps I gave too much weight to my commands."

"Logic at last." Then, because she couldn't bear

not knowing for another minute, she asked, "Where have you been?"

"Spoken like a true wife." His lids drooped as if he were amused. At her, or at himself. "And like a true English husband, I've been at my club, gambling and thinking. Do you know what thought I came up with?"

She didn't know, but she suspected she wasn't going to like it. "No."

"I'm married to you. We have spoken our vows in front of God and witnesses, and we are as surely wed as any old married couple in London. Divorce would take years, a fortune, and an act of Parliament. There's no grounds for an annulment. So there's no escape. We're married."

"I know. I'm—"

"Don't." He slashed the air with the knife of his hand. "Don't insult me by saying you're sorry. You manipulated me every inch of the way, with your artless blushes and shy adoration. I thought I had won all . . . a duchess I could love and sweet revenge at the same time. Instead"—he crumpled his imaginary winnings in his hand—"I have nothing."

She wasn't nothing. She was a de Lacy. Straightening, she said, "You have everything. You have more than most people ever dream of."

"Enlighten me, dear girl. What do I have?"

With his cynical gaze on her, her mind went blank. "Well . . . you have your health."

He laughed, short and sharp.

"That's important." She thought frantically. "Your fortune is intact, is it not?"

"Very much so, to your relief, I'm sure."

"You're young, you're handsome, you're intelligent"—taking a breath, she dared as she had never dared before—"and you have me."

He plucked off his shoes and, one by one, threw them at the door.

Eleanor jumped each time the leather smacked the wood and rattled the lock.

"Ah, yes. My dear wife, who has made me the laughingstock of London. Did I say of London? Of England. Do you know what they were saying in the club tonight?"

Beneath his insults and his seductions, she hadn't been able to detect his feelings before, but he was angry. Of course.

"At the club, everyone was saying that all it took was the whiff of English pussy to entice an American cock to follow."

She was shocked. Even in her travels, she had not heard such vulgarity. "How horrible. How dare they speak so about us? Use such language?"

"They're men. That is how men talk." He was more than angry, she realized. He was furious. She could almost see the shimmer of heat as waves of rage rolled off him.

Heat . . . she could warm herself by that much heat. "What did you reply?"

"I laughed. I said they were right. I said I was so anxious to get under your skirts that I would have wed you no matter who you were."

She wiped her suddenly damp palms along the silk on her hips. This warmth she felt was more than embarrassment. More than the heat from the fire. "You were saving face."

"I was telling the truth." His lips, his magical, wonderful lips, eased into a self-mocking smile. "Ever since I met you, all I can think about is your breasts, your thighs, your . . . pussy."

Her pussy quivered as if he had stroked it.

"Worse, I've been worried about your moods, your happiness, your pleasure. No wonder I let you lead me down the aisle without another thought in my head."

Her mouth dried. He made his intentions clear. He would take her, make her his whether she willed it or not.

He had the right; he was her husband. But rights meant little when it was her body, her self who faced the beast with the untamed eyes. "You said you thought you had a duchess you could love. You were talking to me. You were looking at me. You can still love me."

"No. I can only love a duchess."

His answer stuck at her heart, and finally she made the move to leap away.

His hand shot out and caught her arm. "But I want you. Furthermore, you're my wife." He held her gaze. "I can have you."

Chapter 24

$\mathcal{E}$leanor's heart began a slow, strong thumping. Her chest rose and fell as she tried to get her breath. Remington wanted her. He had every right to take her, to use her as he pleased, and she had no doubt that if she ran, he would chase her down.

But her knees felt too weak to move, for . . . she wanted him, too. If only she didn't feel this cowardly uncertainty about joining with this man. He was dangerous in a way she didn't yet understand. Dangerous to her.

"Come here."

Two nights ago, she had heard his voice caress smoothly, but he didn't bother with such subtleties now. "Come here," he repeated, pulling her toward him, "and pay the price for your deceit."

Stumbling forward, she looked down at him. Why should she struggle? The first time she'd seen him, he'd caught her in his web. She had never wanted to escape. Yet to take this man into herself would involve a surrender of being, and she might never get herself back.

"You little fool." He pulled her into his lap, tugged her gown up, arranged her to face him, bare legs tucked on either side of his hips. "It's too late to have second thoughts now."

He was right about that. Beneath her strained a man enraged by his fate, driven by lust, and it was up to her to tame him.

Yet he was dressed. She was not. She was vulnerable. He was not. The material of his breeches rasped against the tender tissues between her legs. With his hands on her hips, he fitted himself into the notch between her thighs. Beneath his breeches she could feel the stiffness of his manhood, and when he moved her back and forth, the throbbing she had experienced from his mouth on her began again.

Placing her hands on his shoulders, she steadied herself. His face was right before her, and his eyes watched her unceasingly. She tried to hide her expression; she didn't want him to think he could arouse her with a touch.

But it seemed that he could, for that constant, back-and-forth movement made her hands grip him more tightly.

"Do you remember the things you said to me the other night?" he asked.

It was tempting to lie, to say no, but she couldn't concentrate. Not while he rocked her back and forth. "I remember."

"You said you wanted to take out my cock and bathe it in your mouth."

Her desire was growing. Breathing was difficult, thinking worse. She was moving on her own, now.

He shifted one hand to cup her bottom, to encourage her hips, while the other traveled over her skin to her breast. "I didn't let you do that."

"No." He used his fingertips to circle her breast, defining the shape with his touch.

"I bathed you with my mouth, instead."

"Yes." The memory of that pleasure contributed and combined with this pleasure until she could scarcely tell where one left off and the other began.

"I put my finger inside you." He laughed a little. "Inside your pussy." His hand slid beneath the silk of her gown, along the warm, dark cleft of her bottom. He circled the entrance to her body. "You were damp then, too."

She tried to press her knees together, but he was between them and she accomplished nothing. Nothing, except the effort further inflamed her senses.

His finger slipped inside, exploring deeply, rasping the tissues in a slow and steady motion. "You're so tight. When I push my cock inside, you're going to let me in slowly. Then I'll settle in, and nothing you can do will dislodge me."

She had trouble forming the words. "Will I want to?"

"I think so. You're a strong woman, and I'll be in you, making you mine."

A strong woman. He thought she was a strong woman.

"Will you like to have me control you, set the pace, teach you delight?"

She didn't want to think. She wanted to float along on a flood of passion.

"Tell me," he commanded. "Do you want my possession? Do you want to know that no other man will ever have you? Do you want me every night, inside you, reinforcing my claim until you live in a world bounded by bliss, and all you can think of is me?"

The way he said it—it sounded like a threat, not seduction.

Yet at the same time, his hand caressed her breast, while the other moved inside her.

He observed her every expression, capturing her thoughts like an eagle captures its prey. "Tell me."

"I want you. That was why—" Before she could finish, to explain why she had married him, he pulled his finger out.

Disappointment took her, and she whimpered.

Then slowly, he worked his finger back in. But this time she shuddered. The sense of intrusion increased. The pressure increased, and she froze, afraid to move—for pain threatened.

"Two fingers. I'm making a place for myself." He smiled, baring all his teeth. "But it seems as if I'm doing all the work. Why don't you . . ."

She held her breath, wondering what he would require.

"Kiss me."

Kiss him? So insignificant an intimacy, yet so important. Face to face, mouth to mouth, exchanging breath . . .

"You kiss very well," he murmured. "You kiss like a woman in love."

She sucked in a startled breath. He didn't know that. He couldn't. He'd accused her of marrying him for his money, and to her surprise, she preferred that to the truth—that she wanted him, loved him with all her silly heart.

No, she didn't want him to realize that, for that would make her vulnerable to every torment he chose to dole out.

She could tell—he was thinking. Maybe he was realizing he had touched on the truth. That wouldn't do.

So, taking handfuls of his shirt in her fists, she leaned forward. At the last minute, he closed his eyes, giving himself over to passion. She pressed her lips to his. His unshaven chin scraped at her tender skin. She probed with her tongue. He tasted of mint and brandy, manly and delicious, and as she kissed him, she showed him the love she dared not confess.

Again he tucked his hand under her bottom and lifted her. His lips moved on hers, his words were a breath in her mouth. "Move on me."

"But your fingers . . ." He scattered little kisses across her face, but not even that could distract her. "It might hurt."

He pulled away enough to smile mockingly. "And it might be ecstasy. Move."

Carefully, she lifted herself, lowered herself. The motion was right, somehow, the ache of fullness easing.

She lifted herself again, aware that excitement worked its way along her nerves—

And he said, "That's enough. There's no more time." Abruptly, he took his hands away, clutched her against him, and stood.

She caught a glimpse of his face before he turned away from the light, and his expression frightened her. All the time they'd spent together had been a lie. He wasn't a civilized savage. He was simply a savage, and he would feast on her now.

Wrapping her legs around him, he strode toward the shadowy bed.

She clung for fear he would drop her, and when he laid her on the cool sheets, she shivered. "Mr. Knight . . . Remington, please." She lifted herself on her elbow as he peeled himself out of his shirt.

Muscles corded his shoulders and rippled across his chest and down his abdomen, a fine froth of blond hair, like cream on a golden peach. The firelight licked him as she longed to do. He unbuttoned his breeches, and as he dropped them, she turned her head away.

"Afraid?" His voice was smoky with mockery. "You should be. I'm angry. I'm angry at you. And I don't hurt women, so I'm going to force you to climax again and again."

"Perhaps the concubines were not clear in their explanation. Is climax supposed to be disagreeable?" As she mocked him, she looked at his face. Yet as hard as she tried to focus only on his expression, still she saw the strength of his long flanks, the ripple of his muscled belly . . . the length and breadth of his erection. The smooth skin was blushing, the cap was light purple, and it was long, so long. "Oh, my."

Climbing on the mattress, he positioned himself between her legs.

Irresistibly, her hand was drawn to his spike of manhood. Brushing her fingers from the tip to the base, she reveled in the ridges and veins, the strength beneath the silky skin. "In the harem, I saw paintings and statues, but this is really magnificent."

He braced his hands beside her shoulders and closed his eyes, his arms shaking as she explored him.

The concubines were right. Men liked to be touched—and she liked touching him.

When he opened his eyes and stared down at her, there was nothing of ice in their shadowed depths. They burned. *He* burned. Taking the neck of her nightgown carefully between his hands, he tore it. The fine lace resisted, but the silk gave way with a thin, violent sound.

Silk and lace, expensive and beautiful, and he'd torn it away as if she didn't deserve it. She wanted to strike him. "Why did you do that?"

"It was in my way." He pulled the shredded pieces back.

He looked at her body, and seeing the gleam in his eyes, she realized he meant it. He'd torn her nightgown because it had been in his way—and that was a lesson she should remember.

"You've never had a man before. You don't know what I can do to you. How I can make you feel. How I can withhold pleasure, and how I can give it." Holding himself above her, he lowered his head and suckled on her nipple.

Sensation replaced shock. She arched beneath

him. Clutching at his hair, she held him there, wanting him to feed with a strong suction that sent her halfway to heaven.

He moved to the other breast, circling her nipple with his tongue, teasing her, denying her. His breath whispered against her skin as he said, "Your skin is like satin, sensitive, gorgeous satin."

Did he realize what he was doing to her with a simple compliment?

She pressed her hips up toward him, wanting his weight on her. Wanting more than that.

He descended atop of her, and everywhere their skin touched was a flash point of heat. Her breasts nestled in the hair on his chest. The weight of his hips pressed her into the mattress. His manhood nestled between her legs, and for the first time she understood why he had used his fingers to arouse her.

Because now she knew what it was to be full, and she wanted to be filled again—in any way possible. What had seemed natural before, to be empty, to be solitary, now seemed lonely and anguished.

Pushing herself against him, she sought relief from the isolation.

But he didn't oblige her. Instead, he took her face between his hands and held her still. "Tell me what you want me to do."

She whimpered. Tell him? Didn't he know?

"Tell me," he said. "Instruct me. I'll do whatever you crave, but you have to say the words."

Now she understood what he demanded. He demanded that she capitulate mentally as well as physically. He demanded that she think about what they were doing and give him permission to do . . . whatever he wanted to do. In her whole life, she had never sworn at another soul. She did now. "Bastard!"

"You're wrong. My parents were married before I was born." His thumbs met under her chin and nudged her face toward his. "Possibly even before I was conceived. Eleanor . . ."

It was the first time he'd called her by her own name, and she well understood the significance of *that*.

His hips rolled in a languorous, inciteful wave. "Eleanor, tell me what you want." They rolled again.

Deep in her womb, she felt need building.

"You're not going to win. You're going to do as I wish. Surrender, Eleanor. Surrender."

He was right. He knew too much, understood her body better than she understood it herself. With a sigh, she yielded. "I want you . . . please . . ." She wrapped her legs around his hips. Tried to position herself to receive him.

His hands slid down to her breasts, cupped them, caressed them. "Please, what?"

He had perfected the art of torment. "Please, Remington." She used his name deliberately, appeasing him. "I want you inside me. I want you to take me away . . . for a while. I want you to make good on your promise to give me pleasure."

He chuckled, deep in his chest, and she felt the rumble in hers. "Demand that I fulfill my promise, will you? I knew you were a clever girl. Now you've proved it with your challenge. Very well." With one hand, he spread her nether lips and positioned himself to thrust.

But he didn't blunder so crassly. He held his hips

away. He touched her only with the head of his manhood, and that with no force. No hurry. She needed . . . she needed movement, struggle, speed to ease this ache, and he was slow and careful.

"Hurry," she begged. "Oh, please. Hurry."

He laughed, a quick laugh, and didn't increase his speed at all.

She rolled her head against the sheets. She grasped his hips and dug herself into his flesh.

"A little more, then." His rod pressed harder, entered her, stretched her, and what had been a slight discomfort became pain.

"Wha . . . ?" She struggled to sit up. "But you prepared me!"

He held her hips still, managing her with his greater strength and size. "My fingers aren't long enough."

"Or wide enough!" she flashed.

"Did you think this would be easy?" Slowly, he pulled back, easing her pain.

She relaxed, sighing. "I thought it would be satisfying."

Straight away, he was back again, stronger, giving no quarter.

She tensed. He was occupying her as if she were a conquered country. Regardless of the advice she'd heard, the words the concubines had spoken, she wasn't prepared for being taken. *Invaded.*

And he didn't stop. He didn't care about her virginal reluctance. His body quivered as he moved, and in the shadows of the bed, she saw his face in leaps of flame. His brows knit, his lips were folded together. The fire etched his cheekbones and jaw in sharp lines, and he stared down at her as if he could see her every thought—her rebellion, her uncertainty, the gradually eroding control she had over her body, emotions, mind.

The mattress swayed beneath her. The scent of him surrounded her: warm, sensual. The pain grew as he worked his way inside, and she put the back of her hand to her mouth to stifle a moan.

Just when the anguish was at its height, he paused and held himself very still. It was as if he were bracing himself for some great event.

Then he surged forward.

Something snapped within her. She rose off the mattress, ready to fight her way free.

But now he dominated her with his power. His groin rubbed against her, inciting sensations all too briefly abandoned. This time, as he withdrew, she caught her breath on a bright spark of desire, and when he surged back, that spark became a blaze. She thought she might like this, might with time adjust, but he didn't give her time. He set a pace that demanded and explored, and she found herself struggling to keep up. She was like a ship on the ocean, catching surge after surge, ruthlessly driven toward some unknown destination and at the mercy of the elements. It wasn't that the burning within her didn't matter, but pain and pleasure mixed until she couldn't tell where one ended and the other started.

Remington would enforce his will on her, and she, who had never known a man, would pay the price for deceiving him.

She was in a different world, where everything was strange; his weight, his scent, the way he handled her, as if she were his to do with as he wished. The rhythm he set was quick, yet smooth, and her tender tissues yielded to each intrusion, then released him with reluctance. Her body knew what her mind only suspected; this claiming was as old as mankind, yet unique to them. Brought together by fate or happenstance, it didn't matter. Their two bodies fit and formed one.

Bracing her heels on the bed, she moved her hips in his rhythm. Her hands slipped across his shoulders.

The concubines had told her it was the woman's duty to ensure the man's fulfillment.

Eleanor didn't care a ha'penny about his fulfillment. Not now. Not when each thrust grazed the deepest part of her and pleasure, the pleasure he'd promised her, rushed toward her on the winds of possession.

She embraced him, hands slippery with sweat, his or hers, she couldn't tell. His muscles stretched and tensed with his movements.

No grandeur of travel or art could compare with this excitement, and she gloried in every moment.

Each moment, it seemed he grew heavier, more domineering. As the speed of his thrusts increased, he said in a guttural voice, "Yield to me."

"What?" Yield? No. No, how could he ask that she think? Now? Tonight? To yield, to surrender, when all she wanted was to reach that pure level of sensation that would sweep her away.

Sliding his hands behind her head, he cupped it, enfolding her, all of her, in his essence. He looked into her eyes, held them, challenged her. He kissed her with his tongue, pushed his manhood inside until it touched her womb. He filled her with himself, and he commanded, "Eleanor, give me what I want. Yield . . . *now.*"

And as if she had awaited his command, her body convulsed in glorious climax. It started deep in her womb and spread heat through her veins, through her skin, through her breasts. Her legs and arms clutched at him, trying to draw him deeper inside—when he could go no deeper. Love and fear, triumph and passion swirled through her until she was moaning and sobbing. "Remington. Remington."

And at last, he loosed his own passion, his head thrown back, his eyes closed, ecstasy etched on his features.

Together, their passion gathered force, driving them to a sweet madness that went on and on, fusing them together, creating one person, one soul.

Together, the madness faded, and at last they came to rest on the mattress in the master's bedchamber.

Still he held her head in his hands. Still he looked into her eyes as if weighing the depth of her surrender. Still he was hard and thick inside her while she . . . she was exhausted, amazed, overwhelmed. She had given him everything, all her passion, all her love.

But there was no use in telling him that. He wouldn't believe her, because he believed nothing but the worst of her.

But she would get her revenge.

She hadn't spent a fortnight in a harem for nothing.

Chapter 25

*B*lasted by lust, Remington lay with one foot hanging off the bed, the other tucked under Eleanor's thigh, and he stared into her eyes.

She stared back, as defiant as if he weren't still inside her, pressing as deeply as he could.

What did it take to possess this woman? She was exhausted; he could feel it. Her body trembled beneath him, and she had climaxed in rolling waves of passion that had pulled him along like a great undertow. Yet already she challenged him, silently demanding that he yield to her as she had yielded to him.

That was not going to happen. She wasn't the wife he'd won, and she needed to be taught the penalty for duping Remington Knight.

He would do that as soon as he recovered his strength. Right now, he could scarcely summon enough energy to lift himself off her before he crushed her.

Yet he hated to exit her body. Tonight, he had done everything in his power to mark her as his, and yet . . . and yet . . . he wanted her again. In some sane corner of his mind, he knew that was ridiculous. She had been untouched. Despite his preparation, he'd hurt her. She couldn't accept him again, yet it seemed as if this woman, with her diffidence and flashes of bravery, could so easily slip away from him.

Equally ridiculous was to imagine he could manage the act again. He had climaxed so violently that tears of pleasure had come to his eyes. He'd emptied himself inside her. He, who could pleasure a woman five times a night, had nothing left with which to fill her again.

Carefully, he separated himself from her. At last, as if she could hold them open no more, her eyes closed, and she gave a faint moan as her tissues reluctantly released him. His chest heaved as he rested beside her. He needed to cover her with the blankets, for despite the now-blazing fire, it was cool in here, he'd just driven the woman to orgasm, and the shreds of her nightgown were no protection against the chill.

He gazed on the expanse of fair skin beside him: the peaked breasts, the flat stomach, the ruff of hair that hid the entrance to paradise. Her legs were slightly apart, open and inviting, and he saw a dark smear on the pale skin of her thighs.

Blood.

He'd wanted a de Lacy sacrifice on the altar of his

vengeance. He'd gotten it—although not in the way he'd imagined.

Her eyes were closed, her expression serene—and that irritated him. He'd just endured a ground-shaking event. She had to have been impacted, too.

He wanted to take her and shake her, demand she show how deeply their joining had influenced her. Instead he found himself sliding his arm under her shoulder and leaning over her.

Her eyes opened. She looked stupefied, and he enjoyed a bone-deep satisfaction. Yes, she'd been overwhelmed.

She stared around, then down as if astonished to find herself in such a state. Her gaze slid up his body, and all that she had learned came blazing to life. Oh, yes, she had liked what he'd shown her, for in the depths of her eyes he saw interest and aware-ness. She wanted him again, just as he wanted her.

In a soft tone, he said, "I'm going to get you out of this gown."

Automatically, her fingers rose to cover her breasts.

He wanted to tell her it was far, far too late for modesty. Instead, he brushed her hands aside and eased the sleeves down her arms. As the shattered silk and lace slid off her hands, she caught at it, then let it go.

"I'll buy you another." Because he wanted to see her posed before him again, the firelight flickering behind her. She was his, to dress as he wished, to obey his will.

Blood marked the nightgown, too, and he placed it on the foot of the bed. Barbaric, yes, but he would save the evidence. Tonight had not been the triumph he had imagined, yet oddly, it had been more satisfying than his greatest fantasy.

"We're going to move up on the pillows," he told her. Sliding his other arm under her legs, he lifted and shifted her toward the head of the bed, covered her with the blankets, then slid in beside her.

"Go to sleep," he murmured, and his eyes closed.

She pressed her palm over his heart. "Already?"

His eyes opened. He stared at her. What did she mean, *already*?

Her voice was sultry, knowing, and she challenged him with a look. Sliding off the other side of the bed, she moved into the darker shadows of the room.

"What are you doing?" He could see her pale form moving but could discern no particulars.

"Preparing myself to worship my master," she said.

Master? Hm. He rather liked that.

"The concubines told me that a virile man would wish for many rides in an evening."

Ah. Now he understood. She wanted to put the lessons she'd learned in the harem to use. "It's not necessary tonight. We can have many rides . . . soon."

Going to the fire, she dipped a cloth into the pot on the hearth and wrung it out. "The concubines taught me how to revive a man's flagging interest, also."

"My interest is not flagging!"

She cast him a sidelong glance, a glance that flirted and enticed.

For the first time in what seemed like years, his sense of humor stirred. "You little witch. Did the concubines happen to mention that challenging a man's capabilities was one way to revive a man?"

"They might have," she said demurely. Her body gleamed as if, shielded by darkness, she'd washed herself.

He surveyed her as she came toward him, holding the cloth in a basin. She was outlined by fire, her hips swaying seductively.

His certainty that he was done for the night began to fade.

She put the basin on the bedside table. Taking three of the pillows, she placed them behind him. Then she leaned against his chest and plumped them into a cozy, relaxing mass. With her hand on his shoulders, she pressed him back. "Are you comfortable?" she asked. "Can I get you anything? A drink? No?" She slid the covers away from him so shyly, she might never before have seen him naked. "Then if I may, my master, let me cleanse you after your exertions." She didn't wait for his permission, but with the warm, damp cloth, she began to bathe his genitals.

Sweat broke out on his forehead. With three pillows behind him, he could watch everything, and the sight of her pale hands on his swarthy skin was strange, erotic, glorious. Her fingers were warm, and she handled him tentatively, but her mere touch on his balls, on his cock, made him want to writhe and groan. The cloth reached over and around, and his skin cooled as she drew it away. He gritted his teeth in pleasure and anticipation, and his shaft grew and swelled, proving without a doubt that, brainless thing that it was, it did not realize he had come his last drop.

She placed the cloth on the basin, then slipped onto the mattress.

The sight of her, smooth, bare, blushing, kneeling between his hairy legs, was male and female in its essence. Power coursed through his veins, yet as she reached for him he was helpless. She rested her hands on his knees, then slid them up the inside of his thighs. Her fingers caressed his balls as if fascinated by the textures, then wrapped around his erection. Holding the length against her palm, she used her thumb to circle the head.

A thick, white drop oozed from the opening, and his testicles tightened in anticipation. He wanted inside her again.

"You're very large, my master. No wonder my body struggled to accommodate you." Her soft, wondering tone encouraged him to grow yet more.

Yet her words made him remember . . . she was right. Damn it, she was right. She could barely take him the first time. She could not do it again. Someone in this little twosome had to show some responsibility, and apparently, it was him. Harsh with disappointment, he said, "You can't accommodate me again tonight."

She smiled slightly, her gaze on her hands as she smoothed the drop over and around, using it as an emollient. "There are other ways to satisfy a man."

This woman, this inexperienced woman, gave him more pleasure than ever he had imagined—and he had imagined a lot. Now she was offering a delight of which most women had never heard. For a marvelous second, he was tempted . . . but no.

Responsibility. He had to show responsibility. "Not tonight. If you torment me tonight, I'll have you on your back and your legs in the air."

She rose onto her knees. Taking his hand, she guided it between her legs.

He wanted to think, to be sensible, but how could he when this woman guided his own fingers into her? She was damp and slick, and his fingers slipped right in. Red lust obscured his vision.

When it cleared, he saw her smiling at him. "As the concubines taught us, I cleansed myself, then applied an oil to ease your way, should you again wish to . . . have me on my back with my legs in the air."

She had prepared herself to receive him. At the mere idea, he had trouble getting a breath.

"Or perhaps," she said, "I could mount you. In this manner, I could control the motion. Then it would be impossible for you to make me uncomfortable."

Mount him? Control the motion?

Gently, she drew his fingers away, eased herself down on his chest, and smiled into his face. "In the meantime, you must rest and recover from your previous efforts, while I try to revive your flagging interest."

She thought she was so damned amusing.

Actually, he might think she was amusing, too, if she wasn't resting on him, her breasts pressed to him as she searched out his nipples and tasted them. Bit them. Sliding down, she kissed his belly, his thighs. Everywhere she stopped, her smooth lips caressed his skin and heightened his desire, making his loins beat with the rhythm of his heart. He recalled what Eleanor had said just two nights ago. *A woman can bathe a man's genitals in her mouth.* Was that what she had planned? And would he survive the ecstasy if it was?

He had never wanted anything so much in his life.

But he knew that was a lie, because more than that, he wanted Eleanor. He was as struck down with bliss as ever he'd hoped to make his bride. It was as if he were a lad, a virgin again, overwhelmed with the novelty of occupying a woman.

And what a woman! Eleanor had made a royal fool of him all across England and soon, when the story was carried on his ships, all across the world. If she had happened to anyone but him, he would have admired her.

Clasping his hips in her hands, she leaned down and licked the length of his cock, from the base to the head. The rasp of her tongue brought him right off of the bed.

In a demure tone he didn't believe at all, she asked, "Did I hurt you, my master?"

"No," he said hoarsely. "Please. Go on."

Delicately, she slipped her lips around the head and sucked it into her mouth. She seemed amazed, for she used her lips to apply different pressures, then circled him with her tongue, over and over, roughly, then more gently.

"Deeper," he whispered. "Harder."

Lifting her head, she said, "Master, I did not give you advice when you rendered a like service for me."

He wanted to laugh, but he couldn't move the

right muscles in his face. "I humbly beg your pardon."

"Another day, I'll ask what you like best. For now, if it pleases you, I wish to experiment."

"Yes. That pleases me. Experiment." He watched as her head dipped again, and he felt the sweet, wet warmth close on him. "The worst you could possibly do is wonderful."

Sliding her mouth all the way down, her tongue moved around the length of him.

The pressure built inside him. His discipline roared away. The vision of her as she had looked when he was inside her arose in his mind: mindless with ecstasy, desperate for climax. He loved having her bathe him in her mouth, but more than that, he loved giving her pleasure.

And abruptly, he had to have her.

Taking her under the armpits, he lifted her away. She cried, "Wait!" but he had no more patience.

He placed her atop him, opened her, positioned himself to enter her—then, using the last of his waning restraint, he waited.

She lost her show of confidence. No longer the handmaiden but an almost completely inexperienced female, she trembled. Her face flushed, with embarrassment or excitement, he didn't know. Taking a fortifying breath, she held herself above him, her spine straight, her chin lifted as if she faced some unfamiliar ordeal. Tucking her tongue in the corner of her lips, she held his cock and slowly pressed downward.

He entered her, and she was still so tight. So tight. But the oil smoothed the way, and again, in slow increments, he was enveloped by her. Her heat. Her body.

She was nervous, he could tell. Her hands clenched his arms, her legs flinched, and inside she tensed, as if fearing the repeat of the pain.

But he let her set the pace. She rose and she fell, never quite taking all of him. Her thighs worked beside his hips. Her breasts bobbed gently above him. Her shorn hair floated around her pinkening cheeks.

He wanted so badly to take over, to show her how to move, to pump his hips and bury himself inside her. But the torment was somehow even better, knowing he could conquer her at any minute and didn't.

Little by little, her trepidation slipped away and fascination filled her face. The best stroke, for him, was when she finally pushed herself all the way on him, and he was bathed in her essence. Catching her, he held her still, for just a moment, to savor the intimacy, to taste the knowledge that soon another magnificent orgasm would shake him.

Then he let her go.

She smiled. She actually smiled at him, now, as if everything about him delighted her.

And he, who wanted to smile back, could not. He was too stricken by the lightning of divine delight.

She experimented: she swirled her hips, she slid up until he was barely inside her, then down so he was lodged in her all the way. Her hands caressed his chest and belly, and even reached between them and grasped his organ, and worked her fingers on him as she rose and fell.

He responded. He couldn't help it. He groaned aloud. He shook with the effort of holding back his climax. And finally, he took his turn. He ran his fingertips over her skin from her shoulder blades to her waist, giving special attention to the sensitive underside of her breasts. He rocked his hips, scarcely moving them at first, concentrating on putting pressure against that feminine nub, which was so sensitive.

The absorption she showed in this new activity changed. She no longer tried out new movements; she concentrated on the simpler rhythm, rising over him like a Venus rising from the waves. Every time he reached her deepest point, he watched as her eyes opened and closed, lashes fluttering as she absorbed the sensation of having him inside her.

Small moans broke from her with each of his thrusts. Inside, she was molten heat and rough silk, drawing from him a response that built too quickly. The thought flitted through his mind that a few short minutes ago, he'd been convinced he couldn't again rise to the occasion. Now he was having trouble holding back. This wife of his had bewitched him—and he rejoiced in the spell.

She begged, "Please. Remington. Please."

Did she even realize what she begged for?

"Now," she whispered. "Please. Remington. Now."

Oh, yes. He wrapped her in his arms and rolled her over. Holding her close, he moved powerfully on her. With each stroke, he moved more strongly, more quickly, letting the gusts of passion lift them both, and when she cried out in his ear, when she

shuddered with completion, he released his fever—
and came again, as intensely as if he had never taken
her at all.

She panted in his ear. She trembled in his arms.
She was as weak and helpless as he could have ever
desired, and he found his anger had slipped away—
but his infatuation had not. Even though she had betrayed him, he still thought about her, wanted her,
more than he'd ever wanted another woman.

Would he forgive her? When he thought about the
death of his hopes, he knew he would not. Yet in her
arms, he didn't think of hopes, only of pleasure,
pleasure so great as to overwhelm his senses.

Maybe pleasure would be enough.

Chapter 26

The next morning, Eleanor opened her eyes to find Remington, fully dressed, leaning over her, his fists braced on either side of her head.

His expression was not in the least loverlike. "Why didn't you tell me the duke of Magnus was here last night?"

She blinked, trying to focus on his furious face, but he was very close, and she was still wrapped in the pleasurable cocoon of last night. "I . . . never thought about it." She pushed a wisp of hair off her cheeks. "Why?"

"I don't want that man in my house when I'm not here."

"He's my uncle. I can't deny him entrance!" Remington's manner confused her.

He wore a traveling suit of dark blue, perfectly fitted on his perfectly formed body. His blond hair had been perfectly brushed back from his perfectly shaved face. He smelled perfectly wonderful, like soap and fresh, clean man, but his distinctive, pale blue eyes were perfectly distant.

While she was naked, disheveled, and disconcerted. There was nothing perfect about her, and she found herself resenting him and the fact he could rise from their marriage bed without a care to the tender passion they'd exchanged, while she . . . she was still in love with him.

In a sharper tone than she'd yet used on him—indeed, than she'd ever used on any other human—she said, "I'd like to point out, I hardly had time to tell you a list of our guests. Furthermore, if you'd married Madeline, Magnus would be here quite often. He's her father, you know."

"I do know. I know exactly who he is, and I know exactly what he is."

Most men liked Magnus. He was bluff, hearty, a gambler, a drinker, and generous to a fault—a man's man in every way. But despite Remington's win over him at the card table, Remington obviously despised Magnus—and more important, he acted as if he didn't trust him.

Remington had said something last night, too, something that had puzzled her, but which had gotten shunted aside in the rush of desire. From the depths of her memory, she called up the phrase he had used. "What did you mean, you've escaped death at the hands of my family before?"

"Ah." The corner of Remington's lips curled in a sneer that mocked and hurt. "That finally got through to you, did it?"

In her mind, she put together incongruities, bits and pieces that hinted Remington had a greater plan than he'd yet admitted. Lifting her head from the pillow, she gazed at him. "Did you cheat at cards when you won Madeline's hand in marriage?"

"No," he said flatly. "I don't cheat."

She eased into a sitting position, keeping the blankets around her. "You must have wagered a great deal on the hand yourself."

Remington straightened up and watched her, arms folded across his chest. "I wagered my shipping company."

"The whole thing?" Yet he wasn't a compulsive gambler. Lady Gertrude had expressed that belief, and at the Picards' ball, he'd been not at all interested in the card room. In measured tones, she asked, "Why did you want the duchess?"

He watched her, cynicism in the depths of his eyes. "You know why."

"Money. What other reason could there be? Money and power." Eleanor didn't believe it.

"Power. Yes. Power over the most important de Lacy in the land. The power of life and death. The power to make the duke of Magnus dance to my tune."

She blinked at Remington's intensity. Her mind raced, and she said shrewdly, "So few people care one way or the other about controlling the duke of Magnus. He's like a faulty pistol. There's never any certainty he'll do as he's supposed to do. For instance—he gambled his daughter away to a chance-met stranger. Is that the act of a loving father? Yet I think he loves Madeline."

"I was not a chance-met stranger," Remington said. "I very carefully arranged the meeting."

He had confirmed her suspicions, and she repeated, "For the money and the power."

He looked forbidding, not at all like the enthusiastic lover of last night. "Why do you care?"

She ached at his casual dismissal of her, but she was proud. If he could be indifferent, so could she— or at least, she could pretend to be. "I think it very odd that an American man, a man of wealth and distinction in his own country, should come to England specifically to enter society and wed a duchess."

His lids lowered, shielding his expression from her. "You're very inquisitive this morning."

And why would he want to shield his thoughts? *Because he had something to hide.*

Disillusionment filled her. She had thought, hoped, imagined, that last night, they'd formed a bond between them. Not of love, at least not on his part, but of pleasure. Now Remington effectively rebuffed her, and hostility took the place of her regret. "As you said, we are well and truly wed, with no way of escaping the confines of the matrimony. Should I not understand what my husband thinks?"

"You want to know what I sought with marriage with the future duchess of Magnus?" He smiled, a smile with all the chill of a northern winter. "I was seeking revenge."

What had he done?

Worse, what had she done? Into what scheme had her foolish love for him propelled her? "You lied to me."

"What?" There was a scratch at the door. He flung a puzzled glance at her, then went to open it.

Lizzie bounced in, tail wagging, ears up, thrilled to see them and impervious to the hostile atmosphere.

"What do you mean, I lied to you?" Remington demanded.

Eleanor patted the bed, and the dog made a flying leap onto the mattress. "You lied to me. I asked you why you wanted to marry Madeline, and you said money and power. If you'd told me the truth, if you had said vengeance, I would have never wed you."

"Are you saying I should have blithely confessed I wanted vengeance on the de Lacys? Woman, that's the most ridiculous thing I've ever heard."

She fended off a doggie morning kiss and scratched Lizzie's head. "I'm saying you must take at least partial responsibility for our marriage."

"I do, my dear. Believe me, I fully recognize the depths of my—" He hesitated.

Stupidity. He was going to say stupidity.

"Culpability." Striding to the windows, he flung back the drapes. "Do you know the tale of Lady Pricilla and her lover?"

Outside, the sun was shining, the clouds had disappeared. But here, in Remington's bedchamber, dark emotions obscured the obvious, and Eleanor felt as if she were groping through old passions and old hates. "I know . . . some of the tale. And how odd you should bring it up. Nothing has been said in my hearing for so many years, and now twice within a week, I'm reminded of the tragedy."

Remington swung on her, and the light showed a harshness to his face she had never seen before. Even the dog subsided with a whine. "Who else spoke of it? The duke of Magnus, I'll wager."

"Not at all. 'Twas Lord Fanthorpe. He was betrothed to her."

Remington's eyes narrowed. "So he was."

"He speaks of her in heartbreaking tribute." *The poor man.*

"He was one of the suspects in the murder. Did you know that?"

With a shiver, she pulled her knees to her chest and wrapped her arms around them. "That wobbly old fellow? Absurd."

Her dismissal of Lord Fanthorpe's guilt obviously irritated Remington. He paced toward her, then, as if he feared to come too close, he paced away. "He wasn't then wobbly or old—and she was going to run off with someone else."

This situation got more peculiar and more disturbing with every word Remington spoke. Carefully, she observed her husband as he stood, large, intimidating, back to the light. "How do you know that? And why do you care?"

"I'm the son of the someone else she was going to run off with."

"Ohh." Enlightenment dawned. Eleanor stared at him, assimilating the information, and she believed him. For if his father had looked like him, every woman in the world would abandon good sense to have him. After all, wasn't that what Eleanor herself had done?

"You don't seem surprised," he said.

"I am. I just . . . I begin to understand. Not everything, but the pieces are falling into place." No longer did Remington's obsession seem so unusual. "I must confess, that's not the story Lord Fanthorpe told. He said a commoner fell in love with Lady Pricilla, and when she would not return his affection, he murdered her."

Remington smiled unpleasantly. "Fanthorpe didn't like knowing his betrothed preferred another."

"I suppose no man likes that." And Lord Fanthorpe, with his disdain for commoners, probably more than most. "So you think *he* murdered Lady Pricilla in a jealous frenzy?"

"He had no money. He needed to secure the money from Lady Pricilla's dowry."

"Then . . . he wouldn't have killed her." Lizzie curled up on Eleanor's feet, a warm, living thing, delighted to have her ears rubbed, happy to be with them, a contrast to the swirl of ancient, sinister memories that filled the air.

"Exactly. After her death, he had to flee to the Continent to avoid his debtors. He married an Italian countess, quite a lot older than him, and on her death returned to England with her fortune—most of which he has squandered, too."

"Lord Fanthorpe said the criminal was deported to Australia." Eleanor looked him over, noting the confidence that seemed to have been bred into him. "You're an American."

"When my father had served his term, he moved to Boston, where he had transferred some of his fortune, and there started anew."

She wanted all of it clarified, so she insisted, "Lord Fanthorpe said the man's name was George Marchant. Your name is not Marchant."

"The killer was quite determined to cover his guilt—and so he had my entire family murdered."

She drew a horrified breath.

"I changed my name."

"Dear heavens. I am so sorry for your bereavement. I wish . . ." She wished she could hold him, smooth the lines of pain from his face, but he was distant, brooding, remembering events of such loss she couldn't imagine the pain.

"Marchant. Knight," Remington said. "I liked the irony of the names."

Sitting here in the ruin of the bed, where they'd so passionately made love, she cared nothing for irony or even justice. Faced with the facts, she could only think, *I love him, and he will never love a de Lacy, and certainly never one who has so utterly destroyed his hope of retribution.* Her own hopes withered and almost died.

Almost.

Yet hopelessness liberated her. After all, if all was lost, she might as well say what she thought. "You lied about your name, too."

"What?" he snapped.

Her fingers clutched the dog's fur. "I lied about who I was, but so did you."

With a whiplash of scorn, he said, "You needn't worry. I legally changed my last name to Knight. The marriage is binding."

She dared yet again. "I wasn't worried. I was

pointing out that you haven't been, in the most basic of ways, honest with me."

"In the most basic of way, with my body, I've been totally honest with you." He gripped the mantel, his long fingers caressing the wood, and his pale blue eyes glowed like the hottest coal. "I want you. I would have wanted you even if I'd known who you really were."

His admission took her aback—and shook her to the core. She'd lived in Madeline's shadow for so many years, that she hadn't thought anyone ever saw her. "Well . . . I do look like Madeline."

"Or Madeline looks like you." He swept an impatient hand toward her. "And no man finds his woman interchangeable with another. Don't imagine you can play another such trick on me."

A silence fell while she considered his words, and she petted Lizzie. She thought . . . it seemed . . . he had called her *his woman*. He was inscrutable to her: demanding, tender, furious, kind. He cherished the memory of his family and wanted to destroy hers. He carried her to heaven in the night, and plunged her into hell the next morning. She needed to understand him, what had driven him to make a fortune, and be willing to spend it in the pursuit of vengeance. "Tell me more about Lady Pricilla's murder. You've discounted Lord Fanthorpe as a suspect."

"Yes, whoever destroyed my family had to have enough money to trace my father from Australia to America, investigate him and hire thugs capable of murdering a prominent merchant." Crossing the room, Remington tilted her chin up and looked her right in the eyes. "I considered your father a possibility, too, but he doesn't have the income to pull off such a plan."

Bitterness welled in her. "Nor does he care. Lady Pricilla's murder marked both of her brothers in different ways, driving Magnus to live a life of irresponsibility in order to escape the memories. Driving my father to shield himself from emotion. He wants never to care for another woman as he cared for his sister, and he is successful." Eleanor tried to hide her pain as successfully as Remington hid his. "He doesn't care for me at all."

Remington saw through her brave facade, for he looked on her with pity. But pity was the last thing she wanted from him. So she pushed him aside and rose from the bed, blatantly naked. Pretending a casualness she didn't feel, she walked to her dressing gown. Back turned to him, she inserted her arms in the sleeves. "That's why you wanted Madeline. You wanted to force the daughter of the duke of Magnus into your bed. You wanted control of her estates in vengeance for your father's deportation."

"And for Lady Pricilla's murder. Yes, you're right. There's more to my plan than the glory of having a de Lacy in my bed. Although the pleasure involved was acute." He bowed, and from the expression on his face, she knew he had noted her nudity and appreciated it.

She didn't care, and humiliation lent her voice a flick of scorn. "Am I supposed to be honored by your condescension?" She knotted her tie with a savage yank. "Tell me the rest. Tell me everything. I don't even understand how a gently bred young lady like my aunt Pricilla met the commoner George Marchant."

Absentmindedly, Remington petted the dog and watched Eleanor, and that sensual awareness was back in his eyes. "Easy enough. Forty-five years ago, your grandfather was on the verge of losing everything. His debts were gargantuan, his income from his estates not enough to cover the interest. George Marchant came to him and offered him a deal. He had an idea for supplying food for His Majesty's Navy, but he didn't know the right people who could ensure that he would receive the contract. George would give the old duke half of all the profits if the duke would use his influence in the court on George's behalf. Magnus agreed, and within a year, he had earned enough off my father's hard work to settle his debts. In less than five years, he owned a fortune, and best of all, no one knew he had anything to do with sordid commerce." Sarcasm rang in Remington's tone. "Your grandfather was consulted at every step, but my father did the disreputable business as a merchant, protecting your grandfather's reputation as a worthless aristocrat."

Eleanor sat on a chair by the fireplace. The ashes within were cold; so was she. "You haven't yet told me how Lady Pricilla met your father."

He walked toward her, stood above her, and watched her broodingly. "The men became good friends. My father was an educated man. Magnus was a scholar, and so George was often a visitor in Magnus's homes. There he met Lady Pricilla. He sang her praises to me. Beautiful, kind, intelligent . . ." Lizzie leaped off the bed and trotted to Remington's side, sniffed his polished boots, then gazed up at him in adoration.

Stupid dog. To look at him as if the sun rose and set in him . . . Eleanor hoped *she* never looked at him that way.

He continued, "I don't know how much was infatuation and how much was true. But he loved her, and she loved him enough to fight her father for him. When the old duke insisted she marry Fanthorpe, she made an assignation with my father and waited for him in the garden. They were to run away that night, but when my father went to fetch her, he found her stabbed to death, blood all over her." Remington's voice had grown harsh, so harsh it seemed that the light dimmed. Shying away from him, Lizzie hurried to Eleanor and cowered at her feet. "He held her cooling body in his arms and howled his grief to the moon—and that's how they found him."

Remington's vivid description raised goose bumps on Eleanor's arms. She could see the broken body, the grief-stricken lover, and imagine the horror of the onlookers when they found him covered with blood. Sliding off the chair, she knelt beside the dog, rubbed her fingers into the fur at Lizzie's ruff and clutched it as if Lizzie, cheerfully oblivious Lizzie, could somehow make things better.

"When the hired thugs burned down my home and my father's business in Boston, my sister ran screaming from the house. They caught her and beat her to death." Remington stared into space as if seeing things better forgotten. "Abbie was nine years old."

"Abbie . . ." Eleanor whispered. She could imagine a skinny little girl with pale blond hair, a sister who adored her big brother.

No, the bond between Remington and Eleanor could never strengthen. There were no words to soothe his pain. He held her family accountable, and he would never forgive such grievous offenses.

Remington took a long breath, then dragged his attention back to Eleanor. "When my father was deported, Magnus took over the business. Society didn't notice, they were too agog with the murder and the trial. Magnus also received the estate my father had bought in a futile attempt to make himself acceptable. The de Lacys still own it. There the shambles of my father's home still stands."

"Magnus holds no estate like that," she said.

"But he does. My father's estate was adjoining Lacy Hall outside of Chiswick not far from London. Do you not remember—"

"The old ruin against the hill." A shiver ran up her arms, and she rubbed them. The estate at Chiswick was huge—two estates together, she now knew—the wrecked house reputed haunted. And perhaps it was.

"Your grandfather had the building demolished even before my father was deported. They say he did so in a frenzy of grief." Remington's voice grew hoarse. "My father thought it was a frenzy of guilt. He was convinced your grandfather had killed Lady Pricilla."

She shook her head decisively. "That's not possible. Grandfather mourned Lady Pricilla to the end of his days. His mind wandered those last few years, and he used to talk to me. Clasp my hand and call me Pricilla, and he said . . . he said it wasn't George who did it. He said . . . it was so much worse. I didn't know what he meant."

"So that leaves only one suspect. The duke of Magnus."

She laughed, brief and amused. "No."

"In the months before the tragedy, the current duke of Magnus had men sniffing around my father's business. He wouldn't rest until my father and all his family was destroyed."

"You've made a mistake." She stood and faced him. "I know my uncle. I've lived in his house. I've been the companion to his daughter. He is ineffectual, genial, and scatterbrained. I don't approve of him—I think the way he treats Madeline is shameful. But I like him. It's almost impossible not to. He could no more concentrate long enough to deliberately carry out a plan such as you describe than he could fly to the moon. He hasn't a drop of malice in him, but neither does he have a drop of familial responsibility. You've made a mistake," she repeated. "I don't know who killed my aunt, nor do I know who killed your father and sister, but I know who it wasn't. It *wasn't* the duke of Magnus."

Remington seemed to grow larger, and his voice grew menacing with fury. "The only mistake I have made, my darling, is marrying the wrong woman."

Her anger leaped to meet his. "I have the same blood flowing through my veins as Madeline, so if it is for my family that you wished to wed, then you should be very happy. But you wanted the duchess. You wanted the best." Her heart thundered in her chest. She stepped closer and glared into his eyes. "And you got me. I'm not my family, to be blamed for whatever crimes or honored for whatever tributes came before." She might as well say what she thought. What had she to lose? He already thought the worst of her. "This is the first time I've been on this earth, and I have as much right to grasp happiness as anyone else. I'm not Madeline. I'm not my grandfather. I'm not my aunt, who died for love of your father. I'm me. I won't die for you. But I'll live for you. So make your choice and let me know what you decide."

She would have stormed away, but he caught her arm. "A touching speech, but you forget. I'm not the kind of man who cries over spilt milk. I'm married to you now. I'll find another way to revenge myself on your uncle. I'll make sure you don't interfere. And in the meantime, darling"—he slid his hand inside her robe and cupped her breast—"I'm going to enjoy myself with you. Over and over and over again."

He curved her over his arm in a kiss that bent her like a reed beneath a great wind. He fed her passion and fury in equal amounts, and she clutched his hair and answered him. The taste and scent of him were addictive, glorious, and her blood leaped to answer his call.

Putting her back on her feet, he held her while she grew steady. "Now get dressed," he commanded. "I'm taking you on a honeymoon."

* * *

That afternoon, before she left for the seashore with Remington, Eleanor sent a request to the housekeeper at Lacy Hall. She wanted Lady Pricilla's diaries. She wanted to know whether her aunt had feared for her life, and if she had, whom she'd feared.

Eleanor had to get to the bottom of this mystery before Remington took vengeance on the wrong person, ruining her life, and his—and leaving the murderer free to strike again.

Chapter 27

On their return the next week, Eleanor had barely discarded her bonnet and sorted through the stack of mail, looking for the package from Lacy Hall, when a knock sounded on the outer door. At the sound of a well-known voice, she rose and hurried into the foyer. A familiar face and form, much like her own, stood there.

"Madeline!"

"Eleanor!"

The women rushed to each other's arms and hugged, and tears sprang to Eleanor's eyes at the comfortable scent and feel of her cousin. Drawing back at last, Eleanor asked, "Where have you been? I expected you that whole week before the wedding, and you never came!"

"So you married Mr. Knight anyway?" Impatiently, Madeline shed her pelisse into Bridgeport's hands. "Eleanor, have you lost your mind? I assure you, Dickie thinks you have."

"Bring tea, please, Bridgeport. We'll have it in the library." Hooking her arm through Madeline's, Eleanor drew her into a more private place. "I wanted to marry Remington"—she lifted her chin—"so I did."

Madeline stared at her cousin, jaw dropped open. A slow smile spread over her face. "Well. Eleanor. Timid no more."

"There's something about him that makes me . . . I don't know . . . I'm not afraid when he's around. I do what I want." Eleanor looked around the library, where she had first seen Remington, and felt a rightness. "He makes me a stronger person."

"Impossible. You were already the strongest person I'd ever met." They sat on the sofa, and Madeline surveyed Eleanor with a twinkle in her eyes.

Eleanor wanted to laugh, except Madeline sounded serious. "I'm not strong. I've always been such a coward, not like you at all!"

"No. Not like me at all, with all my privileges and the memory of my mother who loved me so dearly and my sweet nanny and my kind governess and my father—who I know you think is unpardonably neglectful—but in his way, he loves me." Madeline discarded her gloves. "You grew up without any kind of support at all, without a father's affection or even the memory of your mother's love."

"I had a perfectly wonderful governess," Eleanor reminded her.

"Until you were ten and your father remarried and Lady Shapster sent her away! Lady Shapster is a menace, and you were a lion to defy her as you did! If I had had the difficulties you've had, I wouldn't be bold, I'd be afraid of my own shadow." Taking Eleanor's hand, Madeline held it tightly. "No, dear cousin, I remember your serenity in the face of every crisis in our journeys, and I refuse to listen to you call yourself a coward. You've overcome obstacles that would have crushed most people. You're the bravest woman I know, and I'm so proud of you."

Eleanor didn't know what to say. She'd never thought of her life that way.

Bridgeport entered with the tea tray while she mulled it over. Slipping into their old ways, Eleanor poured while Madeline selected biscuits and cakes for both of them.

"Now." Madeline looked around. "Is *he* here?"

"Remington? No, after his time away, he had business that required attention." Eleanor nibbled on a lemon tart. "He is in commerce, you know."

"We won't tell the snobs about that, will we? When you reenter society and sweep all before you with your beauty and your kindness, we want nothing to mar your triumph." Madeline sipped her tea. "Since we've returned to Town, that is all we've heard. How sweet you are, and how much everyone likes you. They tell me that, then they eye me as if to say, why can't you be more like your cousin?"

Eleanor chuckled. "Madeline, you're teasing me."

"Unfortunately, I'm not, and a lowering experience it has been. But never mind that." Madeline flipped society's opinion aside. "Confess all that has happened to you."

"No! You first. Where were you?" Eleanor sat back

and looked Madeline over. She saw nothing wrong with her cousin. Madeline looked healthy, with rosy cheeks and a smile that wouldn't go away. "You said you would come to London in only a few days. Were you injured?"

"My husband was shot."

Eleanor froze.

"Oh, I *forgot* to tell you." Madeline giggled, obviously delighted with Eleanor's bug-eyed reaction. "Gabriel and I are married."

"Married? Married? *Gabriel*?" Eleanor could scarcely stammer. "The earl of Campion? Your former betrothed?"

"Yes, the very same."

"He was at Rumbelow's gambling party?"

Madeline frowned. "But my father wasn't."

Pleased to be able to speak with authority about *something*, Eleanor said, "About that, I can reassure you. He was here the day of my wedding. He heard about it—heard you were marrying Remington—and rushed to your aid."

"Well, bless the old noodle." Madeline looked thoughtful. "I would have never thought he cared enough."

"I own, I was surprised. But never mind him. Relate every detail about Gabriel. He was shot? He's fine, obviously, or you wouldn't look so blooming."

"Rumbelow's party was a scam, and Gabriel was almost killed protecting me." Madeline's eyes filled with tears, and Eleanor's self-confident cousin trembled. "That's why we couldn't come when we got your letter. He was wounded, and even if I could have left him, the roads were flooded in that dreadful storm."

"You must tell me all."

Madeline sat straight up. "First, *you* must tell *me*—are you happy? We came to London as soon as we could, sooner than Gabriel should have traveled, only to find you gone on your honeymoon."

Eleanor put down her plate. She picked up her neglected needlework. She stared at the design, at the needle threaded with gold thread. Since the last time she'd touched the frame that held the canvas, she'd taken a man to her bed. Her husband—and sometimes she knew him so well. And sometimes he was alien to her. When she woke in the morning, she never knew whom she would meet, the thoughtful husband, the distant stranger, or the passionate lover.

But to discuss him with Madeline, even as close as they were, seemed wrong somehow, so she bent over her embroidery to avoid Madeline's gaze. "Remington took me to a cottage on the seashore. It was lovely and quiet. The inn had wonderful food, and we enjoyed ourselves." She could feel her face heating as she spoke.

"Oh, dear." Madeline sounded dismayed. "He's angry with you."

Eleanor peeked up at her. "Yes, for he did very much want to marry *you*, my dear duchess, and he was rightfully perturbed at my deception."

"You're far better than he deserves," Madeline said angrily, "and if he doesn't know it, he's a fool. Is he cruel to you?"

"Do you mean, does he beat me? No. I don't think he could bear to raise a hand to any woman." The memory of his sister's death must haunt him.

"There are other ways for a man to be cruel to his wife." In a lower tone, Madeline inquired, "Is he mean to you . . . in bed?"

Eleanor scarcely knew how to reply. She thought about the last week. The walks on the beach, the way he'd hungrily watched her, the times he'd fed her with his fingers, the hours spent in bed, exploring each others' bodies. She almost laughed. She almost cried. After many tries, she looked Madeline in the eyes and said, "If it is possible for a man to try and kill a woman with pleasure, I believe that is his plan."

Madeline stared at Eleanor, her blue eyes wide and shocked. Then, gradually, merriment grew in her face and she sputtered with laughter.

Eleanor sputtered with her, embarrassed and almost proud. "I give as good as he does. Everything the concubines taught us, I utilize, and I've even made up a few things on my own."

Madeline leaned back against the sofa and released peals upon peals of mirth, her laughter as pleasant a sound as Eleanor had heard for weeks. "Then I will stop worrying about *that*." Wiping her eyes on her napkin, Madeline asked, "When will I meet this husband of yours?"

"Tonight? We're dining in. He says I'm tired from traveling, although I've never felt better."

Madeline started giggling again. "You are an inspiration to me, dear cousin. You come to London on a mission you much despise, and before a fortnight is out, you're married to a wealthy man and teaching him to love you."

Eleanor's smile faded. "I fear that the latter is not the truth, but I have hopes that someday, he'll at least tolerate me again."

With the innate wisdom of a new wife, Madeline asked, "Because you love him, do you not?"

"So much, Madeline. I love him more than I have ever loved another living soul, and even if he never knows, I'm happy." Because she was honest, Eleanor added, "I am almost perfectly happy."

As Remington sat alone in his club, whisky in hand, Eleanor's doubt chewed at him. She was so sure that the villain who had killed his family wasn't the duke of Magnus.

Could Remington have possibly made a mistake?

But no, it was Magnus's men who had been investigating his father's business, and that had led to the fires and the murders. Pervasive evidence, surely.

Yet Remington himself had had doubts when he had met Magnus—doubts Eleanor had called up again. Magnus was either a magnificent actor . . . or the wrong man. And if he was the wrong man, then someone else had killed Lady Pricilla, and who was that someone? Lord Shapster? Lord Fanthorpe? The old duke of Magnus?

Or, God forbid, a stranger who killed for pleasure.

But no. It was too unlikely, that she would plan to run away with his father on the same night she was killed.

And worse, Remington had to wonder if his doubts about Magnus had surfaced because Eleanor had weakened his resolve. Because it was easier to loll in bed with her than to rise and seek vengeance on the man who had killed his family.

The other men in the great room played cards, rested in great leather armchairs, and gossiped about politics and society. But they skirted around Remington, who was ensconced before the window, shunning him and the aura of menace that surrounded him.

One man stopped and stared.

Remington ignored him, but the stranger didn't take the hint. Remington glanced at him and saw a man about Remington's age and height, with his arm in a sling and the drawn look of a recent convalescent. A man apparently indifferent to Remington's need for solitude, a man Remington had met once before—Gabriel Ansell, the earl of Campion.

So with a curt nod, Remington acknowledged him. "Campion."

"Knight." Gabriel indicated the easy chair across from Remington. "Mind if I join you?"

"Actually—"

"I understand we're now cousins-in-law."

Nothing else Gabriel could have said would have startled Remington quite as much as that. "You married the duchess?"

"When you won her, but didn't come and get her, I decided to settle the matter in my favor."

So Madeline was no longer single. Remington couldn't have wed her anyway, and he experienced a great, unacknowledged relief to know that his plan could never have come to fruition anyway. Observing Gabriel's pale complexion, Remington said, "Sit down, before you fall down."

"Thank you." Gabriel subsided in the chair, signaled to the footman, and ordered a brandy. "Madeline just got back from visiting Eleanor. I'm to dine at your house tonight."

"I'm delighted."

"No, you're not. You wish I would go to hell. But you can forget that. We might as well decide we're best of friends, for our wives are—and nothing will separate them."

At Gabriel's blunt speaking, Remington grinned and relaxed. "Truer words were never spoken, and I suspect you're a good man to have as a friend."

Gabriel made a seated bow. "Thank you. But there are disadvantages to having our wives be so close. For instance, Madeline sent me out to find and speak to you." He accepted his drink. "She's worried about Eleanor. Eleanor doesn't seem completely happy."

Remington's brittle temper snapped. "Not completely happy? Did she tell Madeline that?"

Gabriel snorted. "Do you know Eleanor at *all*? I've never heard the woman utter a word of complaint! Of course she didn't tell Madeline. As I understand it, Madeline inferred that from a twitch, or some such damned silly feminine thing."

The two men's gazes met in perfect understanding. They would never be able to keep a secret for the rest of their lives.

"Eleanor made me a laughingstock," Remington said.

"The first time we were engaged, Madeline did that with me." Gabriel took a drink and rested his head on the high back of his chair. "While she was gone, I discovered a few things. The people who'll laugh to your face are either your friends or your enemies. You can cuff your friends, and as for your enemies—it's good to know who they are."

Remington thought back. It was true. Since the wedding, the men he'd come to know, to game with, to drink with, to do business with, had laughed loud and long at his foolishness and still teased him about his precipitous rush into marriage with the wrong woman. But their laughter held no malice.

The men who hated him because he was more handsome, because he had more money, because he outwitted them in cards or business, sneered or made rude comments meant to be overheard, and of those men he had taken note.

But there was one gentleman . . . Remington had run into him at the club. The gentleman had stopped in his path, pointed a long, slender finger at him, and stared. His short laugh had rung with triumph. And why? Remington knew the gentleman's name, of course. He knew his name very well. But they had never had dealings of any kind. They had never even spoken.

Remington stared at Gabriel. "Interesting," he murmured. "Interesting, indeed."

And the memory of his conversation with Clark popped into his mind.

"Would he have killed Lady Pricilla?"

"Only if he could have had his secretary kill her."

Lord Fanthorpe.

Grimly, Remington stood. "Excuse me, Gabriel. I'll see you tonight. Right now, I have business to attend to."

Chapter 28

*T*wo evenings later, Remington danced the
quadrille with the duchess. Not *his* duchess—
Gabriel's duchess. Remington didn't have a duchess,
and much to his surprise, he no longer cared. "Your
Grace, this is a grand party." He watched as Lady
Gertrude danced past with Lord Bingham. "How did
you organize it in so little time?"

"I didn't," Madeline confessed. "Lady Georgianna was going to have a ball tonight anyway, and
with the excitement of two such important marriages in so little time, she saw the sense in convert-
ing her ball into a party honoring us." She flicked a
glance at Eleanor and Gabriel, dancing in a separate
set across Lady Georgianna's large and crowded
ballroom. "All of us."

Following the pattern of the dance, Remington

and Madeline made their way to different partners, then returned to each other. "How did my marriage to your cousin become an important marriage?" he asked. "I'm not noble, nor is my bride."

Madeline shot him a smile. "In the ton, everything is perception. You have an aura of excitement. Eleanor is now perceived as being witty, and clever enough to capture a dangerous man, as well as being the diamond of the first water."

The ways of the English were inscrutable to him. He suspected they always would be, but tonight, in the midst of the laughter and the music, he felt at home. At home—because of Eleanor. His gaze sought her out. Her face was alight with her delight in the music, and his body ached with the need to be with her. To talk to her. To take her. To hold her.

This wasn't infatuation. This was love.

Love. For a de Lacy.

He was enmeshed in Eleanor's net, and he was glad to be there. "She *is* beautiful."

"Very much so." Madeline sounded amused. "A hint—you're supposed to be showing interest in *your* partner."

With his most charming smile, he returned his attention to Madeline. "So I am, and so I do. I have thanks to render to you, too, since our close association with the future duchess of Magnus and the current earl of Campion lends us a patina of respectability."

"Of course, that helps, but make no mistake. If not for the sensation you create as a couple, you would be shunned and discarded. As it is, you're the toast of London."

"Of course, there is my money," Remington said cynically.

Madeline laughed warmly. "Of course."

Again, the figures of the quadrille separated them, and Remington took the moment to look for Fanthorpe. The old man was dressed in his best togs, chatting with his friends as if he hadn't a care in the world. Remington knew better. His investigation had not yet confirmed Fanthorpe's guilt in the murders of Remington's family or Lady Pricilla, but it had turned up other crimes. The more Remington found out about Fanthorpe, the more he despised him, and the more convinced he was that this man had murdered Remington's father and sister, and killed Lady Pricilla. God rot Fanthorpe, he'd done a world of harm with his hatreds, but Remington would get his revenge.

For his investigation had turned up yet another interesting fact. Fanthorpe had completely run through his second fortune, and the weight of his debts made it necessary that he flee to the Continent. He had barely been hanging onto the remnants of respectability—and Remington wanted him out of England.

So Remington had pulled strings. Merchants were repossessing their goods, foreclosing on Fanthorpe's properties, and it hadn't been difficult to convince Clark to cut Fanthorpe's credit.

Remington and Madeline met again in the intricate dance, and as smoothly as a woman who regularly made threats, she said, "I want to give you a word of warning. I don't know you well, but since Eleanor's father cares nothing for her, I must advise you that she's my dearest cousin, and if you ever hurt her, I will use all my resources to hurt you in return."

Remington held up his hands to stop the duchess. "I can safely assure you, Eleanor is my wife. I'll take only the best care of her. I've pledged my life on it."

"Well. All right." Madeline grinned. "Actually, I believe you. You bring out the best in her. All the fine attributes only I've seen before, she confidently shows to the world—because of you." The music ended, and Madeline hugged him. "I'm proud to welcome you into my family."

Wrapped in the embrace of no less a personage than the future duchess of Magnus, Remington again looked at Fanthorpe, and he smiled. In fact, he gloated. The ton had accepted him, feted him, made him one of their own, and Fanthorpe hated it, and him.

Deliberately, Fanthorpe turned his back on Remington.

If he knew who Remington truly was . . . but he didn't. Remington hadn't yet told him who now took his place in English society. But he would. Tomorrow, he would.

In the meantime . . . Remington walked to take Eleanor's hand, and reflected that he could not have imagined such happiness could be his. Leaning close to her ear, he said, "It's late, and I want you. Let's go home."

She laughed, low and deep in her throat. "We came with Madeline and Gabriel. We can't leave without them."

Remington glanced up at Gabriel.

Gabriel stood with Madeline, and the two of them gazed at each other as if they were the only two people in the world.

"I don't think that's going to be a problem," Remington murmured.

The two couples profusely thanked their hostess and made their way toward the door. There they found Clark and his wife waiting for their carriage.

"The newlyweds are leaving early!" Clark proclaimed with a twinkle.

"At least we have the excuse of being newlyweds." Remington tipped the butler, who sent a footman for their outer garments.

The color rose in Mrs. Oxnard's cheeks, and Clark looked as guilty as a boy.

Gabriel grinned and rested his palm on Madeline's back. "Marriage is a great institution."

"Yes, if you want to live in an institution," Remington retorted.

Clark and Gabriel guffawed.

"Remington!" Eleanor tried to look severe, but in the last few days her smiles had come more frequently, as if she couldn't resist displaying her joy, and she smiled at him as if he were the greatest man in the world.

And when she was smiling at him, he felt he was.

"Men," Mrs. Oxnard said with affectionate disgust, and the women moved away into a huddle to complain about their husbands.

The men gazed after them, then Clark turned to Remington. In a low, serious voice, he asked, "How is your plan progressing?"

"Fanthorpe bought a ticket on a ship to Italy, leaving tomorrow on the afternoon tide."

"You have more connections than anyone I've ever met!" Clark exclaimed. "How do you know that?"

"I own the ship."

Clark laughed. "B'God, how clever of you."

In the few short days Remington had known Gabriel, he had come to trust him as a man of action and good sense, so Remington explained, "Fanthorpe has caused a problem for my family, and I'm making sure he doesn't cause another one."

Gabriel's face hardened in contempt. "I'm not surprised. The old villain has a penchant for running down children with his coach and raping his maids, and he suffers absolute contempt for any but his own kind—men born to the aristocracy and bred for idleness. He rather despises me for a bit of work I did securing the defenses against Napoleon."

"Did you?" Remington surveyed Gabriel with interest. "That's good to know. Before Trafalgar, some of my ships were involved in the effort—I don't like despots."

"Another of the reasons to dislike Fanthorpe," Clark said.

"Yes," Remington agreed. "Once Fanthorpe's in Europe, I'll have him watched on his road to hell, and I will rest a little easier."

"Do you fear him?" Gabriel asked.

Remington spoke quietly. "Yes. I can't guard all of my holdings every second."

Gabriel got right to the heart of things. "Are you afraid for Eleanor?"

"I don't think Fanthorpe could hurt her—with his world tumbling around his head these last few days, he's been busy." Remington had made sure he was busy. "But when she is out, she stays in public places, and she's accompanied everywhere by her maid or a footman, and I've talked to them seriously about their duties."

Gabriel watched Eleanor as she laughed with the other ladies. "Madeline says that even when bandits attacked their carriage, Eleanor talked the robbers into letting them go. That's an extraordinary woman."

"An extraordinary talker, anyway." But Remington knew what Gabriel was saying. Eleanor was too gentle, too kind to defend herself against a threat. She needed to be instructed, and she needed to be protected. "I sent my men into the pubs to find Fanthorpe's men and buy them a pint or two. My men discovered that Fanthorpe had ordered the attack on my carriage after Picard's ball, and again on my wedding day. He's got to go."

The footman arrived with an armload of cloaks and hats, and Eleanor returned to Remington's side. "What are you gentlemen discussing so seriously?"

As Remington helped her into her cloak, he said, "We were discussing the regrettable tendency of modern women to ignore the proprieties."

All three women looked at him as if he'd lost his mind.

"When did the man who gambled for my hand

start worrying about proprieties?" Madeline asked as she tied the ribbon under her chin.

Remington subdued a grin. "It's a matter of deep concern to me."

"What has Eleanor done that you should be concerned?" Mrs. Oxnard asked.

"Nothing!" Eleanor protested. "I'm so proper I'm boring."

"That you are not, my darling." Remington pitched his voice to a suggestive tone.

Eleanor didn't blush. She fluttered her eyelashes at him, and he wanted to curse. Damn the woman, she led him around like a docile puppy.

"Come now, gentlemen," Madeline said in a rallying tone, "you didn't start this conversation for no reason."

"London is a dangerous place, and I would that Eleanor always take her maid when she walks the dog." Remington shrugged his way into his own cloak and doffed his hat.

"I . . . do," she said, her irritation plain. "I'm not a fool."

"But I would like you to be doubly vigilant." He took his cane in hand.

In a clumsy effort to defuse the situation, Clark said, "Yes, b'God, I hear there's a wave of robberies sweeping the city."

The women exchanged skeptical glances.

"Better to be safe than sorry," Clark added.

Mrs. Oxnard took his arm. "Come, dear, you're making things worse, and here's our carriage."

He harrumphed but went quietly.

The ducal carriage was next in line, and the two

couples climbed in and settled into their seats, Madeline and Eleanor facing forward, the gentlemen facing behind.

As the coach started, Eleanor looked across at Remington. "What *is* wrong?"

Should he tell her? She had liked Lord Fanthorpe. More than that—she was his wife, delicate and fragile. She deeply cared about Lady Pricilla's fate, and she'd been horrified by his loss. He'd already distressed her enough.

Until he had proof that Fanthorpe was, in fact, the villain of so many murders, he would say nothing. Within a few days, he should have confirmation. He would be glad to lay the ghosts of Lady Pricilla, and his father and sister, to rest—for all their sakes. "Clark had the truth of it. There have been a great many robberies around the Town lately, and Clark, Gabriel and I have been discussing how best to keep you ladies safe."

Gabriel took Madeline's hand. "You already almost got killed at Rumbelow's. I want you to be careful."

Neither one of the women appeared convinced. Remington didn't care. In a conversational tone, he said, "It's always a good idea to carry with you something you can use as a weapon, but which looks innocuous. For instance, my cane." It leaned in the corner of the carriage. "It's an accessory men carry."

"Older men, usually," Madeline observed.

He shrugged. "So for me, it's perceived as an affectation, and I take care that no one should suspect any different."

"Yet I saw you using it." Eleanor turned to Madeline. "You should have seen him. He was brilliant, beating five attackers."

"With help," Remington said dryly.

Eleanor showed an enthusiasm that surprised him. "So it's not difficult to be prepared for attack as long as I use something womanly, like . . . I don't know . . . a heavy stone in my bag."

"That would work." Madeline sounded interested. "Of course, you could never carry one of those charming net reticules. Too flimsy."

"True, it would take a heavy material. Hm, velvet, perhaps."

"You could start a new fashion."

Remington stared at the dim outlines of the women. They had taken his suggestion and worked to make it elegant.

Beside him, he heard Gabriel mutter, "I'll never understand."

Remington muttered back, "Thank God they're on our side."

Although she'd imbibed nothing but Lady Georgianna's punch, Eleanor was as giddy as a drunk. "Wasn't that fun?"

Remington followed close on her heels as she entered their home, and she knew very well what he wanted. The same thing he wanted every night, and the thing she loved to give him.

She headed up the stairs and, deliberately enticing, she discarded her gloves, dropping them as she walked. "I used to hate having people notice me, but everyone smiled and seemed to think me a wit. And you know what?" She tossed her pelisse into the window seat. "When I'm not afraid, I *am* a wit."

"I noticed." He did not sound pleased.

She walked backward in front of him. "Do you think I'm a bore?"

"Never." He was more handsome now than he'd ever been, with his fair hair and pale blue eyes that scrutinized her. "I preferred it when all the men weren't in love with you."

"All the men?" she teased.

"Once you were wed, I thought they would find another maiden to flatter, but they insist on sniffing about like dogs on the scent."

"Are you calling me a dog?" She fiddled with the buttons on her bodice.

"A flirt would be a better word." With a rush, he caught her around the waist and bent to capture her mouth.

His kiss was now familiar, yet as always, it tempted her anew. He poured all the passion of his dark soul into the worship of her body, and she reveled in each glance, each touch.

Lifting his head, he gazed down at her. "What an odd circumstance brought us together."

"It was fate," she confessed solemnly. "I decided to wed you if Madeline didn't arrive to stop me, and I declare it to be fate that kept her from that church."

With a crooked smile, he put his finger on her lips. "My darling girl, I would have wed you regardless of who appeared at that church. If Lady Shapster had made her announcement early, I still would have dragged you up the aisle and made you mine. I was that far gone with lust, and—" He stopped.

Don't stop now! But it appeared he was going to. "And what?" she asked breathlessly.

He held her closer, then walked her backward toward their bedchamber.

She laughed at his intensity, at the awkward position, and out of sheer happiness.

He kicked the door open.

Lizzie barked once from her position at the foot of their bed, then rolled over and went back to sleep.

Remington snorted. "Watchdog."

"She's braver than you think," Eleanor protested. "Given the chance, she would defend you to the death."

"Don't be ridiculous." His fingers were busy on her buttons. "She hasn't a brave bone in her body."

Eleanor wanted to argue, but Remington pressed his face to her head. In a grudging tone, he said, "I like your hair."

"Do you?" Heavens, how she loved the man, and never more than when he worked so hard to make her happy. "I'm glad, because I like it, too."

"It was a matter of getting used to it."

"I know what you mean. I like you, too. It was a matter of getting used to you." She laughed while he pounced on her, tickled her ribs.

Looking into her face, he grew serious. "I've written to Magnus."

"The duke? Really? Why?"

"I want to talk to him. See what he knows. See if he"—Remington hesitated—"he still has explaining to do. His men *were* in Boston before my family was murdered, and I want him to explain why. But I wish you to know—you're right. The duke of Magnus isn't the man I'm seeking."

"Oh, Remington." She hugged him. "I am right, I'm sure of it. I don't know who killed Lady Pricilla, but it wasn't Magnus."

When Eleanor rose the next day and descended the stairs, Bridgeport said, "Mr. Knight is off to the bank for the day, but he begs you honor his request of last evening."

"I honor all his requests." Even the ones where he pretended nothing was wrong. It didn't take a fool to know he was worried about something, and had been for the last two days.

He still didn't tell her everything. He was a man used to keeping his troubles to himself. It would take time, but she would train him to understand that she was no frail flower to be protected. In the meantime, she would continue to behave as she always did, and take Beth or one of the footmen everywhere she went. It was no more than good sense—although apparently he believed she possessed none.

"Oh, and madam, you have a package from Lacy Hall." Bridgeport presented her with the paper-wrapped parcel.

"At last!" She carried it with her into the breakfast room. Seating herself, she tore the paper and found a book, worn and scratched, and a note from the housekeeper, apologizing that it had taken so long to find the diary. Eagerly, Eleanor opened the pages and looked on the delicate handwriting of a woman dead long ago. Eleanor's heart clutched; to think of Lady Pricilla, young and beautiful, on the brink of a new life with her lover, brutally murdered . . . and why? This book would answer all.

Cook bustled in with a plate. "Here's yer breakfast, mum. Beautiful morning." A scratch on the door made Cook sigh and go to open it.

Lizzie bounced in, all energy and exuberance.

"Will mum be taking the doggie fer a walk?" Cook asked.

"It seems I have no choice." Eleanor put the diary aside and dug into her food. "Tell Beth I'm going to Green Park. I need her to accompany me, and please, bring my reticule with my needlework. I like to stitch while I'm waiting for Lizzie to finish romping."

Chapter 29

"*Y*ou're the luckiest girl I've ever heard of." Horatia turned from her own path to join Eleanor as she took her constitutional through Green Park, Lizzie trotting happily at her side, Beth trailing behind, complaining of her shoes. It was a beautiful day.

"Yes, I am, aren't I?" The sun was shining, Eleanor wore one of the new costumes Remington had bought her, and she could scarcely keep an unladylike grin off her face.

Last night . . . last night had been a living embodiment of her most secret dream. She had been feted by London's finest, she had danced and been complimented, then at two the handsomest man in the world had taken her home, and there made sweet love to her—and more important, sweet conversation. There hadn't been one acrimonious word between them. Quite the opposite.

Now Eleanor bowed and smiled as she passed people she had met the night before, and she even found Horatia to be a charming and enjoyable companion.

"When I heard the duchess's cousin had been pretending to be her, I said to Huie—that's my husband, Lord Huward—Huie, I said, that girl's going to be shunned by everyone in society, and Her Grace is going to send her into exile. And I said, Huie, that luscious Mr. Knight has been courting her, and now he's married her, and he must be *furious*. I said, that man has an aura of danger about him, and I wouldn't be surprised if Miss de Lacy turns up dead one day. Well, Huie agreed with me, but Eleanor—I may call you Eleanor, mayn't I?"

Eleanor wanted to think about that, but Horatia didn't wait for Eleanor's consent. "Eleanor, last night you proved Huie completely wrong. The duchess still loves you, the ton loves you, and that luscious Mr. Knight loves you." Envy dripped from her tone. "How did you do it?"

"I'm lucky, I suppose." Very lucky. They were headed for the gazebo. There Beth could go off and visit with the other maids, Lizzie could chase rabbits, and Eleanor could sit in the sun and do her needlework and dream about Remington.

"I suppose." Horatia lowered her voice. "What about your stepmother? That awful Lady Shapster? She's the one who told everyone that *you'd* married Mr. Knight, and not the duchess, and she said awful things about you. What are we going to do about her?"

We? "Lady Shapster is not a problem for me," Eleanor said.

"No, I suppose not. Lady Georgianna made it quite clear last night that she wished Lady Shapster would fall off the face of the earth, and everyone feels that way. I said to Huie that Lady Shapster has gone beyond all that is decent in her persecution of Eleanor, and she'll get her comeuppance, you'll see!" Horatia nodded vigorously, and her corkscrew curls bobbed.

"I think she already has." Last night, as Eleanor had danced with Remington, Lady Shapster had stood and watched, her face a mask of jealousy and spite. She was drowning in hate, and nothing she could do would ever salvage her reputation. Now, at last, she would have to go back to Eleanor's father and live in the house with him, a victim of her own cruelty and a captive to his indifference.

"I suppose you're right," Horatia said. "But it seems so unfair that she should get away with—"

From behind them, Beth's voice broke in. "Excuse me, Mrs. Knight, but there the ol' witch is, 'eaded straight at us like a ship under full sail."

"So I see, Beth." Lady Shapster wore a silver walking gown and a billowing cloak, and her golden head was bare except for a blue feather bobbing above her head. She looked beautiful, and she looked deadly, and all of Eleanor's brave defiance faded away. She wanted to curl into a ball and hide her head.

Horatia grasped Eleanor's arm. "Do you want to walk the other way and pretend we didn't see her?"

"No." No. Eleanor had spent far too many years hiding from Lady Shapster. Lady Shapster would not vanquish her now.

Lady Shapster planted herself directly in the path in front of Eleanor.

Lizzie growled.

Eleanor slipped her fingers under Lizzie's collar. "Sit!"

Lady Shapster's feverish eyes ignored Horatia, ignored Beth, ignored the dog, and gleamed viciously at Eleanor. Only Eleanor. "So you think you've succeeded in achieving every one of your hopes. But I assure you, when society hears that Mr. Knight has left you everything in his estate, they'll draw away from you as decent people must."

Lizzie growled again and lunged.

Eleanor held her back.

Lady Shapster's little foot swung out. "Keep that vicious bitch away from me."

Infuriated, Eleanor said, "Don't you kick at my dog."

"Oh, you're brave now. You think you've vanquished me. Well, wait until I tell the ton what you really are. I tried to warn your father about your murderous tendencies. He didn't listen to me, but everyone else will. For shame!" Lady Shapster backed away as if she couldn't bear to be close to Eleanor. "To have your husband killed so you can have his fortune."

Horatia gasped loudly enough to frighten the birds in the trees.

The blood drained from Eleanor's head, and a buzzing filled her ears. "What do you mean?"

"As if you don't know. Do you think no one will be suspicious that a runaway dray just *happens* to be in front of the solicitor's office as Mr. Knight leaves from changing his will in your favor?"

"Mr. Knight is dead?" Horatia squawked.

"Lawks!" Beth exclaimed.

Distantly, Eleanor noted that her hands shook. Her head buzzed. Remington, dead? *Dead?* He'd made love to her last night. She'd seen him this morning, when he had kissed her good-bye. That vital being couldn't be dead. He *couldn't* be.

This was—had to be—Lady Shapster's idea of retribution. "You're lying."

"Lying." Lady Shapster laughed low and long. "That's rich, coming from you. Couldn't you have waited to have him killed? Did you hate to have him touch you so much you couldn't have let him swive you one last time?"

Eleanor didn't even know how it happened. One minute, she was almost fainting. The next, her palm stung and she was staring at the mark of her hand on Lady Shapster's cheek.

Horatia gawked.

Lady Shapster gazed at Eleanor as if she'd never seen her before.

Lizzie, free from Eleanor's restraint, sprang at Lady Shapster's skirt, bit into a mouthful, and tugged, ripping the beautiful, light cotton right at the empire waist.

The paralysis that held Lady Shapster silent ended, and she shrieked, "Eleanor!" in exactly the same tone she used to use in the old, horrible days when she drove Eleanor to tears.

Eleanor was not intimidated. She stepped up to her, toe to toe. "If I find out you're lying about this, I'll make you sorry. And you'd better be lying." Whirling, she left the ugly scene behind, almost running with her need to find him. Find Remington.

Lizzie followed, keeping up in a determined doggy trot.

Beth lagged behind, keeping up a running lamentation on the master's death and the sad state of her feet.

It's not true. It's a lie. It was not true. Eleanor chanted the words over and over, as if that would make them real. Remington couldn't be dead. Before him, the world had been empty, with no place and no one for Eleanor. She had found love and home in the being of one man; God couldn't be so cruel as to separate them before she'd even told him how she felt!

She reached the road and looked up and down for a sedan chair or a hired carriage. As if by a miracle, a handsome coach drove up with footmen clinging to the sides. The coachman tipped his hat. "Take ye somewhere, lady?"

She opened the door. She lifted Lizzie in. "Berkley Square, at once." She climbed into the dim interior, its windows covered with cloth, settled into the seat, and waited for Beth to catch up.

Four things happened simultaneously.

The door slammed shut. The coach started with a jerk.

The dog growled, low and threatening.

And Eleanor realized she was not alone.

"If I were you, I'd keep my dog under control. I hate to stain my velvet seats with its blood." The tall, thin gentleman in his old-fashioned clothes gave her a supercilious smile. "You do have a regrettable fondness for mongrels, don't you?"

She stared across the interior at the seat opposite. "Lord . . . Fanthorpe?" Lizzie growled more, and Eleanor caught her collar as she lunged. "What are you doing here?"

"Your husband's not really dead, my dear," Lord Fanthorpe said. "But he will be."

In a flash, Eleanor understood. She understood everything, and her blood chilled. She glanced toward the door.

His cane snapped across the seats, smacking the blue velvet so hard that she sprang backward, away from its lash. "I've gone to a great deal of trouble to acquire you. Don't imagine I'll let you go so easily."

Lizzie's low growl was continuous now, her chest vibrating beneath Eleanor's hand. "Remington is still alive?"

"Very much so, and I shall enjoy finishing him."

Eleanor gripped the dog's collar harder, her palm slippery with sweat. "You . . . killed Lady Pricilla?" She held her breath, praying he'd deny it.

"For the exactly same reason I'm going to kill you."

"Kill me?" Eleanor wet her lips. The carriage was careening through London, headed for the countryside. "Why?"

"Like Pricilla, you have no sense of propriety. No sense of honor. Just like you, Pricilla mated with a commoner." He rubbed his fingertips together. "That night, I found her in the garden. I could have raised the alarm, kept her from her Mr. Marchant, and her father would have forced her to marry me. But I didn't want her."

Was Lord Fanthorpe delusional? Driven to madness by the loss of his dear fiancée? "You couldn't have murdered her. You had no blood on you."

He waved his lace handkerchief in airy dismissal. "I prefer the word *executed*—and I had my footmen with me. They did the job, and adequately."

She remembered the footmen riding on the coach, and she swallowed. "Adequately? Everyone who saw the scene said she suffered horribly."

"I had a lesson to teach. I wanted it taught well. She was a traitor to us. To noble people everywhere. As you are." His narrow chin lifted, his narrow lips sneered. "I tried to save you the night I met you."

"Save me? Oh." She remembered. "With the attack on the carriage."

"My men had strict instructions to kill Knight and leave you alone. But Knight's a devil with his cane."

"Yes." Her mind lingered lovingly on the memory of Remington's cane, the weapon he carried because it appeared to be harmless. "You tried again on my wedding day."

"Right you are! I'm not usually so inefficient, but"—he flushed—"I'm short on funds, and the best assassins cost money."

Lizzie sat on the seat beside Eleanor, staring at Lord Fanthorpe through narrowed eyes, and Eleanor wondered how a dog sensed his rot and she had not. "How is Remington supposed to find me?"

"He's a smart young feller. A Marchant." Fanthorpe leaned forward and whispered, "You see, I know who your husband *really* is."

A cold trickle of sweat crawled down her spine. "How?"

"His father had dark hair, he was stocky, he was freckled, but he had those freakishly pale blue eyes, just like Knight's." Lord Fanthorpe shuddered. "Did Knight think I wouldn't notice?"

"Why would he care? He didn't know that *you* were a murderer."

Lord Fanthorpe smiled with every evidence of pleasure. "I love the irony of this. Yes, your Remington will get there eventually, and find your body, and whimper over it. But I won't be the fool I was last time. I won't trust to the law for justice—I'll kill him, too."

"You'll kill him yourself?" Because this old man had no chance against Remington.

Lord Fanthorpe sighed deeply. "I realize you don't have a title of your own, but you're a member of one of our most noble families. Kindly remember a true aristocrat never dirties his hands with menial tasks."

She petted Lizzie and thought. This old man was going to have her killed.

She didn't believe it. Remington would come for her.

But the dog was a problem. Remington couldn't defend her and Lizzie, and Lizzie would do her best to get into the thick of things. She already hated Lord Fanthorpe. She would try to bite him, and Fanthorpe's henchmen would have no problem killing a dog.

Keeping one hand on Lizzie, Eleanor opened her reticule and produced her needlework. "Where is *there*?" As she freed her long, sharp needle from the canvas, she watched Lord Fanthorpe across the carriage. He was old, and he stank of evil.

"Lacy Hall. We should be there within the hour." He leaned his head back against the seat, a dreadful smirk on his painted lips. "I needed someplace close, and I liked the touch of killing you both on Marchant's old estate."

Eleanor tied the end of the thread into a noose, then looped it around her fingers. "But won't Magnus get the blame for the murders?"

"Possibly." Lord Fanthorpe chuckled. "The old duke of Magnus thought it was Marchant, at first. That was so grand. He persecuted Marchant to the fullest of his ability."

She tensed. Clutched the dog's collar.

"But apparently the current Magnus convinced him someone else had done the deed."

She measured the distance between her and the door.

"So the old duke made Magnus promise to find George Marchant and do some kind of reparation. Magnus was so helpful in tracking Marchant to Boston." Still in that dreadfully amused voice, Lord Fanthorpe said, "That ridiculous fool told me all the details. All I had to do was hire the men to take out Marchant and his family."

With all the force of her arm, she plunged the needle into the back of Fanthorpe's hand.

He roared in pain.

With the thread, she jerked the needle free.

He snatched his hand back.

The dog made a lunge for him, but Eleanor propelled herself against the door, opening it. "Go home," she whispered in Lizzie's ear, and tossed her out onto the road.

Eleanor heard a yelp as Lizzie hit the ground.

Grabbing Eleanor, Lord Fanthorpe slammed her back against the seat.

Gripping the needle, she swung her hand at his face in a great arc. The needle sliced through the skin under his eye.

From outside, a footman shut the door. Popping open the hatch, he shouted, "M'lord, shall we stop fer the dog?"

"No. Let it go." Stunned by her attack, Lord Fanthorpe touched the cut, then looked at the blood on his fingers. His eyes were thin slits of hate. "You slut." His voice trembled with rage, and he lifted his arm to strike her.

"Don't!" she shouted. "That's a menial's work."

As he swung, he said, "I'll make an exception for you."

"Remington, they're saying on the street that you were killed by a speeding dray." Clark stood in the door of his office, where Remington was going over the profits from his newest shipment.

"Never felt better," Remington said. Then it struck him—how odd that Fanthorpe should be leaving England at the same time such a rumor was circulating. A prickle of warning ran up Remington's spine. "Who says so?"

"Lady Huward is screeching over half of London

that you went to your solicitor, changed your will in Mrs. Knight's favor, and within an hour, you were killed."

Remington's sense of unease grew. "That's a very specific rumor. Where is Lady Huward?"

"She *was* in Green Park. Now she's home, surrounded by ladies and almost fainting from shock."

"Green Park?" Remington rose. "That's where Eleanor walks. Does rumor say where Eleanor is?"

"I believe she was there, too."

"Hell!" Eleanor would have chided him for swearing if she'd been here. Eleanor, who had so sweetly kissed him good-bye this morning. Her lips had clung, and he'd thought, for a moment, that she was going to tell him that she loved him.

She hadn't.

But surely a woman like her wouldn't give herself so freely unless she loved him. Maybe she didn't realize it. Maybe she was afraid to say the words. But it was the truth. It had to be.

"I'm going home," Remington said. "I want to see that Eleanor is safe."

"Henry, order Mr. Knight's carriage. Remington, I'll go with you." At Remington's lifted brow, Clark said, "I did promise, as your best man, to watch your back."

Remington nodded and ran toward the outer door, Clark puffing beside him.

Fanthorpe had to board that ship today. He should be there now.

But what if he were truly mad? Eleanor looked much like Lady Pricilla. What if Fanthorpe sought to destroy Eleanor?

Or what if he wasn't mad but knew Remington's true identity? In his drive to wipe out Remington's entire family, would he include her?

And what if he was on board but had hired the job done? The carriage was pulling up as they descended the steps. "Home," Remington shouted. "Hurry!"

"Does anyone walk with her?" Clark asked as they swung inside.

"Her maid. That dog. I don't like this. The rumor is so blatantly untrue, so easily disproved, and Horatia is such a fool—I don't believe she made it up. I think someone told her." Remington's hands trembled as he fingered his cane. He kept a knife hidden in the carriage, too, and he drew it out and fingered the nine-inch blade. Sharp and made for slashing . . . he strapped the sheath to his arm. *Couldn't John drive any faster?* "I didn't think he would go after *her*."

"Fanthorpe," Clark said. "Of course."

The rest of the ride to his home was silent, their arrival grim.

Beth sobbed in a chair in the foyer.

Bridgeport stood wringing his hands, and at the sight of Remington, announced, "Madam is missing."

"With Lizzie . . . ," Beth quavered, her eyes red and swollen.

Remington turned icy cold. His brain began to work as it always did in crises—intelligently, coolly. "How long ago was she taken?"

Beth gulped and said huskily, "An 'our, sir. Just like ye instructed, I screamed and screamed, but the coach rolled away so fast, no one could catch it."

An hour's head start, but in a coach. "Bridgeport,

get me my horse. Clark, follow with help."

Clark nodded. "But where?"

Remington knew exactly where he was going. "To Lacy Hall, to the ruins of the old house on the estate. And Clark—for the love of God, hurry."

Chapter 30

Remington raced through the London traffic. Pedestrians shouted imprecations and scurried out of his way. Vehicles maneuvered aside as rapidly as they could. And still he couldn't move fast enough.

Terror rode with him. Would he get to Eleanor in time? Fanthorpe had murdered before; he would murder Eleanor out of evil pleasure, because she was Remington's.

Remington left the outskirts of Town behind. On the open road, he could allow the horse its head, and he bent over, galloping so hard the wind brought tears to his eyes.

A single bark brought him wheeling to a halt.

Lizzie stood beside the road, an expression on her face he'd never seen before. Her eyes gleamed red, her lips lifted in a snarl, and she looked at him as if to demand he make things right.

"I'll rescue her, girl," he said. "I promise."

He rode on, and behind him he heard ever-diminishing, reproachful barks. He couldn't take Lizzie up, so she was following him as fast as her gangly legs could run.

Eleanor was correct. Lizzie was a brave little dog, and she would be all right. She'd better be, for Eleanor would murder him if something happened to that dog. . . .

Murder.

Grimly, he passed the gatehouse to Lacy Hall and continued down the road, to a faint, old trail through the grass that had once been the entrance to his father's house. When Remington had first arrived in England, he'd visited here on a pilgrimage of bitterness. He had stood among the trees that had marked the drive, and stared at the jagged ruin of the house. Ivy grew over the rubble of bricks, and birds nested in toppled chimneys. He had hated every de Lacy ever born, and on his sister's grave, he had vowed revenge.

Now he raced to rescue a de Lacy, the woman who had cured his wounded soul. "Hurry," he whispered to the stallion. "Hurry." He wound his way along the lane, through the tortured trees, following fresh wheel marks in the grass.

Taking the last turn to the house, he saw the coach standing before the wreck of the front steps, as if death were visiting. He saw Fanthorpe, dressed in his old-fashioned, garish garb, leaning against the coach and watching. He saw six men, dressed like footmen in their blue satin costumes, and looking like thugs. They were standing in a circle around . . . Eleanor.

Remington had arrived in time.

She looked beautiful in the dappled sunlight, fresh and joyous, and he loved her so much he didn't dare consider failure. Two women had already died because of Fanthorpe's evil. Remington would not allow him to take Eleanor.

He was slowing the horse even before Fanthorpe pointed the pistol at him.

"Get down, Mr. Marchant," Fanthorpe shouted. "Or I'll shoot you now."

A searching glance showed Eleanor's face had lit up at the sight of him. The brutes surrounding her held cudgels, but she seemed blissfully unaware of the danger. She cared only for him.

Remington measured the distance between Fanthorpe and his men. Forty feet, probably. Perhaps Fanthorpe didn't want blood spattered on his clothes—and perhaps he didn't trust these bastards to stop once they'd gotten started.

Remington cantered to a spot halfway between the old man and Eleanor.

"I told them you would come for me," Eleanor called. "I warned them."

"I'm glad you have such confidence in me," he answered. He hadn't been so sure—he'd been scared to death.

He was still scared to death. Fanthorpe's men were dangerous, scarred and grim, the dregs of the slums who had nothing to lose.

Worse, something had made Fanthorpe lose that

sneering self-assurance that usually imbued his every move. Hectic color filled his cheeks. He had a scratch under his eye, deep, red and puckered. He leaned heavily on his cane, and the hand holding the gun shook. "You got here earlier than I expected—Marchant."

Hell. He knew who Remington was.

Remington didn't like the trapped expression on Fanthorpe's face. Men who were trapped shot wildly, without forethought, and that would set off a massacre. The whole situation was as dangerous as a powder keg on a burning frigate.

In a calm voice, Remington said, "My lord, you're missing your sailing."

"The captain will wait for me. *I'm* the earl of Fanthorpe."

"Perhaps you haven't heard." Smoothly, Remington swung out of the saddle. "The tide waits for no man."

"Then I'll take another ship." Fanthorpe no longer sounded suave and cold, but sharp and thin. "Marchant, are you carrying your cane?"

"No. Why?" As if Remington didn't know.

"I had to hire new men after the last time you used your cane." Fanthorpe waved the pistol toward the circle. "Go there. It'll be very touching. You can die in the arms of your lover."

Remington moved toward the circle, gripping the knife in his sleeve.

A cold-eyed thug slapped his palm with his cudgel and eyed Remington with pleasure. Speaking out of the side of his mouth, he declared,

"M'lord, this is a big un. 'E'll cost ye another ten quid."

In a patient voice, Eleanor said, "I told you. Lord Fanthorpe doesn't have any money. You're not going to get paid. None of you are going to get paid."

Remington recognized her tactics. Eleanor talked her way out of trouble, and that was what she was trying to do now. She'd held the brutes off—good, although Remington suspected these men would finish the job for the pleasure of it, then start on Fanthorpe until they *were* paid.

But Fanthorpe was looking harassed, and in a vicious tone, he said, "I told you to shut up."

Remington noted a bruise darkening her cheek, a smear of blood under her swollen nose. That was Fanthorpe's work.

Remington caught her gaze, sliced a glance at his horse, and silently spoke to her with his eyes. *Escape when I give you the chance.*

She nodded, the serenity he'd admired intact, and in a sweetly reasonable tone, she spread her hands and asked the men, "Why do you think Lord Fanthorpe is catching a ship today? Why do you think he wants me to shut up? He's escaping his debts."

Fanthorpe's patience snapped. "Trollop!" The pistol swung from Remington to point at Eleanor.

Eleanor threw herself to the ground.

Remington slipped his knife free and drove the glistening blade onto the arm of the cudgel-wielding thief.

And all hell broke loose.

The thugs jumped on Remington, swinging their

cudgels. Without his cane, the odds were impossible, yet he fought back, slicing at them, taking two down before the sheer numbers broke his defense. A cudgel cracked his skull. They ripped the knife out of his grip and caught his arms. Before their first blow landed, he saw Eleanor running toward the horse.

"Get her!" Fanthorpe shouted, the pistol wavering.

One man broke away to chase her.

And she stopped—and lifted her skirts to her waist.

The men froze. *All* of them froze and stared at the display of her long, bare legs and her pale, curved bottom gleaming in the sunlight.

Remington's mouth dried. He wanted to kill the other men for staring, but he couldn't tear his own gaze away.

Then she ran at the horse, swung herself into the saddle, and rode straight at Fanthorpe. The old man scrambled backward onto the step for the coach.

At the last moment, she swerved and headed toward the road.

Fanthorpe hobbled out, aimed his pistol at her back, and shot. "Bitch!" he shrieked.

She rode on, unscathed.

Released from their paralysis, the blackguards swung their cudgels. Remington felt a rib crack. The air blew out of his lungs. He kicked one man in the groin, freed an arm, grabbed a dropped cudgel and laid about him smartly. But he fought a losing battle. He faced a slow and painful death, yet the thought sprang into his mind that his last memory would be of Eleanor, sprinting for the horse, her skirts held high.

They had his arms again and were using their fists, taking turns, shouting as if they were at a boxing match. Each shout was punctuated by another blow, another agony. He felt his nose break, his lips split against his teeth, and he tasted blood. The sound of their enjoyment grew in intensity; these brutes relished their work.

Suddenly, all shouting stopped.

Remington heard a thundering in his ears. Felt the ground shaking. He looked up through swollen eyes to see the cudgel-wielding bastards turn and stare in terror.

Eleanor was riding hell-for-leather, right at them, swinging a stout branch and yelling words much worse than his simple *hell.*

The men dropped him.

He fell to the ground with a groan.

The men scattered, running for cover.

She chased them down, riding Remington's huge stallion like an avenging goddess.

Remington staggered to his feet.

Fanthorpe. What about Fanthorpe? Where was he?

A quick glance showed the old nobleman crouched in the door of his coach. He held a rifle against his shoulder.

It was pointed at Eleanor.

Remington shouted a warning.

She didn't hear him.

He started running.

But although he stretched out his gait as far as possible, although his heart pumped as fast as it could, he couldn't make it. He hadn't the speed. He hadn't the time.

Fanthorpe was going to kill her.

When the shot rang out, Remington jerked as if the bullet had hit him, too. "Eleanor." He wanted to crumple in agony. "My God, Eleanor!"

But Eleanor was still in the saddle, using the branch on two of the fleeing thugs, an implacable smile on her face.

And Fanthorpe was falling, tumbling out of the coach, blood spurting from a wound in his chest.

With dread, Remington looked around for this new threat.

In the lane, Magnus sat on his horse, a smoking rifle in his hands and a deadly expression on his face. He looked at Remington, and in a chill voice said, "He killed my sister, too."

Justice had finally caught up with Lord Fanthorpe.

Galloping up were Madeline and Gabriel, and behind them were Dickie Driscoll and Clark. While they followed Eleanor's example and relentlessly rode down Fanthorpe's men, Remington staggered to a halt. He was hurt, and he was furious. "Eleanor!" he shouted.

At once she turned from her pursuit and rode to his side. Sliding out of the saddle, she caught him around the waist to support him. "Oh, no. Look at you." Her lovely eyes were horrified as she gazed at his face, and her tender fingers caressed his throbbing forehead. "My poor Remington, how badly have they hurt you?"

"Never mind that!" He scowled at her. "What were you doing, exposing your legs for those men to see?"

She blinked at him as if *he* were the crazy one. "Didn't you figure it out? I was trying to distract them so you would have a chance to fight your way free!"

His voice rose. "How the hell did you expect me to fight my way free? I was too busy staring at your ass!"

Her voice rose, too. "Don't say *hell*, and you've seen it before."

"When I don't look, you'd better call the undertaker, because I'll be dead." He was shouting now.

She shouted back, "Next time someone's beating the stuffing out of you, I'll let them do it."

"And that's another thing. Why the hell did you come back? You were supposed to—"

"Ride away and let them kill you? Just because you're a damned idiot?"

"Don't say *damned*," he mimicked.

"I'll say whatever I like. I'm your wife, and I love you, and . . . and they hurt you . . ." All her fine fury faded. She looked down as if she were guilty, and mumbled, "I didn't mean to tell you that."

All his pain abruptly faded. Sliding his arms around her waist, he said, "You didn't mean to tell me you loved me?"

"I didn't think you'd believe me." She fingered his torn, bloody cravat. "You think I married you for your money."

"No, I don't."

She looked up indignantly. "You said you did."

"I said a lot of stupid things." He pressed their bodies together, although not too tightly—his bruises were making themselves known. "Saying stupid things is what I do when falling in love with the most wonderful woman in the world."

She considered him, her face serious, and for a moment, he wondered if he'd made some kind of mistake. Was there some English etiquette for telling your wife you loved her?

Had she not really meant what she'd said? Did she not love him?

Then, like the sun rising, her eyes lit up. Her smile blossomed. "You love me?"

Breathing a sigh of relief, he said, "For how many other women do I let myself get beaten silly?" He brushed her hair back from her forehead. "I love you. You make me whole."

Sliding her arms around his neck, she tried to kiss him.

But his lips were swollen and one of his eyes was swelling shut.

Lightly, she pressed her lips to his forehead. "You poor darling, we've got to get you home."

Looking up, he realized they were surrounded by a circle of riders, all watching without a bit of discretion. Magnus, Gabriel, Madeline, Clark and Dickie observed them as if captivated.

Remington pointed his thumb at the torn and huddled group of thugs nearby. "Did you get them all?"

"How many were there?" Gabriel asked.

"Six," Eleanor said.

Magnus looked disgusted. "We only have five."

In his Scottish accent, Dickie Driscoll said, "I don't think ye have to worry about number six." He nodded toward the drive.

Lizzie trotted toward them, a mouthful of shredded blue satin in her teeth. Coming to Remington, she laid her offering at his feet, then sat and thumped her tail on the ground.

Eleanor laughed aloud.

Remington tried hard not to smile—it was too painful. In fact, now that the excitement was over, everything was too painful. "Good dog." He went down on one knee to scratch Lizzie's ears. As if she knew what he was thinking, she nudged him meaningfully and looked up at Eleanor.

Remington could take a hint. He looked up at Eleanor, also, with just as much adoration as the dog. "Will you marry me?"

"We're married." She was still grinning, not taking him seriously.

"I want to do it properly. I want to marry you, in a church, with my mother's ring, knowing full well who you are." He offered her his hand, bloody knuckles and all. "Will you marry me?"

Madeline gave a stifled sob.

Tenderly, Gabriel drew her into his arms.

In a disgusted voice, Magnus said, "Oh, for God's sake."

And Eleanor realized Remington meant it. Taking his hand, she knelt beside him. Looking into his eyes, she said, "My darling Remington, I would be honored to marry you."

"Thank you. Now." He tried to look pleasant when the world was whirling around him. "I'm afraid I'm going to faint."

Epilogue

"*My* favorite part of the whole brawl was when Remington fainted like a girl." Downstairs in the foyer, the duke of Magnus slapped his knee and roared with laughter.

Gabriel put his hand to his forehead and pretended to collapse, and the rest of the men roared, too.

Remington stroked the adoring Lizzie's head and waited until the laughter had died down. With a superior smile, he said, "You're jealous because *I* rode back in the coach with my head pillowed in the ladies' laps."

The men all laughed again, nodded and affectionately thumped Remington on the back.

Annoyed, Eleanor turned to the ladies gathered in the upstairs gallery of Magnus's home in Sussex. "Listen to them. They're cackling like fools. Don't they know he took a concussion to the head and almost died?"

"To say so would indicate compassion." Madeline dismissed them with a wave of her hand. "Compassion isn't manly."

"They're men, what do you expect? Logic?" Lady Gertrude looked lovely in her green satin gown, and her cheeks were rosy with excitement.

"I think they're nervous." Mrs. Oxnard's eyes were wise. "It's not every day you stage a double wedding for two such distinguished couples."

The ladies fell silent as they considered that great truth.

Magnus had decided that if Eleanor and Remington could repeat their vows, he wanted a chance to give his own daughter away, and so the single wedding grew to a wedding for Remington and Eleanor, and Gabriel and Madeline. In an hour the event would take place on the estate in the de Lacy chapel.

Eleanor looked at Madeline. She was lovely in a gown of pale blue muslin, which showed her arms and bosom to an advantage. Eleanor wore a matching gown in pale pink, but the straight line of her Empire waist skirt draped over the slight swell of her belly.

"You look beautiful," Madeline said, proving again that the cousins thought alike. "I envy you. You're done with this dreadful nausea." She pressed a hand to her still flat abdomen. "It would be dreadful if I was ill during the ceremony."

Eleanor laughed. "But memorable."

Their children would be born two months apart. Remington and Gabriel were convinced they would be girls and, they said, as much trouble as their mothers.

As usual, the men would be wrong.

With an upwelling of affection, Eleanor hugged Madeline. "Who would have thought eight years ago, when you took me in, we would come to this?"

It had taken four months to organize the wedding Remington had proposed. Four months of upheaval and excitement. Word of Lord Fanthorpe's demise at Magnus's hand swept the ton, leaving them open-mouthed with shock. That Fanthorpe had killed Magnus's sister made the elders nod and claim they'd always suspected it was so. That Fanthorpe had gone after Magnus's niece left everyone disavowing any association with him. Everything about his memory was now tainted.

When Lady Shapster's part in Eleanor's kidnapping became common knowledge, she received the cut direct from every hostess and slinked home to her husband—who didn't care to attend his daughter's wedding. It was grouse hunting season, and anyway, wasn't she already married?

So Magnus would give Eleanor away, too, and she found herself indifferent to her father's neglect. After all, she had Remington.

The day was fine, the morning sun shining as everyone waited for the call to go to the chapel. Only family and close friends had been invited, so the guests would number a mere two hundred, and Eleanor couldn't help a clutch of fear as she thought of facing all those staring eyes. After all, she was still Eleanor, shy and quiet—except when those she loved were threatened.

When Remington had recovered enough to sit up in a chair and receive visitors, Magnus had paid him a visit. When Magnus had lost Madeline in a hand of cards, he had decided he'd had no choice but to recover the family fortune. He'd been investigating the old business of providing supplies to His Majesty's Navy. He had pulled strings; he had the contract, and he wanted Remington to handle it and take the profits. Because, he'd said in his bluff manner, he'd promised his father he would make reparation to the Marchants for the great injustice done to them. And because Remington had given Magnus a great gift—the truth about his sister's death. All those years, Magnus had been convinced it was his brother, Lord Shapster, who had killed Lady Pricilla. Now he knew the truth, and both Lady Pricilla and Abbie could rest in peace.

Remington had agreed to take the business, on the condition Magnus continue to use his influence in the government for a percentage of the earnings. They had shaken hands on it, and it wasn't until Magnus had left that Remington had found the deed to his father's old estate on the table beside him.

The animosity between the families was over.

Stepping to the banister, Eleanor looked down at Remington's fair head. The hours he'd been unconscious haunted her still, the lump on his head and his swollen face giving witness to the beating he'd taken. The healing had taken weeks, and she had guarded him fiercely from too many visitors—and from himself, when he'd tried to get up too soon.

She'd almost lost him. She would never forget.

As if he felt her gaze on him, he looked up at her and smiled.

With the sunshine falling on him from the atrium above, his blond hair glowed and his eyes crinkled at the corners. He was still the most handsome man she'd ever seen, and she could scarcely believe he was hers—and that he loved her.

But he did. He expressed it in every way. And when she'd told him about the babe, he had sat down with her in his lap and held her as if she had given him a miracle.

"The carriages are here," Magnus called.

"Oh, the carriages are here. Girls!" Lady Gertrude clapped her hands. "You need to don your bonnets and your pelisses." Leaning over the banister, she called, "And Remington, dear boy, the doggie cannot go to the church with us."

Remington laughed and handed Lizzie over to her own special footman.

Since acquitting herself so admirably in the fight four months ago, Lizzie had gone from being a stray to being an honored member of the family, and she adored Remington with all her canine devotion. And Remington, although he wouldn't admit it, adored her, too.

"Do you know," Lady Gertrude said in a low voice to Mrs. Oxnard, "that Remington actually asked if Lizzie could carry the wedding rings? I think he was jesting, but really, I'm not sure."

Madeline and Eleanor submitted to being dressed by Horatia and Mrs. Oxnard. They accepted their bouquets. They started down the foyer.

Gabriel and Remington came to the foot of the stairs.

Gabriel stared proudly at Madeline as she descended.

Remington held out his hand to Eleanor as if he couldn't wait to hold her again.

On the last step, she gave him her hand.

Lifting her fingers to his lips, he kissed them and in that dark, dangerous, beastly growl she loved so much, he asked, "Eleanor de Lacy, will you marry me today and be mine forever?"

Her joyous smile broke forth. "With all my heart."